## More praise for *A Trick of Nature*

"A perceptive, unnerving account of the fault lines destabilizing contemporary family life . . . Matson has written an absorbing, elegant novel that feels hauntingly familiar but remains surprising to the end."

—SUZANNE BERNE
Author of *A Crime in the Neighborhood*

"So skillfully does Matson describe the calm before the marital storm that it's possible to be lulled right along with them into their own blind harmony."

—*Boston Book Review*

"Here is a novel peopled with characters so intimately and empathetically drawn that we feel like we're reading about our friends, or ourselves. Combined with Suzanne Matson's splendid instincts for plot, they make *A Trick of Nature* a thoroughly engrossing and moving book."

—MARGOT LIVESEY
Author of *The Missing World*

"[An] eloquent second novel . . . Describing the sustenance derived from family is Matson's métier, and she portrays it here in an especially tender, emotionally revealing way. She effortlessly shifts the narrative between Greg's point of view and Patty's, beautifully illuminating the inner lives of a family stubbornly held together by a persistent love."

—*Publishers Weekly*

Also by Suzanne Matson

*The Hunger Moon* (a novel)
*Durable Goods* (poems)
*Sea Level* (poems)

# A

# TRICK

# OF

# NATURE

*a novel*

**Suzanne Matson**

BALLANTINE BOOKS · NEW YORK

A Ballantine Book
Published by The Ballantine Publishing Group

www.ballantinebooks.com

Library of Congress Cataloging-in-Publication Data: 2001117932

ISBN 0-345-44456-6

This edition published by arrangement with W.W. Norton &
Company, Inc.

Manufactured in the United States of America

First Ballantine Books Edition: November 2001

10  9  8  7  6  5  4  3  2  1

FOR JOE, NICK, HENRY, AND TEDDY

Thanks go to the Massachusetts Cultural Council for fellowship support during the writing of this novel, to Elizabeth Graver and Paul Doherty for their attentive close readings of the manuscript, to Steve Matson for contributing his memories of high school football, to Jill Bialosky for her insightful editing, to Henry Dunow for his always supportive advice, and to Joe Donnellan—reader, sounding board, fact-checker, reality tester, and all-around sharer of both the angst and the fun.

I

I t was a perfect June day: clear, windless, hot without being sticky. Mitch was on the driving range when Greg arrived. Greg waved, then went inside to buy his own bucket. He found a place on the line and began briskly sending the balls down the range in long, hooking arcs. Mitch kept trying to correct Greg's swing, but Greg didn't have the patience to be a real student of the game. When anyone gave him pointers, he knew he acquired a glazed, unlistening attitude. Greg's reason for golfing was to get his butt off the couch, plain and simple. He found that after a round of nine holes he usually had the energy to take care of some little chore like changing the oil in the car, or stopping at the hardware store to buy a set of hinges for the basement door that hung askew.

He whacked away at the golf balls, not really caring how far or straight they were going. He liked the pleasure of swinging the club until his whole upper body felt warm and loose, and hearing in rapid succession the crack of each ball against the driver.

They waited their turn to tee off. The foursome they were behind was going to slow them down today, that much was sure, a quartet of grandfathers in pastel slacks—jocose, relaxed, and none too spry.

They moved as if they had all the time in the world, which Greg assumed they did, in their respective retirements. During summers Greg had time to waste, too. He just wasn't able to accept it like these geezers. Maybe that was his problem: summers felt too much like retirement to him. But retirement represented the end; and at thirty-eight, what had he accomplished? What had he even begun?

Every summer vacation he experienced this uncomfortable feeling of being without compass, adrift on a raft of days he was expected to steer in some purposeful way. At the end of each school year he forgot what summer felt like, and he behaved like the rest of the teachers, like the students, even, as they all leaned forward into June, their collective longing for freedom seeming to actually tip the school toward the powdery dust of the baseball diamond, the mowed football field, the empty, sun-heated bleachers.

This year was like the others. When the weeks arrived he had been so impatient for—time he would spend fixing things around the house, reading, lifting weights every afternoon in the cool of the basement—he felt obscurely abandoned, confused by the falling away of routine and hurry. He washed up the breakfast dishes after Patty and the girls left the house. He puttered through the morning until it was time to make a sandwich, the radio he turned on for company playing rock from twenty years ago, songs that still felt fresh to him. Some mornings he couldn't even wait until noon for this ritual, not out of hunger, but out of impatience to move to a new thing.

As soon as he had the time to begin his projects of self improvement and home improvement, they ceased to interest him. He knew that Patty expected to hear about something he did that day when she returned home from work—lumber bought, a trip to the library, a shrub uprooted and moved farther away from the house—and he resented what he imagined as this wifely investment in how he spent his time, her interest in his days making them seem less his own. They spent the summer envying each other. Her complaint, voiced often enough so that he knew when it was coming, a particular little sigh of fatigue preceding it, was that she never had enough time to catch up on things at home.

For his part, Greg envied his wife her alarm set at six, her ten-minute allotment of shower time, the fact that she had to put on real clothes and not just shorts and a T-shirt, and her last-minute dash around the house to gather up her keys and bag. He disliked how when he gave her a peck of a kiss and wished her a good day, he saw that in her mind she was already in the driveway, on the road, settling into her office chair and booting up her computer. She would have her neat In box, her neat Out box, and at the start of every day In would be empty, or nearly so. She would have her computerized calendar, with little chimes and bits of music periodically reminding her to leave her desk for meetings and appointments. By the end of the day Out would be fairly bulging with accomplished tasks.

Even the twins had a tight schedule now that they worked as summer baby-sitters, which meant they left the house earlier than their mother, and returned later. Their days were regimented by the needs of the children they tended: naps and mealtimes, snack breaks and play periods, and afternoon walks to the playground that they synchronized with one another. He pictured the twins with their charges approaching the playground from opposite directions, meeting at the slides like the wings of a butterfly coming together. But with or without their jobs, the twins wouldn't be company for their father during the summer. They were fifteen now, not old enough to drive places by themselves but old enough to have friends who could drive them. They strove never to be seen in his company outside the house.

Greg had his odd summer employments. He taught Driver's Ed in June, and coached for the football team in August. During the trough of five weeks or so in between, Patty would usually take a week off for their vacation, but never more than that, because July was the beginning of the fiscal year for her accounting firm, and there was too much work to do.

Those weeks he was at loose ends felt too long to be unoccupied, yet too short to begin a new way of life. Of course, if it had been Patty's time off she would be up early, throwing rugs out of the house to air, taking down venetian blinds, plotting neat little rows of marigolds and petunias. Greg meant to be like that too, disciplined and focused, but somehow he always wound up watching cable reruns of *Star Trek* in the afternoon, the lazy, secret glow of daytime TV imparting the same mix of pleasure and malaise it had given him as a kid.

The ebbing of his self-worth corresponded to the ebbing of his desires in general, and he seldom reached out for Patty at night during the season of midsummer. When everyone else he knew seemed to look younger than usual in summer shorts and tan, and to delight in the aphrodisiacal mixture of slowly cooling patio combined with gin and tonic and the primitive flare of the lighter fluid on coals, he did not. The evening barbecues didn't feel like hard-won snippets of vacation he deserved after a long day. He dutifully handled the tongs, tweezed the charred disks of hamburger onto the toasted rolls his wife and girls held out, drank his beer and stretched out on the lounge chair, listening to Patty talk about her meetings as the stars gradually appeared, first one at a time, then in a great swatch, like the rhinestones Patty had punched into her denim jacket when they were both in high school.

The girls would wander off, leaving the two of them alone. Patty would wind down, high on her day, her drink, the soft breeze blowing through their yard. She would murmur something about the twins, which meant she had tuned her radar in to find them—whether they were doing their nails in a lighted bedroom upstairs, or sprawled in the dark family room blued from the TV, waves of sitcom laughter surging from the open window. Then she would reach over and lightly put her hand on his thigh, sometimes edging the tips of her fingers inside the legs of his shorts, and he would almost unconsciously flex a muscle there, but he wouldn't reciprocate, wouldn't reach over to rub her neck, or even rest his palm on her arm. Weirdly, he desired his wife most when she wasn't there, when he was lying by himself on the couch watching an old episode of *Love, American Style* or *I Dream of Jeannie*. That was when he remembered himself as a person with appetites—flashes of the taut, hungry boy he had been, stretched out on his mother's rug in front of the TV. There was no irony then to the watching, just the cramped longing that came from seeing Barbara Eden's legs outlined beneath her filmy genie pants, teasing him with the exotic freedom of adulthood. Greg had idolized Major Nelson: his razor-sharp uniform, the fact that his work involved missions, and the lovely, unbelievable secret of his girlfriend in a bottle. When the Major was in one of his frequent welters of confusion—caught between the sexual pull of Jeannie's charming chaos and the inflexible demands of his military superiors—the preadolescent Greg had keenly sympathized.

THE OLD guys must have felt Mitch and Greg's antsiness at their heels, because they motioned for them to go ahead on the next hole. Good for them, Greg thought. They weren't about to let anybody ruin their good time.

"Greg! Long time," one of them said. Greg squinted against the sun. He recognized Ned Bennett under the plaid cotton hat, the man who had been his father's internist. The last time he had seen him had been seven years ago in the hospital, by his father's bedside.

"Family well?" Ned asked.

"Everyone's fine, thanks."

"Glad to hear it. We're going to step aside and wait for you youngsters to play through. Wonderful day, isn't it? Give my regards to your mother."

Greg wondered why his old man couldn't have been more like that—amiable and relaxed, a pleasure to be around. Why hadn't he ever just gone out and enjoyed a round of golf with a few friends? For one thing, he didn't have any friends. For another, he would have whined that he was too broke for a ritzy game like golf. Ray Goodman had divided the world into haves and have-nots, and put himself—*nothing but a peon for the fat cats who own the plant*—squarely in the latter category. But the simple fact was that his father had needed to play the victim. He had never been able to admit that he had the power to enjoy his life. And now it was over, and it had been a miserable thing from Greg's point of view, radiating discontent into the lives of everyone around him.

By the time they were at the third tee, Greg had worked himself into the silent fuming which always happened when he started to run through the list of grievances he still had against his father. Mitch interrupted his thoughts.

"I need to say that we're golfing next Wednesday at nine, and that we had lunch after," Mitch said.

Greg was slow to catch on. "You want to golf next Wednesday?"

"No, I only want to be able to say we did. To Sandy." Mitchell wasn't looking at him. He was studying the lay of the fairway, lining up his shot.

"What's up?"

"I'll be seeing someone. A woman." He grinned, then turned away from Greg to address the ball. He made a series of tiny weight shifts on the balls of his feet. Then he twisted in what looked like an almost violent motion, and connected driver with ball, sending it in a deep and perfect arc, its dot disappearing into retinal memory.

Mitch turned back to Greg, his fair skin flushed with satisfaction. The smear of sunblock on his nose combined with his dark glasses and baseball cap gave him the smug mask of a lifeguard.

"How long has this been going on?" Greg asked. The question came out sounding aggrieved, as if Sandy had asked it.

"It hasn't," Mitchell said, smiling again. "It will. On Wednesday."

"Who is she?" This new fact, combined with Mitchell's casual attitude, was changing the whole color and shape of the day—the fir trees lining the course, the high, thin beards of clouds, the carpet of preternaturally green grass—all of it had grown sharp-edged and vivid. A minute ago, Greg had been lost thinking about his father; the grooves of judgment were worn so smooth he could travel them effortlessly. Now he felt a kind of tilt, as if everything he knew were sliding to the side, making room for things he didn't.

"She's a client. She hired me to redo her office's billing system. We had a few lunches, and one thing led to another."

"Wow." Greg shook his head and took his swing. He sliced the ball into a stand of trees. They picked up their bags and began walking.

"So, just in case I need a backup for my whereabouts, can I count on you?" He must have realized what he was asking; Sandy and Patty were good friends.

"Won't you feel like an asshole every time you look at Sandy after this?"

"That's just it." Mitchell stopped him by grabbing his elbow. His blond eyebrows were drawn up with excitement above his aviator rims, and his forehead was faintly beaded with sweat. "It's been a turn-on for me with Sandy, too. The whole thing has got me feeling charged up. Things have never been better with Sandy."

"Then, why?"

"Oh, for Christ's sake, Greg. You mean to tell me you never—"

"Never."

"—even *wanted* to?"

"That's different." There had been Jane, single and in her first year of teaching English at the high school. Jokey, athletic, quoting Shakespeare to him over lunch in the faculty room. Greg hadn't been that far out of college himself; in many ways he had been closer to the randy adolescent boys he taught than the husbands and fathers he lived among in the suburbs. That spring he and Jane had jogged together after school. By late May, when the contagion of reckless-ness from graduating seniors infected everyone at school, Greg had found himself watching Jane's bare limbs on the track—speculating, wanting. It had taken him a while to quell that. But wanting was not getting. It didn't count for the same at all.

"I don't think it's so different," Mitch countered, "if you do it, but don't really get involved. This woman, she's married, too. She wants to be as careful as I do. My marriage will come out of this fine, be-lieve me. Better, even."

That's when it occurred to Greg that Mitchell had done this before, and he hadn't seen. Did Sandy see? He couldn't believe that she would stay if she did. But then they had two kids. Maybe she knew and stayed anyway. Maybe—but he couldn't imagine it—she did it, too.

"I didn't know you were such a prude, Greg," Mitchell said mildly, after sinking his putt and retrieving the ball. "Forget I asked."

Somehow this irritated Greg more than the original request. If he said no, he would be taken out of the loop. He wouldn't hear any more about Mitchell's affair, and he suddenly realized that he wanted to, needed to even. Was he really a prude? Or was he simply a more honorable man than Mitch? He had always thought they were a lot alike—men who did their best by their kids, felt settled and lucky in their marriages. When had Mitch become this other person? And where did that leave Greg?

"You can say we're going golfing," Greg told him.

"Okay, I will." Mitchell clapped his hand on his shoulder.

THAT NIGHT in bed he rolled over and found Patty, her skin cool and moist from the shower. She smelled like a complicated medley of fruits and herbs from the various potions she rubbed on her skin before coming to bed. Her hair was wet. He wasn't looking at her face, but he knew it would be pale and luminous from the moon shining in their room.

"Kind of hot, isn't it?" she murmured, as he pushed her T-shirt up, feeling her familiar curves and hollows, as known to him as anything on earth. He didn't answer, but slipped her panties off and continued to travel the lines of her body with his hands. She played possum for a few minutes, waiting, he knew, to be persuaded. Finally she rolled toward him. When he closed his eyes he saw blue like the sky over the golf course, immense and dizzying. He shifted and pushed inside his wife; only then did he feel himself bound by gravity again.

This year his daughters asked to stay home from the family vacation because of their jobs. Kiley took the lead in the negotiations one night at dinner, her shoulders hunched slightly forward as she ticked off good reasons for not going: they would be leaving their employers in the lurch; they needed all their income to buy school clothes; and hadn't Dad himself stressed the importance of being dependable employees? Wasn't all that more important than a week's vacation? Kiley let her voice rise incredulously on the word "vacation," as if she, with her serious work ethic, disdained the very thought.

Melissa sat beside her sister at the kitchen table nodding every once in a while for emphasis, but letting Kiley do the talking. Greg was sure the plan had begun with Kiley anyway. It was Kiley who made it her job to test limits. When the girls were toddlers, Kiley had mastered a complex and athletic set of moves to vault out of her crib at will, while Melissa remained behind clutching at the rails in hers, calling *Mommadadda COME!* As a first-grader it had been Kiley who rode her bike without permission to the Dairy Queen—a journey requiring the crossing of two busy intersections. The transgression had come to light when Patty overheard Kiley taunting Melissa about her cowardice and boasting of the dip cone she had enjoyed; the episode resulted in the first of Kiley's many groundings. Greg wasn't sure why they had kept grounding Kiley all these years; the punishment seemed to faze her not at all. It was almost as if she gathered fresh energy from the imposed seclusion in her room, an eagerness for the next flight. Yet she hadn't been a defiant child. Rather there had been something sunny and uncontainable in the way she ignored rules, a birdlike tendency of hers to swerve past snares and soar into open, dissolving sky.

In this case, though, Kiley knew that a deal would have to be worked. Greg gave her credit for not simply declaring that the girls didn't *want* to go on vacation with their parents anymore. Instead she was cool and strategic, her rap delivered at a pace that left no opening for parental interjection until she had concluded.

"Well, we can't leave you home by yourselves," Greg said, twirling the last of his spaghetti around his fork with miscalculated force and spattering his white polo shirt with specks of red sauce. "And you know I can't take time off next month. August practices are in my contract." He didn't add that even if they weren't he wouldn't give them up. Coaching football was the highlight of his work at the high school. He much preferred the students' company when they were working with him outside the classroom to when they were being jerk-offs in his social studies classes.

"But you *can* leave us home, that's the whole point," Melissa said suddenly, untwining her fingers and spreading them before her, as if to show she concealed nothing. Because she had been silent up to now, she gained everyone's full attention. "Give us one good reason why you think we couldn't handle it," she demanded. She curled one fist on the tabletop, ready to bang it down and rule him out of order.

Greg could think of plenty, but to list them would be to make it sound as though he didn't trust them. It wasn't *them* he didn't trust, it was being fifteen going on sixteen. It was being let loose with too much freedom. He saw it all the time at school, kids running wild.

"Let your father and me talk about it," Patty said, surprising him.

He had assumed she'd feel as he did. But she rose to clear the dishes, officially curtailing discussion. The girls exchanged veiled triumphant looks.

"We'll *talk* about it. I'm still against the idea," Greg said peevishly. But the air in the kitchen had shifted. It no longer gathered around him and his opinion, but seemed to be circulating among the women.

Later in their bedroom, Patty folded laundry from the basket into their dresser. "They're fifteen, old enough to take care of themselves for a week," she said.

"Old enough to get into real trouble," he said. He flicked through the channels on the tube.

"But we trust them, don't we? Haven't we taught them rules?"

Greg snorted. "We had rules. We broke them."

Patty smiled. "Do you think they still call them keggers? It seems so different when we talk about us. Different times." She shut the drawer. "Then there's the fact that our parents were unreasonable, whereas we're so open and understanding." She sat beside him on the bed, watching the images fly by as he kept clicking.

"Open and understanding does not have to mean saying, 'Okay, girls, here's the house, here's the liquor cabinet, and here are the beds. Have an orgy. Just make sure the place is clean by the time we get home.' "

"You'd actually expect that from your own daughters?"

He pictured them: Kiley plugged into her earphones, smiling and shaking her head to show him she couldn't hear a word he was saying; riding her bike on "an errand" after supper that kept her away for an hour and a half. Melissa blowing on freshly painted nails as she pinned the phone to her cheek with one shoulder, glaring at him and clapping a hand over the mouthpiece if he happened to walk past.

"They're teenagers," he said. "They're powder kegs ready to blow."

"I forgot, you're the expert," she said. She snatched the remote away from him, used it to switch to the news, then put it down beside her on the nightstand.

"You're going about it all wrong," he said.

"Yeah?"

"Those things are meant to be held constantly ready for action. Here, you'd better let me take over." He patted her knee consolingly.

Patty kept the control out of his reach until he had to wrestle her for it—a cinch, of course, since she was a flyweight and he was a light-heavy. He could feel her using every particle of strength to try to unpin herself. He actually had to work a little to keep her held down, and felt himself getting aroused in the friction of their struggle. Patty felt it too, and narrowed her eyes.

"It really is a guy thing, that clicker, isn't it?"

"Don't call it a clicker. That's my gun." He heard a tread on the stairs and released her, both of them sitting up against the pillows but still breathing a little heavily when Kiley poked her head inside their door to say good night.

SINCE THE girls were staying home, they made reservations at the coast. The Oregon coast was not really Greg's idea of a good time; the water was too rough and cold to swim in, and even in July you were as likely to get rain as you were sun. He much preferred it when they drove to Santa Barbara, or Lake Tahoe, or flew to Vegas. But the coast was only a two-hour drive from Portland, which meant they could come home quickly if there was an emergency. They wanted to ask an adult to check up on the girls, and Patty suggested Sandy. Greg mumbled something about Sandy's probably being too busy and suggested Patty's mother.

Cass welcomed the plan as a way to see more of her granddaughters. And Greg was spared the thought of Mitchell having access to his house keys through Sandy, and the possibility of one of the girls coming home from work early to discover her father's friend screwing some strange woman on the couch in the family room—or make it on his and Patty's bed, as long as he was having this nightmare. That wouldn't happen now, since Cass had come through. He didn't even mention to Mitchell that he and Patty were spending a week away. Not that he had much opportunity. Only about one out of three of their golf dates now was real. Greg was suddenly leading a double life, thanks to Mitch Brown. He didn't actually tell Patty he was going golfing on the fake days, he was just careful not to say anything specific about his mornings at all, so details could be filled in later if Mitchell called upon him to corroborate a game. This busy non-golfing schedule left Greg with more dead time than ever throughout July, and he couldn't wait to get away.

LYING BY the pool at the Devil's Cove resort, he couldn't quit thinking about Mitchell's affair. They had known each other as long as they had each had children. The fact that their wives had been friends first, through a baby-sitting co-op, had long since washed away in the mutual history that Greg shared with Mitchell. It was one of those friendships easily sustained because it was part of a web: the guys hung out, the women lunched, the couples double-dated, and even their kids had enjoyed each other's company when they were small. Everybody meshed. True, Mitch could get on Greg's nerves. He was a little show-offy, a little too self-congratulatory about the success of his software consulting business. He'd make calls from the golf course on the cell phone. He sang loudly with the radio when you rode in a car with him, as if you were dying to hear his voice drown out the professionals. Whenever Mitch encountered waiters or janitors or checkout clerks he demanded their first name and called them by it, which no doubt to him seemed progressive and generous, but struck Greg as patronizing. On the other hand, there wasn't a favor the guy wouldn't do for you. A few years ago he had picked Greg up every day after school when Greg's foot was in a cast and he couldn't drive. Mitch had set up Greg's first computer and loaded it with programs. After a blizzard he would drive over with his snow blower.

But despite the hundreds of hours they had spent shooting the breeze, the two of them didn't spend a lot of time talking about intangibles. They talked mortgage rates, election results, car trade-ins, play-off scores, kid milestones—all things solid and quantifiable.

Marriage as a subject *per se* didn't much come up. Sure, together they joked about their wives: harmless little sallies that were as much about being guys together as they were evidence of mild and fleeting feelings of matrimonial rebellion. Mitch made the occasional sour remark about Sandy's extra pudge (a roundness Greg had always found sexy, that cushiony bottom in stretch pants which he had sometimes had a crazy desire to grab). Greg made fun of Patty's militarily precise routines, her tendency to try to take charge of him, but these criticisms were delivered without malice; he offered them mostly to keep his end up. The joking was a way to blow off steam; what mattered was how fundamentally loyal both were to their families. Greg thought he knew this. So he was stunned by his friend's casual, even offhand, transformation from family man to—what? Greg couldn't think of a word.

At the coast it took Greg and Patty a day or two to get used to the fact that the girls weren't going to come bursting through the door any minute to announce how bored they were, or to ask permission to disappear with some new friends they had made by the pool. At first there didn't seem to be enough mess, or enough noise. After it sank in that they were really and truly alone, they settled into an adult routine. They bought newspapers and read them over breakfast, they lay around baking inside the glass-screened pool area, they soaked in the whirlpool, lunched in robes on their deck, showered and dressed late in the afternoon, walked on the beach, and drove a half hour up or down the coast highway to find a new dinner spot every night. They drank a lot of wine, and somehow didn't wake up with headaches. They called the girls every night and nothing seemed to be different in their children's voices, no guilt or secrecy seeping through the phone wire, no sound of breaking glass or drunken shouts in the background. Cass said everything looked normal on her visits and that Greg and Patty should leave her to supervise her granddaughters more often. She had had the idea of bringing over a different dessert every night, and the three of them had sat out on the patio after dark gossiping and eating Sacher torte or angel food cake with fresh berries and sipping cordials.

"Cordials?" Greg asked.

"Oh, you know Daddy's weird collection. I'm sure it's just a thim-bleful of apricot brandy or crème de menthe or something."

"Your mother is bringing alcohol over?"

"*Greg.* She's *bonding* with them. It sounds as though they're hav-ing very ladylike, very adult little parties."

"Yeah, and then she's leaving two buzzed teenagers alone every night after her 'supervisory' visits." But he said it in a tone meant to show he thought it was all right. Cute even. Because Cass was a good grandmother. Much better than his own mother, who could never much be bothered to show an interest in the girls unless it was to extort some kind of servitude or fawning declaration of affection from them. They had wised up to iron-haired Grandma Goodman by about the age of five, and Greg had never tried to talk them out of their instinctive aversion to her. He thought it was healthy, in fact, how she couldn't get to them, how the distance of a generation made his girls immune to her plaintive manipulations.

Because they were both on vacation, Greg felt that things were equalized between him and Patty. She wasn't busier than he was, or pissed off because of it. Away from her own house, she could be still. She abandoned her list-making, she let the maid clean the room. With the little tucks of concentration and irritation gone from her forehead she looked smooth and young again, a woman untrou-bled by domesticity. From under his baseball cap Greg watched her as they lay stretched out on lounge chairs by the pool. A large hat shaded her face, and she wore black oval sunglasses. As she read her novel, she pursed her lips slightly. She was in shape: stomach flat from sit-ups, nice muscular legs. She was sitting with one knee drawn up so that the top of the thigh was defined and lean, the un-derside a jiggly little handful of flesh he would like to cup his palm under. Small breasts—no flesh rounding out above the bikini top, no shadow where a cleavage would be. Nursing had almost completely flattened them, never large to begin with. There had been that star-tling and almost freakishly huge swelling when the milk first came to her. The breasts had filled to the size of extra-large grapefruits and jutted out in front of her like a parody of a sex goddess—except that they were woodenly solid and she couldn't bear to have them touched. Engorgement, they called it.

Her mother had thought she was crazy for even trying to nurse twins. Greg had not offered an opinion; the whole birth and sudden doubling of his family had left him in a wordless daze. But the nursing thing had become a crusade to Patty. She had called on some league of milking experts that did nothing but give advice over the phone to weeping new mothers. The league had proposed remedies for her discomfort: he had found her on the second day wrapping her by then bowling-ball-sized tits in cabbage leaves; another time he came upon her bending forward to launch them like Japanese floats in a sink of steaming hot water. When the alien breasts had finally softened, and Greg felt an erotic stirring at the sight of his wife curled topless in an armchair, suckling their newborns, Patty shielded herself from him and turned away. "Can't you see that I'm bleeding?" she accused him after he had made a tentative overture. And she had been, right from the nipples, which were cracked and raw. The insistent little mouths never released her. He had watched her give in to it, their offspring's rhythmic, tugging need. He had watched her curve over their hungers patiently. If he had felt forgotten, he didn't think he had shown it.

Instead he had waited for the babies to consume less of her, waited for her to regain some patience for his touch. He couldn't remember now when it had come, if it was when the babies were finally weaned (for Patty had taken the milking leaguers seriously and had had her goals to reach: had it been eight months? Twelve? Fifteen?) or after. But he did remember how when he finally got her back, when the milk had gone completely from her, she was changed. She was a different woman in his hands. The breasts moved loosely up and down as he rubbed them, like empty packets sliding over a rib cage. And as he squeezed and rolled the nipples in his fingers she had seemed indifferent, exhausted by sensation.

The body stretched out before him now wasn't one he could be entirely objective about; he had shared in its history for more than twenty years. But it was a good body, although he had given up trying to convince Patty of that. Despite the fact that she managed it like an investment portfolio he knew that, deep down, she didn't like it.

She had let him talk her into buying the bikini she was wearing, a lime-green thing tied with strings they saw the first day in the resort shop when they were looking for T-shirts for the girls.

"That's for teenagers, Greg," she said as he held it up for her to see.

"Why? It would look great on you. When did you start thinking you had to wear those one-piece jobs? Those are for women who don't have your abs of steel," he said, goosing her at the waist.

He had been shaving in the bathroom when he caught sight of her putting it on the first time, tugging at the bottom in back.

"You'll need help with the sunscreen," he said, moving up behind her, running his hands up and down her back, around the front of her belly, up the soft part of her thigh that she was self-conscious about.

"I feel so naked," she said.

"Good idea," he said, pulling on a string. "Hey, what a concept. Like opening a present. I knew there was a reason I liked this bathing suit."

Greg thought by the time they wouldn't have to worry about children interrupting their lovemaking he would be too old to want to do anything. But here they were, not old yet, Patty not even past the point where she looked good in a bikini. This week Greg had been running every morning on the beach at low tide, shirtless. Now he was brown from the sun, his muscles ached pleasantly, and he buzzed from the sudden surplus of endorphins in his system. Midmorning sun streamed over them on the bed. Fucking in daylight on top of the covers. Even Patty seemed to be fully present for this, her eyes opening to see him, then closing again, a little hint of smile on her face, her fingers kneading the back of his shoulders. He had a sudden flash of what things used to be like, her old eagerness for him that through the years had paled, like a rug gradually and invisibly bleached of its vividness. Then when you shifted something, a heavy piece of furniture, the glowing patch of color underneath showed you how much had been lost without your even noticing.

AT HOME Patty was grouchy shaking sand out of their dirty clothes, even though Greg said he'd do the laundry in the morning. But Patty couldn't stand going to bed without a load started. She was grouchy examining her skin in the mirror, declaring that the sun had given her estrogen spots from her birth control pills. She was grouchy because when she turned on her laptop at home her calendar played a few notes of Mozart and flashed the urgent message that she had a meeting at eight-thirty the next morning, and did she want to save or cancel this alarm? Greg saw her cancel it with the stab of a finger.

Greg himself was annoyed because Kiley was nowhere to be found when they pulled in at six o'clock, as planned, and Melissa feigned ignorance as to her sister's whereabouts.

"Get real," he told her. "Since when do you two not know exactly where the other is at any given minute of the day?"

"I don't, Dad. Why are you on my case when it's Kiley that's not here?" Melissa sniffed at the injustice. The twins were forever expecting perfect parity when it came to gifts and privileges, and perfect autonomy when it came to accountability. But in any disciplinary matter, they were a seamless monolith; they had never ratted each other out, and never would.

When Kiley coasted her bike into the driveway at eight-thirty, Greg was ready to meet her at the kitchen door.

"Hey, Ky. Where were you?"

"At a friend's house. Did you guys have a good time?" She opened the door to the refrigerator. A year earlier, she would have flung herself at him in a hug after a week's separation. He suddenly noticed how rangy she was, how her forehead was almost even with the top of the freezer.

"Yeah, we did. Which friend?"

"I don't think you know them."

" 'Them' is several friends—were you with several friends?"

"No, a friend. Why are you grilling me? It's only just after eight."

The girls were experts at changing the line of questioning by filing a grievance in the middle of a conversation. He knew it, and would not be swayed.

"It's a simple question, Kiley, and I'd like you to answer it. I'm your father and I would like to know who you spend time with."

"I *told* you. You don't know him."

"Ah, now we're making progress. A him. If I don't know him, you could start by telling me his name, where he lives, the nature of your friendship, and whether his parents were home. Later we could progress to the niceties of his character and hobbies." He was trying to sound humorous, and could tell by the expression on her face that he had failed.

"Dad, why do you always talk to me like I'm some kind of baby?" she said. Outraged tears sprang to her eyes, and she slammed the refrigerator door (finally—he'd been thinking about the electric bill the whole time she was staring into it), making all the condiment jars clank violently against each other.

"What's going on?" Patty asked, coming into the kitchen carrying the cooler. Greg told her he'd wash it out tomorrow, but she was bound and determined to do it tonight.

"Dad's picking on me again," Kiley said tearfully.

"Have you eaten?" her mother asked her. Greg was amazed. Talk about going over to the enemy.

"I ate at Will's house. I just wanted to pour myself some soda, and Dad started giving me the third degree."

"Who's Will?" he asked.

"I'm sure your father was just—"

"Who's Will?" he asked again.

"I *told* you. You never listen to me!"

"I listen!" His voice rose. "I was listening for a goddamn name, which you wouldn't give me!"

"Will!" She screamed it, contorting her face, the face that Greg loved to watch when she didn't know he was watching, it's astonishing perfection. At times he glimpsed her lost in thought, already so deeply into her own life that he wanted to rouse her from there, find a way to interrupt.

"Are you satisfied? That's his goddamn name!"

"Kiley!" Patty said.

"Oh fine, Daddy can swear all he wants at me and it doesn't even matter. I'm just supposed to take it. Why didn't you two just stay on vacation? Melissa and I had such a peaceful time while you were gone."

Greg started to answer, but Patty silenced him with a look. "Your father will apologize to you for swearing, and you will apologize to him for your tone."

Greg was steaming. Patty always did this slippery mother thing that tried to put her on the side of everybody and ended up putting her in charge. He banged out the kitchen door and went to scrape down the grill. Over his shoulder he heard his daughter whine, "See, Mom? He'd die before he would say he's sorry to me. He's so unfair."

Savagely he worked the wire brush over the charred remains of a month's worth of dinners. Kiley had fixed it so she ended up a victim of his brutality in Patty's eyes—now Patty would add to her bad mood by acting self-righteous and morally superior about how he handled their daughters. And no one had given him a straight answer about this Will. Apparently *Patty* had been told about Will. But she didn't see fit to mention to him that their daughter had a new boyfriend. That would be the line he would take with Patty, if she dared reproach him. A little righteous indignation of his own.

But Patty didn't have anything to say to him when he came upstairs to bed. It was one of the maddening things about her, the way she would hug a complaint to herself without voicing it, making you pry it from her, which of course he had no intention of doing. They were in bed, backs to each other, when one of their daughters stuck her head in the door and said, "Night, Mom. Dad."

He thought it was Kiley for a second and felt himself soften, words of apology and conciliation coming to him, then saw that it was

Melissa's slightly rounder face. From the beginning he had had no
trouble telling them apart, even before they began developing dis-
tinguishing quirks of dress and hairstyle. Kiley had always been the
struggler, weighed two ounces less at birth, came out last, facing
wrong. She was the more serious twin, her gaze more nervous, her
questions as a child darker and more persistent: *Will we all die at the
same time? If you die first, how will I find you?* Kiley fell into funks
and moods; many of these seemed to have no basis to him. By contrast, Melissa was sturdy and hearty and—making allowances for
adolescence—pretty nearly always in a good mood. Her evenness at
times puzzled Greg; was there something behind it they should be
looking for? It was easy to take a good girl for granted and be grateful for her cooperation while you handled the kid who was acting up.
But he had noticed lately that Kiley had pulled way ahead of Melissa
in the confidence department. Melissa seemed content to let her sister lead, to let her take up more space in the room somehow.

Both girls were beautiful, much more physically ideal than either
of their parents. Greg was good-looking enough, in a normal guy
way, with brownish hair and grayish eyes. Patty was very pretty, but
you wouldn't call her absolutely stunning. She was thin and small-
boned and cut her brown hair in a style that hung straight in a line
with her jaw and flattered her. But Greg was so clearly ordinary, and
Patty so plainly no-nonsense, that you couldn't help wondering where
the twins got this ethereal blondness, this milky skin and corn-yellow
hair. As children they always wanted to be princesses for Halloween,
and Greg couldn't blame them. He, too, would have hated to see
them become something other than themselves, something garish or
strange. They had worn their beauty innocently then, and Greg
feared what being grown-up would do to it, and what it would do to
them. Particularly he feared adolescent boys, and then men, feared
the words they would use to describe the girls' beauty back to them
to ensnare them. He knew how the spell worked, had used it himself
on Patty in high school, so that she seemed to hunger after a while
for Greg to tell her what she looked like, as if only he could unlock

her reflection for her. She had grown out of that, but Patty had always had her store of common sense to fall back on; the twins seemed more vulnerable. Maybe it was because of being twinned, of never, even for an instant, being forced to be only, merely, yourself, and having to make that do.

He had delighted in their beauty when they were small and completely his, two little princesses completing his kingdom. Now he saw it as a dangerous wild card. It was only in the last year that he had realized how little he could protect them, how mercurial their entrances and exits were on purpose becoming, to evade his watchfulness.

Tonight he went to sleep dissatisfied. Dissatisfied with Patty, certainly. Dissatisfied with Kiley's attitude, to be sure. But there was more to it than that, something out of joint he couldn't put his finger on, though maybe it was just the hot, still air of the suburbs they had returned to. Patty dropped off immediately, using her time to sleep as efficiently as she used her time to be awake. Greg felt stifled, even by the one thin sheet that lay over him, and he missed the sound of the ocean they had heard from their open balcony door at night. He wrestled with the heat for half an hour, then gave up. On his way downstairs to the TV he caught sight of himself in a mirror, his white T-shirt and jockey shorts moving through the dark like a ghost.

reg was sleeping in when the phone rang. He had awakened briefly when Patty was getting ready for work and had heard female voices murmuring at the breakfast table downstairs. Usually the sound reassured him, the way the presence of water running in a stream was somehow comforting. This morning it made him feel as if he were far outside the heart of the household, the women in it forever trading information they did not offer him. He had pulled the pillow over his head and gone back to sleep.

When he picked up the phone, his voice had a telltale thickness—obvious that these were his first words of the day.

"You're asleep." Mitch's words were an accusation.

"Yeah. Stayed up to watch a movie. What's up?"

"You could have told me you were going away. You really messed me up, you know that?"

"What are you talking about?"

"With Sandy. I told her we had a golf date last week, and she told me you were on vacation."

"Look, Mitch. When I said you could use me for your cover story, I didn't commit to tell you my whereabouts every minute of my life."

"You could have thought it through."

"*You* could have thought it through. Why didn't you check with me first?"

"I tried to call you, but you weren't home."

"There you go. I wasn't home. You should have left it at that."

"Sandy accused me of lying to her."

"Uh-huh."

"I managed to smooth it over. I told her I must have messed up my dates and that it was for the week after, when you got back. So I'm calling to make sure you'll go along with it."

"You came that close to being caught with your pants down and you're still screwing around?"

"I told you, I fixed it with Sandy. Are you with me or not?"

"Last time."

"Fine, fine. I told her we're golfing tomorrow at ten."

"You're getting involved with this woman."

"No way. It's a fling, that's all."

"Then end it."

"Why? It's not doing anyone any harm."

"What's she like, anyway?"

"She's fun. She's probably a lot more fun with me than she is at home when she's being somebody's wife. The point is, she's not my wife."

"That's the point?"

"Yeah. We both feel different when we're together. It's like going back twenty years and being a teenager again."

"Being a teenager is not so hot."

"The sex is. Don't tell me you've forgotten. Don't you ever wish you could go back to when you never knew if you were going to get any, and so when you did, it was fantastic, every time? That's what it's like."

TEN MINUTES after taking a shower and putting on clean clothes, Greg felt sweaty again. Last night the air had never cooled off, not even ten degrees, and this morning the sky was a uniform bright haze. He would have welcomed a chance to trade places with Patty and be too busy all day in an air-conditioned office. The atmosphere mirrored his inner sense of oppression. Why did summer always do this to him? Why couldn't he take a little bit of freedom and enjoy it like everyone else? Instead he felt like an old screw rattling around in a drawer, one nobody knew what to do with, whose very existence grew to be an annoyance because it lacked definite purpose. Greg decided to drive to the high school and check on the equipment and the practice field.

The building was almost cool, its dark air having been sealed up since June. Only when the halls were deserted like this did the school remind him that he used to be a student here. The locker at the very end of the main hall, just by the entrance to the cafeteria, had been his own senior year; it was prime real estate, and he always had a knot of friends circled around it before and after lunch. Having a locker open to lean against gave you the illusion that you were hanging out in your own territory, an island of selfhood you preserved against the hall monitors and rules. He had been comfortable at school; he was actually glad to come every day, get out of his house with its stale smell of hopelessness. Growing up, it had taken Greg awhile to realize that his father was the wrong one—not the bosses his father complained about, or the neighbors with whom he feuded, or the big, anonymous "they" that he invoked for grievances whose cause he couldn't immediately trace. As a kid, Greg took in his father's bitterness with his morning Cheerios; he assumed that the Goodmans had been somehow marked out for rotten breaks and ill treatment. By junior high and high school he had seen more of the world, hung out with friends whose dads came home cracking jokes and ready to shoot baskets on the driveway as soon as they changed clothes. He had been in kitchens where you could accidentally knock over a glass of milk and nobody exploded, the sky didn't fall, it wasn't the biggest goddamn deal in the world. In those kitchens, if you had been clumsy somebody would hand you a bunch of paper towels and refill your glass.

By high school, Greg hungered for the normalcy of the world outside his family life, and it was with relief that he would come every morning through the double green doors to the row of khaki-painted lockers. As he leaned there exchanging bullshit with his friends, the pressure of the cool metal against his shoulder blades was like touching ground.

Then, too, there was Patty to see every morning at school, Patty, who made the tiled halls and cafeteria feel more like his own home than the house he lived in with his parents. He and Patty had gone together from April of tenth grade. Thus they spared themselves the endless flux and insecurity of wondering who liked them, and with whom they would be going to the next dance or game. Patty always knew he'd be sending her a homecoming mum or valentine rose when the pep committee took orders in the cafeteria. She never needed to sweat it out, like other girls, when the door opened in the middle of algebra and the student making the flower deliveries scanned his list. For his part, Greg didn't have to agonize weeks before getting the nerve to ask someone new out, and he didn't have to be checked out by different sets of parents all the time. Cass and Walter had liked him from the start, and he was so grateful to be approved of that he felt himself slip into an exaggerated version of the Dependable Young Man whenever he was in conversation with them.

But despite the image he had projected to her parents, Greg had worked hard on getting Patty to give in and have sex with him. They had had months of passionate necking, and then months more of serious fooling around, and then she finally said yes, after they had agreed to get married two years after high school, when they were twenty. He was the only guy Patty had ever been with. She would have been the only girl he had had sex with, too, except for a two-month breakup they had had in college. Greg couldn't remember now who started the fight, but he guessed he must have, because one part of him had surely wanted what had happened to happen. He lost no time in finding someone new to date, and to fuck. In fact, there was time to go to bed with two different girls before the inevitable course of his life put him back together with Patty and they resumed their engagement. Patty was the one he had really wanted to be with. Those other girls had seemed all wrong to him—scented differently, their laughs pitched at a strange timbre. But he had been greedy to have those new bodies. He couldn't recall if the sex had been good or not; probably it hadn't really mattered to him beyond the moment of possession.

GREG OPENED the door to the equipment room with his own key. Everything was in order, the footballs hanging in a net bag, the shoulder pads and helmets neatly lined up on the shelf, gold-and-blue Cougars uniforms laundered and ready to be assigned. There was a battered gray metal desk where parent permission slips were stored, and excuse forms for when the boys had to leave school early for an away game. A blackboard, ghosted with the x's and o's of some play from last season, stood ready to be wheeled into the locker room for a play briefing. Someone had circled August 5 on the calendar with a red marker; probably Drew. He was bound to be as anxious as Greg for daily doubles to begin, although he had summer football camps and coaching workshops to keep him busy until then.

Greg was head coach of the JV team, which didn't start practicing by itself until the week before school started, but all the coaches and prospective players turned out for daily doubles in August. During the season he liked having charge of his own team rather than being an underling to Drew Davis, the varsity head coach, who was also the boys' PE teacher. Greg got a small extra stipend for the coaching, but he would have done it for free. On the football field the guys dropped their wise-ass attitudes and their faces took on a purity and hopefulness he loved to see. Even the ones without talent responded to the camaraderie on the field, and said the word "Coach" with the kind of respect that they probably didn't show when addressing their own fathers. When he called them over to discuss a play or give them a pep talk, he always made it a point to make eye contact with each one. It was the least they deserved for all their sweat during practice, and for the way they crouched down to listen to him, taking off their helmets and wiping their faces, then looking at him as if he had all the answers, as if what he was about to tell them was what they most needed to know in order to go forward in life.

It was so hot that Patty had given up on her lotions at night; she said they made her too sticky. Tonight she slept in an undershirt with thin little straps, and a pair of his boxer shorts, ridiculously baggy. She lay on the floor doing sit-ups directly under the fan. When she was through she stayed where she was, looking up at its turning blades.

"Do you think anything's wrong with Mitch?" she asked. "Has he said anything to you?"

Greg's finger froze on the remote. "Like what?" he asked.

"Sandy's been worried about him. She thinks he's got something on his mind."

"Maybe work."

"Could be. She says he's not himself. Not really *there* when he's there."

"Hmm." Greg spun through a few channels, his breathing careful.

"I just thought he might have told you if something was wrong," she said.

"He hasn't mentioned anything being wrong." This was completely true. But he was conscious of how the secret divided them, had put Greg on Mitchell's side somehow against Patty, and not just

Sandy. He wasn't sure why this should be so; Patty was in no way involved, and therefore his responsibility was not to her. He had not set
out to deceive her in any way, and in fact most of his untruths, if you
could call them that, were sins of omission. But he had become nim-
ble with the truth. He scrambled around the little mountain of facts
Patty did not know about Mitchell and told himself that being a loyal
friend was a separate matter from being a good husband.

Patty turned out the light and climbed into bed beside him. She
folded the sheet down so it was around their ankles. Greg flicked off
the TV, leaving only the sound of the whirring fan overhead. Usually
they curled up together to sleep, but for weeks it had been too muggy
to touch each other.

"What's going on with Kiley and this Will?" he asked her.

"Don't know," Patty murmured. She was already drifting off. Greg
didn't know how she did it; she never seemed to lie there sifting
through the scenes of her day, or previewing the next one, as he did.
His wife rolled away from him, her breaths deepening. Then she was
gone.

THE NEXT morning Greg was the first one out of the shower. The
coaches had a seven-o'clock breakfast meeting at the IHOP. By
eight, they were on the field, lining the boys up for stretches and cal-
isthenics in the shade of the bleachers. By nine-fifteen, Greg's fresh
white coaching shirt was soaked from demonstrating running drills.
The season had begun.

After they had the kids dripping and exhausted from a three-hour
practice, Drew gave them his customary opening pep talk. Greg let
the words flow over him; he didn't have to listen to any sentence in
particular to respond with excitement. The worn nature of the
phrases was actually the point of these talks—*giving their all, setting
the bar high, going the extra mile.* Like mantras the words would be
repeated hundreds of times during the season, making their en-
deavors on the field seem large and timeless, linking them to the notion of great champions and great contests.

They broke for midday, and Greg went home to drink a quart of orange juice and to shower. By two-thirty, they were out on the field again, practicing fundamentals in small groups, running some basic plays. Drew stood observing a group of defensive backs tackling the dummies; he was drinking from a can of soda, looking crisp. He was one of those coaches who wore a tie and sweater on game days, never a sweat suit.

"We're in good shape this year, Goodman. Lotta talent out there."

"Looks that way. You've got your quarterback for sure," Greg said.

"Yeah, Malone's come along. What an arm that kid's got." They watched Jeff Malone throw a perfect forty-yard pass, the nose of the ball turning in tiny, elegant spirals. As a sophomore, Jeff had been Greg's quarterback on JV. Back then he had been a spindly boy with a voice that hadn't finished changing. He had always had accuracy and speed, but now he had the power that came with his new body, three inches taller and thirty pounds heavier.

They were putting away the equipment, Greg bringing up the rear with a stack of plastic cones they had used for running drills. A kid Greg didn't know who had been sitting alone on the bleachers approached him. He was wearing jeans, although it was much too hot for them, and a U of O T-shirt.

"Coach?"

"Yep." Greg was having trouble hanging on to the cones. Carrying them in one stack was too high, and two was too awkward. "Here, how about a hand with these?" The boy accepted a stack of cones and fell into step beside him.

"What can I do for you?"

"I want to come out for the team."

"Great," Greg said. He sized him up. "You a sophomore?"

The kid nodded.

"Why aren't you dressing down?"

"My dad won't sign the permission form."

"Gotta have the form," Greg said. He was picturing the cold beer he would have when he got home.

The kid said nothing. Greg glanced at his face and saw that it had that bright, mottled look of a boy fighting tears.

"Why won't he sign?"

"He's mad at me."

"What'd you do?" Greg asked.

"Nothing. He's always mad. That's the way he is."

"What position do you like to play?"

The boy was stringy and lean and had a stubborn jaw. "I'm fast," he said. "Real fast."

"Well, you can't practice without the permission form. We could get sued. What about your mom?"

"She's gone."

Greg didn't know if this meant dead, on vacation, or if she had just picked up and left. Didn't matter. She couldn't sign the form. He reflected briefly that the kid could have forged his dad's signature, but hadn't. They walked along in silence, then they reached the side door of the gym.

"Do you want me to call him?" Greg finally asked.

The boy nodded. Again the choked look.

"Come inside and give me your number."

GREG HUNG up the phone and ran his hand through his hair. The gym office had the odor of burned toast, the way the towels came back smelling from the laundry.

"You're right, he won't sign. What's his problem?"

"He lost his job, he's not looking for a new one, and he spends all his time picking on me."

"What can you do to get on his good side?"

The boy—Tim was his name, Timothy Phelps—shrugged with a sullen look.

"Look, Tim, I'd rather be home right now in my backyard. If you want my help you've got to work with me."

The kid looked at him helplessly. "But I *don't know.* He's unpredictable, you know?"

Greg knew. His dad had been exactly that way: unpredictable, prone to sudden fits of temper that slammed against you from out of nowhere, so that you had to walk around your own house with a poker face, just in case he wasn't in the mood to see anyone smile that day. Greg tried to imagine what would have softened his father.

"Okay, Tim. Here's what you do. Starting now you're a real Boy Scout around the house—mow the yard, help clean up without being asked, take out the garbage. You with me so far?"

Tim nodded doubtfully.

"Will he notice that kind of stuff?"

"He'll notice. He won't say much, but he'll notice. I could do the laundry. Neither of us has any clean clothes."

"Then do the laundry. And get a haircut. You can't practice with that mop in your eyes." Tim's face got a trapped look.

"Money a problem?"

Tim nodded, studying the poster on the wall that had little drawings of a man and a woman doing warm-up stretches. The artist had given them blank, cheerful expressions.

"What will you do about equipment fees?"

"I thought maybe I could pay it off a little at a time."

Greg sighed. This kid was going to mean a lot of extra headaches for him.

"Look, I need someone to help me do some yard work at my house. I could cover your equipment fees and you could work it off. You interested?"

Tim nodded.

"Okay. And in between all your good deeds at home I want you to come watch the varsity practice. You can learn a lot that way, make up for not being on a freshman team." Greg fished in his pocket for a twenty. "Here's an advance on your pay. Use it to get a haircut, nice and short."

"Okay, Coach." Tim's voice sounded happy, the way a kid's should sound.

By the end of the week, Mr. Phelps had still not signed. Tim showed up for at least one practice a day, watching hungrily from the bleachers. He wore a clean pair of loose gym shorts and a T-shirt and had gotten himself a buzz cut at the barbershop. He said he was running four miles every morning and doing a lot of work around his house. Greg put him to work a couple of evenings mowing and cleaning up his own yard, and could see the boy's lean muscles flex with every movement; there wasn't an extra gram of flesh on Timothy Phelps, but what he had was hard.

"Let me give you a hand with that," Greg offered when he saw the boy staggering down the driveway with a metal can of grass clippings gripped in a bear hug. Tim's zeal had left Greg no chores to do when he came home at night, and he felt self-consciously clean and idle.

Tim shook his head without speaking, a greenish dust from mowing streaked across his face. He plonked the can down and spent a moment straightening it.

"What else should I do, Coach?"

Greg spread his hands. "You've done it. My wife says you're the hardest worker she's ever seen." It was true that Patty seemed to have developed a little crush on Tim. She heaped praise on his work to his face and fretted privately to Greg that he was undernourished.

Tim blushed and looked around the yard. "I haven't finished the mulch yet. Mrs. Goodman told me she thought she needed more mulch in the back."

Greg recognized the tone. It had been exactly his own high-pitched eagerness as a kid to please adults. He wanted to take Tim aside, tell him not to work so hard at it. "Look, I know what's eating you," he wanted to say. "Things are rough at home; something's not right there. Too bad. Learn to shrug it off." Because if the kid came off too needy, people were going to back away from him.

"Next week," Greg said. "I'll buy more over the weekend. I'll get you and my wife a stack of mulch bags as high as the house. How's that?"

Tim nodded, either too shy or too tense to smile in response to Greg's teasing. But something in his thin shoulders relaxed; he seemed relieved to hear that he would be coming back.

"Let me give you a ride home, and I'll try your father again."

Greg talked football trivia as they drove. He was afraid of silence with Tim, of sitting quietly with a boy so uncomfortable in his skin, of what he would remember about feeling fifteen: the knee whose unconscious bobbing up and down you couldn't control; the lip you chewed until you had a little raw patch to nervously keep tasting with the tip of your tongue. How the only cure for such an excess of self-consciousness was movement, finding some action like throwing a ball you could do over and over again—all under the guise of practicing. After exhausting the feeling, ridding yourself of the static along your limbs and in your head, you could fling yourself down to earth and rest there, holding on, almost feeling it turn beneath you.

At the Phelps house the boy disappeared into the shadows of his backyard and told Greg to ring the bell. Tim and his father lived in a small, vinyl-clad ranch. It was a lot like the kind of house Greg had grown up in, and nothing like the split-level he and Patty had been able to afford because of their two salaries and the gift of a down payment from her parents. Even when Greg was a child he had been conscious of the difference between the streets with the identical postwar ranches like his own and the ones with the newer split-levels and two-stories. When he had bicycled onto a two-story street he had felt he was crossing over into a more authentic version of American life: RVs or boats out front, snowmobiles in the garages, ski racks on the roofs of the cars. Even the Christmas trees got decorated differently in the two-story neighborhood—with white artificial snow flocking the branches, and Christmas balls and lights all the same color, usually an icy blue. Though he had actually preferred the Christmas tree the way they did it at his house—green branches laden with lots of tinsel and decked out with a colorful riot of balls that his mother picked up at Kmart—he had suspected that the cool blue-and-white approach went along with a superior vantage point in life.

Tim's house looked as if it had never seen a Christmas tree; there was an air of desertion about the place. A waist-high chain-link fence enclosed the lot. A couple of shrubs partially obscured either side of the front door, but no other plants or trees grew. What had once been a flower bed in front of the picture window was now a rectangular patch of gravel. The curtains were drawn and dipped in the middle, where a hook had jumped the curtain rod. A newish black pickup was parked in the driveway.

Tim's father was around his own age, but soft-looking. He didn't look as if he had the physical grace that came from having been an athlete in his youth, and he certainly wasn't one now. His gut bulged against his undershirt over the belt of his khaki work pants, and he had a delta of broken capillaries on his nose. Greg could see a resemblance between father and son, but it was as if someone had soaked the father underwater until he grew bloated and fuzzy, whereas the son was all keen edges. Phelps stared at Greg, waiting for him to speak. His face looked sullen and closed.

"Mr. Phelps, I'm Greg Goodman, one of the coaches at the high school. I called you earlier this week about allowing Tim to play football."

"And I said no."

"I was hoping you might change your mind. Tim is very anxious to play on the team, and I think it would be good for him."

"What do you know about what would be good for my boy?" Phelps demanded. He shifted forward until he filled the gap in the doorway completely. Greg was conscious of disliking him already—his soft, amorphous body, the expressionless eyes, the sarcastic twist at the mouth as though he already knew what you were going to say.

"I just think in general it's good for boys to play a sport. It's a good discipline for them. They gain confidence."

"And you think Tim needs confidence," Phelps said. Greg thought he heard the same mocking tone his father had used to belittle his ideas. Well, he would give this asshole exactly one more minute of his time. After that, Tim would be on his own with him.

"I think most adolescent boys can use it. I don't know Tim that well yet. He seems like a real good kid."

"He's not a bad kid," Phelps conceded unexpectedly, still locking his flat eyes on Greg.

"I thought maybe I could answer some questions for you about the football program, hear your reasons for not wanting Tim to play."

Phelps sagged a little, as if his belligerence were too wearying a posture to maintain. He opened the door a few inches wider.

"You want a beer?" he asked.

"Sounds good."

Inside the house a small tabletop fan whirred ineffectually. The lights were out, and a muted large-screen TV flashed images of mud slides somewhere. Except for some photographs on an end table, the living room was entirely without decoration. It was as if Tim and his father had moved in last week and had only managed to unpack the big stuff. Somewhere in boxes must be the prints for the wall, the vases, the coasters, the candy dish the kid had to have made in elementary school. As Phelps went to the kitchen to get the beer, Greg perched on the scratchy plaid sofa, watching as a filmed aerial view showed Monopoly-sized houses sliding off embankments and then breaking up into matchstick pieces of wood.

In the Phelps backyard there was the sound of a tinny lawn mower engine starting up.

Phelps came back carrying two sweating cans of Miller. He handed one to Greg and allowed himself to smile briefly. "You responsible for that?" he asked, lifting his chin in the direction of the mower.

"I told Tim it might be helpful to stay on your good side."

"My good side." Phelps sat down heavily and stared at the TV. Greg waited for him to speak. He scanned the row of photographs. In one, a female pair of arms encircled an infant Tim, but that was all. No body, no face, no mother. The pictures seemed to suggest that Tim had sprung into the world all by himself; they were close-ups of the baby's round face and of the toddler grinning and reaching for the camera. No family shots, not even one of Phelps holding his son. The picture frames were interesting, though. One had buttons glued all over it, another seemed to be a collage of varnished petals. They looked homemade. They didn't look like Phelps's handiwork.

"Money's a problem," Phelps finally said. "There's a hundred-and-twenty-dollar fee to play football, and I've been out of work for three months."

"Tim mentioned that he was going to have a hard time coming up with the fee. We could let him pay it as he goes, and he said he was going to do yard work around the neighborhood to earn the money." He had to be careful about this part. In fact, the school bureaucracy demanded the check up front, and Greg was prepared to write it. But he couldn't appear to be offering a handout to this guy. "Was that your main concern?"

"Oh, I don't know. Mainly, I guess." Phelps sounded vague, still watching the soundless TV. The graphic for the health feature flashed across the screen, followed by a picture of a headless woman draped in a sheet receiving a mammogram. They cut to a shot of another draped headless woman, this one reclining, her pale legs hoisted in stainless-steel stirrups. Greg felt the slight aversion he always experienced to anything gynecological. He glanced at Phelps, but the man seemed not even to be seeing what he was staring at. Greg took a swallow of his beer.

"I got hurt playing football once," Phelps suddenly offered, crinkling his beer can slightly. "Tim's not that big a kid."

This surprised Greg. Usually the mothers worried about safety, not the fathers. But here there seemed to be no mother to do the worrying, so maybe Tim's dad thought he had to do it himself. Or maybe being alone threw the worry into sharper relief.

"It's a lot harder to get hurt wearing this high-tech equipment we've got now. Every year we see a sprain or a pulled tendon, and once in a while some kid gets a dislocated shoulder. That's about it. I think the risks are about the same as with any sport."

"Broke my collarbone."

"Yeah. It can still happen. We're pretty safety-conscious."

Phelps reflected on this, working his jaw muscle around the problem.

"He must really want to play. That kid's been polishing and cleaning anything standing around here." His father shook his head. "I shouldn't be such a hard-ass, I guess. Sometimes I just focus too much on my own problems, you know?"

"I hear you."

"Tim could maybe use the company—the team involvement and all that."

Greg was beginning to think the guy wasn't a complete jerk. His mouth, released from its sneer, had a crooked ruefulness.

"You said you played? What position?"

"Lineman. You know, grunt work. Nothing flashy. After I took the knock, my mother put an end to it."

Greg let a little silence fall, to give Phelps the opportunity to mention Tim's mother. No mention came.

"You got the form?" Phelps asked. Perhaps he, too, felt the sudden absence in the room, a stirring of something beyond the reach of the small plastic fan.

"I think Tim's been carrying it around in his back pocket all week. I'm glad you changed your mind." Greg stood up to shake hands.

As he opened his car door, Tim's face, its angles blurred by the dusk, appeared at the side of the house. Greg flashed him a discreet thumbs-up, and the boy raised a fist in jubilation before disappearing again into the backyard. Greg thought he knew the scenes that would follow: the father gruffly offering to sign the permission slip, Tim instantly providing the pen and creased form. They wouldn't say anything more about it. There would be no dinner conversations about practice, or the position Tim would be given to play. Phelps wouldn't show up at the games. All of these blanks, these non-things and non-words, would register in Tim's consciousness first as a series of tiny dullnesses, then later as a familiar heaviness. Then at times, when Tim least expected it, the heaviness would melt into flashes of rage, a swelling and solidifying of his body that gave him momentary strength, albeit the kind of strength that wanted to destroy something. If he was lucky, these moments would come to him on the playing field. If he was smart, he would train himself to summon them there.

But tonight he would be simply happy. He would be folding and refolding the permission slip; putting it first into his pocket and then into his notebook, and finally just keeping it beside him on the nightstand so it would be the first thing he saw when he opened his eyes.

GREG DROVE home feeling as if it were he who had gotten permission to do what he most desired in the whole world, and not Tim. He was all set to regale Patty with his piece of successful diplomacy, bask a little in her approval.

He walked in to find her pounding on the bathroom door, and heard the tearful shouting of the twin who had barricaded herself behind it. He couldn't immediately tell from the muffled, hysterical voice which child was locked inside. Then he saw Kiley's bedroom door yawning wide and Melissa's shut.

"What's going on?" he asked.

"Ask your daughter that," Patty said, her face shiny with perspiration and anger. She waved something pink in his face.

"Kiley?" His voice was gentle, fatherly, kind. He was trying to prolong this moment of being the composed parent, the one his daughter would have to turn to since Patty was over the edge.

"Leave me alone!" she screamed from behind the door.

"Patty, what's this about?" he said. "What's in your hand?"

"What's in my hand?" Patty looked like a madwoman, her hair hanging in sweaty strings, her face contorted. "Your daughter's birth control pills are in my hand!"

Greg's gut turned inside out. His first impulse was to go back down the stairs and get in his car and drive away. Maybe back to Phelps's house, where they would drink beer together in silence and stare at the muted TV.

He wouldn't think about what Patty had just said. He slid the words into some compartment of his brain and snapped on a lid, as if they were now neatly sealed in a container from Patty's Tupperware collection. He found it easier at the moment to concentrate on his wife, try to settle her down. After all, the main problem, to anyone just happening on the scene, would seem to be this screaming woman. His daughters were the same as they had always been, prone to little teenage snits, but basically wonderful girls, trustworthy girls.

"Patty, calm down."

"Oh, great! That's a great response!" she screamed, flinging the pink plastic case down on the floor and stomping off into their bedroom, where she slammed the door.

Greg was stuck. He couldn't leave the scene and go down into the kitchen without sending a message of indifference to Kiley, the last thing he wanted to do. He couldn't go into his own bedroom to think because Patty was in there, and Patty was dangerous right now. Melissa was obviously staying firmly out of the way behind her own door. He couldn't go into Kiley's empty bedroom. Especially now, it seemed to emit a kind of force field repelling him, not just because he was a parent, but because he was the male parent. He was stuck in the weird crossroads of this upstairs hallway, with the little pink case seeming to glow there on the carpet.

He knocked softly on the bathroom door. "Kiley? Why don't you come out, honey?"

He heard sniffling behind the door. He had never been able to stand hearing his daughters cry, even when he suspected they were doing it to manipulate him. It was a sound that produced a crushing sensation in his chest.

The door opened and Kiley emerged into the hall light, her face puffy and streaked. She stalked by him majestically, not deigning to look down at the pill case on the floor. Her bedroom door shut and locked behind her with a click that resonated injustice, that announced she had been violated, and was asserting her right to absolute silence and absolute privacy, beginning now.

This freed Greg from his fixed position in the hall. After all, he had moved things forward; Kiley was no longer locked in the bathroom. She was now locked in her bedroom, which seemed more acceptable somehow.

He gave the pink box a wide berth and went inside his bedroom to find Patty stretched out on her back on the bed, staring at the ceiling fan, which wasn't turned on. He flipped the switch for it and joined her on the bed. They didn't touch.

"You okay?" he finally asked.

"I am not the issue here," she said flatly.

"I know that."

"Then why did you make me the issue?"

"Patty, I just said to calm down. You weren't going to get anywhere by screaming like that."

"You're still doing it. Did you even hear what I said? Our fifteen-year-old daughter is taking birth control pills. I'm not supposed to be upset about that?"

"Of course you are. So am I."

"Finally," she said. "A little acknowledgment from her father that we have a major problem."

"Patty, what do you want from me? I just walked in the damn door! It hasn't even sunk in yet!" He didn't want it to. Images of his daughter—a child, really—making love to some guy kept darting in from odd corners of his mind. No matter how hard he kept pressing it back, the top kept popping off his mental container, as if it were one of the lids that had been warped in the dishwasher.

"Oh, Greg." Suddenly Patty was crying. She rolled up against him and gave herself up to it, crying against his chest.

He wrapped his arms around her and relaxed a little. This was more like it. This gave him something positive to do. He needed her to be herself.

He didn't want to say it, didn't like saying it, but he had to say it. "We were sixteen."

"But she's fifteen! And these are different times, everything's so dangerous. And she's only gone out with him a little while! Don't tell me you think it's okay!"

"Of course I don't. I hate it." He stroked her hair, kissed her wet cheek. "I hate it, sweetheart." The words seemed weak, because he was still keeping the images at bay. He was afraid of what would happen to him if he unleashed them.

"I just can't stand it. She's too young to know what's best, and she won't listen to anything we say. She thinks I was snooping through her things. I was putting away laundry, like I've done practically every day of my life since they were babies." She began crying again. "Oh, Greg, she's too young."

"I know, sweetheart, I know. She's our baby girl." As they lay there, silent now, except for the muffled sound of Patty's intermittent sniffs, the picture of his daughter as a toddler came to him as clearly as if he had just plucked her up from wandering too near a stairway and hoisted her high in his arms where she would be completely safe.

Greg's first waking thought was of the heat. Though he lay completely uncovered, his limbs splayed out as if he were an accident victim, though he and Patty were two feet apart in the bed, his body was covered by a sticky film of sweat.

"I don't know why we've waited all these years to get a goddamn air conditioner," he complained as they pulled on their shorts and T-shirts from where they lay crumpled on the floor. "Other people have air conditioners. It gets hot, they plug them in. What's wrong with us?" Patty hadn't bothered to do her sit-ups last night, or wash her face. She had a little smudge of eye makeup on each lower lid like a mime.

"Because we've never needed one before," she said. "Don't swear at me."

"I'm not swearing at you, I'm swearing at this fucking heat wave."

"Stop it!" She faced him, clutching her hairbrush, her unwashed face twisted in a combination of anger and pain. He could suddenly picture her old.

"You are too swearing at me," she said. "Only you don't even know why. It's not the fucking heat, it's not me, it's what's happening with Kiley. You refuse to even think about it."

"Now who's swearing," he pointed out.

"You can't even respond to what I said."

"I'm responding, all right? Kiley. Kiley and her pills. That's the subject. You don't have to lecture me like I'm a moron. If I want to complain about the heat, I will. If I want to swear, I will." It was a relief to let his voice rise.

Patty turned and left the room without speaking. He waited a few minutes and then went downstairs. He noticed that the pink case had been removed from the hall.

By the time he was on his third piece of toast and second cup of coffee, the girls had drifted downstairs, fully dressed and made-up. They silently went about getting themselves something to eat. When Patty appeared, he saw that she, too, had taken time to wash her face and brush her hair before coming down, leaving Greg the only one who still had sleep matter crusted in the corners of his eyes and a greasy shine to his forehead. He felt this put him at a disadvantage.

Last night they had gone around and around about what measures to take. Neither of them wanted to permit Kiley to be sexually active at this age, yet neither of them thought they could actually stop her, especially if she had already had sex. Greg felt an acute sense of failure. He was conscious of how many times he had tiptoed around a ticklish issue with one of his teenagers, hoping to avoid a blowup and keep the atmosphere pleasant in the house. They had conditioned him by their tears and sulks to go too easy on them, leave too many questions unasked.

Patty told the girls to sit down. Then she poured herself a cup of coffee and took the chair opposite them.

"Kiley, do you have anything to say to us about your birth control pills?"

He was amazed that she could just say it like that.

"All I have to say is that I'm shocked you would go through my things," Kiley said to her mother coolly. She looked both of them in the eye, and Greg saw in her expression some of Patty's own toughness.

"I was not going through your things. I was putting back your un-

derwear after doing laundry. I think you *wanted* me to find those
pills, because you know you're too young to have them."

"Excuse me," Melissa said with feigned sweetness as she rose
from the table with her plate.

"Sit down," Greg said. "The rules we're about to set for your sister are going to apply to you, too." He could do his part as long as he
didn't have to talk about the pills specifically, or anything that they
implied. Melissa raised her eyebrows and lowered herself back down
with a dissatisfied scrape of the chair.

Kiley rolled her eyes and looked out the kitchen window.

"Kiley, how long have you had the pills?" Patty asked.

Kiley stared resolutely at the pine tree that filled the view from the
window.

"The prescription says July. Did you just get them for the first
time?"

Greg held his breath. This was their one shred of hope, that Kiley's
plan was too new to have been put into action yet.

Almost imperceptibly, their daughter's chin wobbled. Greg saw a
flash of the seven-year-old in her profile; the time she wasn't allowed to go to a sleep-over birthday party at the nine-year-old's house
across the street—the rage and grief she had shown them in her
held-back tears.

"Kiley, just tell them," Melissa said impatiently. "You haven't
done anything."

Greg and Patty looked at each other. This was completely out of
character, one twin offering information about the other. Patty cocked
an eyebrow, and Greg understood: Melissa must be panicking about
the rules that were coming down and wanted to head off whatever she
could.

"Let them think the worst about me—they will anyway. They treat
us like absolute infants."

"Kiley, just what are we supposed to think when we see that you've
started yourself on birth control pills? There aren't a whole lot of conclusions we can come to."

"It just so happens," Kiley flashed, lifting her chin defiantly, "that I went to the clinic to get them because my skin was breaking out, and some of my friends told me getting on the pill would help."

Greg was out of his depth; he wished they would go back to the rules discussion. Like football: legal and illegal plays, regulations, referees.

Patty looked incredulous. "If that's the case, why didn't you discuss it with me?" she asked.

"Right, and have you freak out, like you're doing now."

"You're damn right I'm going to freak out, if I think my fifteen-year-old daughter is having sex."

Kiley shrugged contemptuously. "It's not like I can't get condoms anytime I want from the school nurse."

Patty looked as if she had been slapped. Greg's teenage bullshit meter told him that there might be some truth in Kiley's story, but a lot of things unsaid as well. Like maybe the pills started out for a medical reason, but she was keeping quiet about them to leave her options open—gauge her future needs. So far they hadn't asked Kiley the real question, the one Greg couldn't find a way to phrase except in the quaint Victorian words that had been running through his head ever since last night: *Do you still have your innocence?*

Instead, he said, "Let's talk about some basic things that have to do with both of you. The fact is, your mother and I realized last night that we don't know nearly enough about who your friends are, who you're dating, and what your activities are. That's going to change."

Just as he finished his sentence, a souped-up car pulled in front of the house and idled deafeningly.

"Daddy, I have to go," Melissa pleaded.

"Who's that?"

"That's Jason. You know. He gives me a ride home from baby-sitting sometimes. He lives right next door to the Millers."

"Where are you going?"

"Oxbow. We're going swimming."

"Jason can come up to the door and meet us."

"Oh, Daddy, please not now. It's the first time he's asked me out. I don't want it to seem like I have really strict parents."

"But you do have really strict parents, starting today. So tell him to get his butt to the door, or you're not going."

Greg almost felt sorry for causing the look of agony that crossed Melissa's face as she rose from the kitchen table. Then he remembered what was at stake. It was in the spirit of negation that he sized up Jason when he came to the door, and he didn't like what he saw. Greg took in the extravagantly torn cutoffs, the tank top with skull and crossbones, the smile crowded with too many teeth. He tried not to see the things that Melissa undoubtedly dwelled on—the golden hair on the forearms and legs, the muscled, tanned limbs, the broad, developed shoulders.

He didn't know if he and Patty had stood before her parents in their kitchen looking like this, at once so young and so sexual, an almost palpable scent of hormones rising off their bare skin. If so, why had her parents ever let them leave the kitchen, get in a car together, go to the river on the hottest days of the year? The kegs had been kept in somebody's pickup under a tarp. Patty didn't even like beer until that summer at Oxbow. They'd fill their cups and then walk up the bank until they found a spot where they could lie flat on a warm rock. They listened to the shushing sound of the current and the whoops of the other kids in the distance. A coolness rose off the river like air from the refrigerator.

The shock of the cold water made them cry out. They grabbed onto each other, laughing. They could barely touch the sandy bottom; they kept losing their footing because of the current. Then they'd pull themselves back onto the rock, and lie side by side, kissing. It was as if they had been born kissing each other, with no problem deciding when to stop or shift or breathe. He remembered pressing himself against Patty, wordlessly asking her to. Finally, she'd take it in her hands, and that was all he needed—her hands cupping him, his cock that had sprung free from the open zipper to meet her cool fingers. When they finally rose from the rock their lips would be bruised and pulsing; Patty would lean into the water to wash the stickiness of his cum off her fingers. The river had been the beginning of everything.

Here was his daughter, asking his permission to go for a drive. Why had Cass and Walter not told Greg then to leave their kitchen and never return? Was it because they had no idea what would happen? Was it because they knew they couldn't hold a daughter to them by making her stay home? Or was it because some part of them decided to relinquish control, allow that it was time for Patty to begin her life? He didn't know any of the answers. But he began asking Melissa and Jason questions just the same, as though learning times, names, and the precise location of things were a charm that could ward off or slow down what lay in store.

They met Will, too, and Greg was surprised to find that he liked him. He had a serious air like Kiley, almost a parson's long meditative face, and Greg could picture the two of them sitting in a Starbucks, talking intensely about life. That was all he tried to picture, because like Melissa's Jason, this boy, too, had an excruciatingly male presence. He was six feet tall and had brown wavy hair that he grew long enough to pull back in a rubber band. The day he dropped by after supper to have dessert in their kitchen he wore loose madras shorts and a T-shirt that said *Jam Cannery*, which Greg guessed was a band, rather than the declaration of a summer job. The fact that the kid wore Birkenstocks and wire-rimmed spectacles reminiscent of Benjamin Franklin did not reassure, since Greg could feel Will's store of edgy male energy beneath the gangly mellow image.

Still, things seemed to be on a smooth footing at home the next couple of weeks. The girls observed the new rules and curfews not exactly cheerfully, but not really sullenly, either. Greg chose to believe Kiley about the pills, because it was easier on him that way, easier to think that he and Patty still had time to exert their influence over the girls' choices. He almost relaxed enough to get used to the predatory growl of Jason's Camaro approaching his house to pick up Melissa.

Meanwhile, football practice was tuning up his body and mind, getting him ready for the school year. On a Monday late in August, Greg parted company with the varsity coaches, and he and his assistant coach, Wilson Perry, the school's history teacher, stood before his assembled junior varsity team, suited up for the first practice of the season. They had only five practices before school started, and then a game scheduled for the Friday of the first week of classes.

After three weeks of working with the whole team, Greg felt his usual initial shock at seeing the smaller frames of his mostly sophomore players. When the boys chanted the counts during warm-up, their voices rose high and reedy in the air, instead of rolling forward in the bass wave he was used to hearing. But Greg was happy to be with his young team. He couldn't help but think that more was on the line for them as less experienced players. Later their paths would be set: they were the star players or the benchwarmers. But at fifteen, who knew what was possible and what was not? Greg could afford to give everyone the benefit of the doubt for a while. No one knew who all the starters were yet, not even the boys themselves. Every once in a while he saw some kid surprise himself.

TIM WAS right about one thing: he was fast. Greg began to see him as a starting wide receiver. He seemed to be able to get his legs under the ball and catch it wherever it was thrown. Greg had grown fond of the boy's stubbornness, too—the way he approached the drills as if they were the game itself, not satisfied until he had run a course perfectly or had succeeded in bettering his time at sprints. The one thing Tim didn't seem to be getting the hang of was belonging to a team. He didn't seem to know what to do with himself during the downtime, when the boys were milling around bantering among themselves. Tim always kept to himself, wearing his mortified look. His teammates, in turn, were a little wary of him. They didn't go out of their way to bring him into their circle. They gave him his space, which was exactly the opposite of what Greg was hoping for. The kid needed some friends his own age. He needed to learn how to make a joke, or at a bare minimum, how to laugh at one.

Of course, Greg couldn't play favorites. Just because Tim had spent time hanging around his own house and Greg had come to feel an almost paternal responsibility for him didn't mean Tim should become his project, or have a head start on the team over the boys he didn't know. In fact, Greg tended to veer the other way to keep things even, expecting just a little more from Tim before he would bark out a "Good job!" But he couldn't help the secret pride that stole over him when Tim caught the ball in a scrimmage and ran like hell.

The weather didn't give them a break. The number of days over ninety degrees had become a media story, and on Wednesday they broke the record for consecutive days of drought. Every lawn in town had been reduced to a rough brown stubble, as if the Willamette Valley had been magically transported to desert latitudes. It was too hot to do anything except lie around in an air-conditioned room, but the coaches and team didn't have any choice but to tote their water bottles and salt tablets onto the field and run until all the water was gone from their bodies, drink up, then run some more.

On Thursday, thunder showers were predicted. Greg showed up half an hour early so he could get some equipment set up and was pleased to see that Tim and a kid named Randy Martin were already dressed down, tossing a football back and forth. Below the hill on the main field Greg could hear the *hunh! hunh! hunh!* of the varsity players chanting during the warm-up of their afternoon practice. Together Greg and the two boys rolled out some tires from the equipment shed for footwork drills, and by that time Coach Perry and the rest of the team were arriving, lining up for stretches and squats.

They slogged through the heat, stopping every ten minutes for water breaks. The white sky pressed down on them like a wet towel, and one kid had to sit down because of dizziness. No one complained. By the time they finished the first half of practice, large dark clouds had edged in from the west, accompanied by a slight breeze.

They were walking through a new play when the rain started—fat, cooling drops that smelled of brass. Then the rain became heavier, drumming on the kids' helmets, and the sky blackened overhead. A warm wind swirled up. At the first clap of thunder, Greg blew his whistle and motioned the guys toward the breezeway. Rain began sheeting down on them halfway there, so that when they reached cover, water rolled off their slick helmets and down their bare fore- arms and shins, forming puddles around each player on the cement. Outside the breezeway the sky flashed brightly and went dark, as if someone were playing with the lights. Then a roll of thunder, osten- tatiously loud. The air temperature had dropped ten or fifteen de- grees.

"Okay, we can't afford to lose the rest of this practice, so we're going to see if we can wait it out. Looks like this storm is moving fast. Meantime, Coach Perry will take you through some plays in the play- book."

Perry had been talking just ten minutes when Greg saw that the ink-colored bank of clouds was moving off to the east and behind it the sky had already lightened to the color of pale ashes. He let Perry come to a stopping point, then said, "Okay, rain's over, let's get back on the field."

They resumed their walk-through. Greg froze the players in a kind of tableau, arrayed according to their positions midway through the play, while he explained what had to happen next. Winters had to fake a handoff to Hildegard, then take a couple stutter steps and fire off a pass to Phelps, who would be open to his right. Hanson and Martin would block for Phelps, who would loop around and, if every- thing went according to plan, run long with the ball.

Greg blew his whistle and saw Winters fake, step back, and raise his arm to throw. Phelps was moving sideways on the field toward Greg's position on the sidelines. Greg was in the act of shouting something to him, some word of encouragement or warning, perhaps, when a sound like the tearing away of a large piece of metal raked his eardrums and Timothy Phelps was suddenly illuminated by a shoulder-wide column of white light. Greg was hurled backward and then—it was curious what drew his attention in the split second it happened—he noticed that his shoes were missing.

Before Greg could open his eyes he became conscious of panic around him. An acrid smell hung in the air—part electricity, part burned soil. There was a confusion of excited voices and through it his name being called. His whole body seemed to be pulsing, and he couldn't free himself from this internal pounding long enough to respond. Then he heard Tim's name being shouted over and over, in a kind of hysteria, and he forced himself to raise his head and try to see what was going on.

"Coach!"

"Don't try to sit up yet!"

"Tim was hit, too."

"Someone went to call the paramedics."

"Give him a little air, move back."

Greg had to lay his head back down—things were too bright and loud. The voice bent over him and said, "You were hit by lightning, and so was Tim. Maybe you shouldn't move until the paramedics come."

Greg tried to sort through the hubbub, but he was having difficulty putting everyone's sentences together. He heard them, but they weren't being processed properly in his brain. Both he and Tim had been hit—hit how, exactly? Maybe if he tried again to sit up. He tested himself with a few deep breaths: he felt fine, really. Lightheaded, ears ringing, and still this crazy pulse thudding against the walls of all his arteries, but everything seemed to be working all right.

He was helped to his feet, and noticed again his lack of shoes. He padded over to where another circle of players were bending low. Wilson Perry was herding them back to make a space. That's when Greg saw the boy's still form. He watched as Perry worked the helmet off and tilted Tim's head back, then bent to administer mouth-to-mouth resuscitation. That meant he wasn't conscious. Greg knew he should be doing something, moving closer to help Tim, but every thought was taking a long time to form, and events were moving too fast for him to keep up. Before he could act, another player, Greg couldn't think of his name, knelt down and said to Perry, "I've been a lifeguard. I know CPR."

The two of them worked in rhythm over Tim. Fear began to knife coldly through Greg's foggy daze; just how bad was all this? Greg noticed how Tim's uniform was torn and shredded, how the skin beneath his football pants was charred by burns. He saw the snaking path of the scorched grass, curving from where Tim had caught the ball to where Greg had been standing on the sidelines. It looked as though someone with a blowtorch had walked between them, connecting their two points with a ribbon of ash.

Greg had no idea how many minutes were passing. The paramedics arrived and took over the CPR. Then they fitted an oxygen mask over Tim's face and lifted him onto a gurney. They looked unusually clean and white next to Tim's blackened clothes. They stayed busy with their machines and paraphernalia for what seemed a very long time. Then the second EMT truck rolled up and two paramedics leaped out and were directed over to Greg. They had him lie down on a gurney, too, though he explained that he was fine. They took his vital signs and must have heard the thundering of his pulse, because they were saying something about his heart rate and BP. Greg wondered if they could hear the ringing in his ears. They shined a light in his eyes, and for a minute Greg saw it all again—the boy running toward him, his head twisted back to find the ball in the sky, arms outstretched to receive it—someone suddenly transformed into a kind of angel, shrouded in light.

WILSON PERRY was already at the emergency room; he had ridden over with Tim. He came over to Greg's hospital bed and stepped inside the curtain.

"You okay?" he asked.

Greg was sitting up, waiting to be examined. He had been going back in his mind to the time before the strike, when they were setting up the play. From there he was trying to fill in their movements, as if he could take a stick of chalk and mark everyone's path with arrows. But the lightning had made a rip in time. For a few seconds or minutes Greg had been absent, and that's when Tim had somehow slipped through the tear the sky had made.

"I'm fine. How's Tim?"

Perry's face was grim. "Still unconscious. They don't know much yet. He took the strike full force. He was in cardiac arrest on the field, but came back from it."

"Thanks to you."

Perry shrugged.

"I'm okay here," Greg said. "Go back to Tim. Anyone call his dad?"

"He's coming. By the way, there are reporters asking questions. You want to talk to them?"

Greg closed his eyes. "No."

"MR. GOODMAN?" Someone stepped inside his curtained enclosure.

Greg looked up, expecting the doctor. Then he saw a woman dressed in red with a microphone, and a man following with a camcorder hoisted on his shoulders. Another light shone in his eyes; the thing was aimed at him.

"Mr. Goodman, I'm Joy Scinterro from Channel Nine. I understand you're the football coach who was struck by lightning on the field today."

Greg held his hand up to shield his eyes. His temples throbbed. "Are you supposed to be in here?"

"It must have been a terrible experience." Joy Scinterro clucked with concern. She had a smooth blond pageboy and wore a suit that looked too hot for August. But she appeared fresh and cool.

"If you're filming, I'd like you to turn the camera off."

The cameraman circled the foot of his bed, crouching slightly for a better angle.

"Do you have any comments about the boy in the coma?"

"Coma?" The word sounded so much more dangerous than just being unconscious.

"You didn't know?" Joy started scribbling on her pad.

Just then a doctor came in, saving him.

"You'll have to do the interview later, I'm afraid. Mr. Goodman is going to be examined now."

"You would be Doctor . . ." Joy said, thrusting the microphone toward him.

"Yes, I would be a doctor. Now you'll have to excuse us."

"Could you tell us about the boy's condition, Doctor? Is it true that he may have sustained brain damage?"

"This way, please." As the doctor was ushering the news crew out of the cubicle, Joy managed one last question over her shoulder.

"Greg, who made the decision to keep the boys on the field during a lightning storm?"

"The storm was over," he said, more to himself than to anyone, since Joy, and the cameraman, and the doctor had all stepped beyond the curtain.

O n the local evening news the meteorologist had computer graphics to show the kinds of lightning—forked, streak, ribbon, sheet, and ball. These could strike an individual in different ways: directly, like Tim, or by way of a "splash" that jumped from one person to another. A "striding" strike was one that traveled through the ground and entered a person through the feet. Greg thought this must have been what happened to him; it explained the burned path between Tim and himself, and also Greg's blasted-away shoes.

But the thunderstorm had passed: no one in his right mind would lead a bunch of kids out onto a field in the middle of lightning. Perry backed him up, and so would the boys on the team. Who knew that lightning could lie in wait like that—springing at you from nowhere? The meteorologist had mentioned—too unemphatically, it seemed to Greg—that lightning sometimes forked obliquely, coming from a storm out of view. If Greg had heard this information last night, he would certainly have waited an extra fifteen minutes before sending the team out on the field. But last night the fact that lightning could strike from nowhere hadn't been headline news.

He flipped the channels and found Joy Scinterro talking from the

JV playing field. On the grass where Greg and his team had been practicing a play just hours earlier, Joy now trod gingerly in high heels, tracing the scar left by the lightning. The camera zoomed to the spot where Tim had been poised to catch his pass. There where he had stood—his upstretched arms making him the tallest thing on the playing field, a target because he was reaching for the ball he surely would have caught—were two blackened footprints stamped in the earth. Joy knelt down, allowing the camera a close-up of her stockinged legs, and inserted a ruler to show that the foot indentations were almost five inches deep.

"The young player Timothy Phelps was driven deep into the ground as the terrible force of the lightning bolt struck him. Tonight, as family, teammates, and coaches gather in vigil, praying for fifteen-year-old Timothy Phelps to regain consciousness, these silent impressions in the earth tell the story of the unbelievable drama that happened earlier this afternoon here at Willamette High School. This is Joy Scinterro for Channel Nine News."

Greg clicked the TV off; he was breathing slightly fast, as if he had just sprinted upstairs. He wondered where everyone was gathering in vigil, or if that was something Joy had made up. No one had told him about any vigil. He had paid a visit to Tim's ICU cubicle before leaving the hospital. Phelps was there wearing dusty construction clothes—apparently he was back to work. Upon seeing Tim's father, their first encounter since their beer together, Greg had had the momentary feeling they should embrace. Phelps, however, seemed moved by no such impulse. At first, he looked blankly at Greg, as if he had trouble placing him. Then he seemed to recoil, and went back to watching his son, his lips pressed together, his stubby fingers drumming on the metal railing of the bed. Together they had stared at Tim. His hair was burned away from a circle of blackened scalp about the size of a dime. There were charred streaks on his neck. Tim was breathing on a respirator, and a heart monitor jerked with pulses. A nurse standing nearby had quietly adjusted an intravenous tube. Seeing Tim's form lie still and flat under the white expanse of hospital linen, his face partially obscured by the machines and paraphernalia, Greg had almost felt a giggle well up in his throat. *Come on!* he wanted to shout. *Coma? Respirator? This is a kid we're talking about!* Greg's mind could not focus; it had skittered past Tim and all that he could not take in like the hamster the girls used to keep caged in their room. The animal had dry, scratching feet that would hurtle it from one corner of its cage to the next in its sudden fits of panic.

Phelps would not speak to him. Greg wondered if he had even noticed the wheelchair Greg had rolled up in. The emergency room nurse had insisted he ride in it. He felt silly being pushed when he was perfectly capable of walking. But after the visit, as she wheeled him back down to the ER, he was suddenly grateful to have it; since seeing Tim the noise in his ears had increased to a dull roar that hadn't yet subsided.

The doctor told him before his discharge that the headaches, partial deafness, and ringing would go away in a day or two. Patty and the girls had received Perry's message and come to the hospital. But Greg hadn't been able to get word to her to bring a pair of shoes, so he left the hospital still in his muddy and grass-stained socks. He was on the point of throwing them away when he got home, but then thought of Tim. It seemed dangerously casual to discard the socks; he would bleach them and try to restore them to their former condition. He wondered if someone had found his shoes and brought them inside before Joy Scinterro got to the field. He would hate for her to have them.

The phone rang and Patty rose again from the sofa to answer it. They had worked out a statement from him, and Patty was the one relaying it to anyone from the media who called.

"My husband was released this evening with minor burns, a severe headache, and some ringing in his ears," Patty was saying. She paused to listen. "He is devastated by what happened to Tim, and is in close contact with his family, hoping and waiting for news that Tim has regained consciousness." The "close contact" part was an exaggeration, but what else could he say? That Phelps had looked right through him? She frowned now, holding the receiver. Then she said,

"My husband saw that the thunderstorm had passed. That's why the boys returned to the field."

He hadn't offered excuses to Phelps. Before taking his leave, Greg had interrupted the man's silence to say, "I'm sorry," and Phelps had nodded, this time without looking toward him at all. Greg would have tried to say more—he didn't know what, maybe just "I'm sorry" a few more times, until it registered—had Phelps simply met his eyes.

Greg's earlier coachlike words about the safety of the new equipment mocked him. Perry had told him how the plastic inside the helmet had melted where Tim's head took the strike. Doctors were worried about damage to the heart, and a scan had revealed swelling of Tim's brain. No prognosis was offered. Greg might have preferred Tim's father to rail at him, to shout, even to come at him with his fists flying. But the man froze him with silence.

Patty hung up and came back to sit, drawing her bare feet up onto the couch and tucking them under his thigh. He patted her leg. "Thanks. I wish we could unplug the phone."

"You wouldn't want to be the last to hear if anything develops with Tim," she said. "Anyway, that should be the end of the calls. It's eleven o'clock."

But the phone rang two times after that, and both times Patty rose from bed to answer, and neither time was it the hospital calling with good news about Tim.

TIM WAS still in a coma on Friday, and Greg thought he should cancel practice. On the other hand, maybe the boys needed to come together, today especially.

He opted to call it a "team meeting," asking Wilson Perry to call everyone. The weather taunted them by being bright and cloudless. Overnight, low pressure had cooled off the air, and they had a perfect seventy-five-degree day to practice in.

He began by briefing them about Tim's condition, though most of the boys knew already, either from visits to the reception area of the intensive care unit or from each other on the phone. Greg could tell from their uneasy faces and fidgety presence that he had done the right thing in bringing them out on the field today. In fact, what they needed to do was run off some of their anxiety.

"Okay, here's the plan," he said. "I wasn't planning to have a practice today, because we all know that Tim is uppermost in our minds right now. But I think he'd want us to feel that we're all in this together, supporting each other. And the best way I know how to do that is to go out and do some playing. This isn't about getting ready for Friday's game, it's about coming together as a team. Are you with me?"

The boys nodded solemnly. Then Todd Winters, the quarterback, raised his hand. He had a blunt square face and straight hair cut in an unfortunate line across his forehead. "What do you want us to say when the reporters call us?"

"Reporters?" Greg asked, his jaw dropping. "They're calling you guys?"

A few of the boys nodded.

"Well, don't talk to them unless your parents want you to. And then, if you go ahead, say . . . say what it was that happened. As you saw it. I mean, that's if your parents think you should even talk to them."

For some reason the boys weren't meeting his eyes as he said this. The collective listening gaze he so depended on from them had suddenly broken up into a lot of individual faces, some of which were looking at the ground or at something floating in space in front of them.

"I'm not worried about reporters," Greg said loudly, trying to get them back, then wondered if that sounded defensive. "I'm worried about Tim."

Randy Martin, a weak player and the one kid who seemed to have taken a shine to Tim, spoke up. "They said on the news he'd probably have brain damage."

Greg tried to make his gaze and voice as level as he could. As level as the bubble of air that a carpenter uses to make a house stand plumb.

"Well, you know what, Martin? You know what, guys?" The boys turned their eyes to him and waited. For a few seconds at least, he had them.

"That's because on the news they have to say something. They have to fill airtime even if they don't know shit. And the truth is, they don't know shit. The truth is, not even the doctors know what's going on, and doctors know a lot more about brains than reporters do. So let's not go jumping to conclusions. This is serious, we all know it's serious. But it's not going to help Tim or anyone if we assume the worst." They held his eyes after he spoke, and he knew he was on solid ground with them again, at least for now.

GREG HAD them dressed down and running laps when the Channel Nine News truck came bumping across the field. By the time Joy leaped out, dressed in a beige linen pantsuit and loafers, Greg was there to meet her.

"You've got to get that truck off this field," he said.

"We just hoped to get some film of the boys. Are some of them too shaken up to practice?" Joy was fumbling with her microphone. The cameraman was getting out of the back of the truck.

"You listen to me." Greg's voice grew loud. "I called the practice because the boys needed to be together. They do not need to be on camera, and they do not need to answer any questions. They need to run. In peace. And your truck is not allowed on this field."

The cameraman was in the act of raising his camcorder toward the players. A few of the faces rounding the lap turned toward the truck. Greg stepped in front of the lens and put his hand up.

Joy said, "That's okay, Bill, we don't need the film. Why don't you take the truck back to the parking lot, and I'll talk to Greg for a minute."

As the truck rumbled away over the grass, Joy turned toward him. She had uncannily blue eyes and a perfect chin.

"Greg, the public is interested in this story. We had I don't know how many calls last night wondering about Tim's condition—and yours, too—as well as how the team is doing, and the families. A lightning strike captures people's imaginations—it's the kind of freak accident people can't protect themselves against, so it fills them with awe. They have sympathy, they're fascinated, but they're also frightened, too, because it could happen to them, or their kids."

When she wasn't sticking a microphone in his face she seemed sweet and earnest. Her face lit up with total belief in what she was saying. No wonder they put her on TV.

"You're made for this stuff," he said.

She blushed, the color suffusing her whole face. It was the way his girls blushed. "You make it sound like a fault," she said, tilting her chin.

Up close he saw that she must only be around twenty-five or -six, though her TV persona was harder, older. Now she had dropped it, and her face was soft and inviting.

"Look, Greg, we just want to get the story out from your point of view. You're the best eyewitness of what happened to Tim—you were standing the closest to him. And you were struck yourself. People want to hear what you went through."

He shook his head. "I'm not comfortable talking on TV," he said.

"But you really should. Keep the public on your side. Do you know that there were lawyers dropping by the hospital to give Mr. Phelps their cards? You never know what may result from that. It could be important that you give an interview now, before there's any lawsuit. Later, it might look too defensive."

"Lawsuit?" He glanced at the boys, doing their warm-ups together under Coach Perry's direction. A lawsuit was absurd. They were a team, they stuck together. No one was to blame.

"You never know. Anyway, what can it hurt? Just a few questions about what you saw, what it felt like. And in your own words you can explain how you thought the storm had blown over."

"The storm *had* blown over," he corrected her.

HE WENT up to the truck and talked, with the camera filming. He didn't look at the camera, he looked at Joy, and she held his eyes and kept nodding to everything he said. Every once in a while she'd interject a small, helpful question, just to get him to fill in all the details. It surprised him that he had so much to say, that he forgot the camera, that he felt so safely suspended in Joy's gaze as he talked. He told her about calling out to Tim—he couldn't remember what— as the boy ran in his direction. He told her how crystallized in his mind was the moment of Tim's reaching for the ball. He told her about his deep amazement at the column of light, how it was suddenly there and seemed to swallow Tim up. Unexpectedly, his eyes teared up as he spoke. He blinked, and swallowed, and the depth of Joy's interest and sympathy kept him talking. He told how his shoes had vanished, and how his head even now echoed with the screeching noise he had heard just before the blast. How he had designed that particular play for Tim. How fast the kid was, how much he loved playing.

Joy was still nodding, even when he had finished talking. Then she said, softly, "And you thought the storm had passed?"

"The storm *had* passed," he repeated firmly. He wondered how many times he would have to say it.


PATTY STARED at him after the story aired that night on Channel Nine.

"I don't get it," she said.

"Don't get what?"

"You didn't tell me half that stuff. How come you suddenly decided to go on television and discuss your feelings?"

"Dad, that's so awesome," Melissa said, bouncing up off the couch. "I wish we had taped it. I'm going to call Sarah and see if she saw you on TV."

Greg turned to Patty. "I wasn't talking about my *feelings*. Just what happened."

"Bullshit." Patty got up and gathered their drink glasses. The glasses clinked roughly together.

"What's the big deal? That reporter was hounding me. I had to give her a statement. A lot of it just came to me as I talked."

She stood glaring at him, glassware in either hand. "That's my point. Did it ever occur to you to talk to us about it? See what came to you then? It's not as if we didn't ask!"

Greg shook his head helplessly. He really didn't know how to give Patty what she wanted. Or why he had had so much to say to Joy Scinterro.

Patty snorted and went into the kitchen. Greg glanced over to Kiley, who was watching him curiously.

"Where's Will?" he asked, to turn the tables.

"Practicing with his band," she said, as if Greg should know all about it. This was the first he'd heard that Will was a musician. She was still watching him. "Dad, were you really scared?"

"I didn't have time to be scared." He picked up the remote and started scanning the channels.

"I know what Mom means," Kiley said.

"What are you talking about?"

"The way you answer questions like that—'I didn't have time to be scared.' It's not really an answer, not like the answers you were giving that reporter."

"Yeah, and you're a great one to be giving me lessons in communication skills," Greg said, irritated.

Kiley shrugged and went upstairs, leaving Greg alone with the news.

reg stopped by the hospital Saturday morning. Tim was by himself in his ICU cubicle, the machines sighing and humming over him. Greg wondered where Phelps was. He wondered if maybe Phelps had seen him on television and now understood how powerless Greg had been and how utterly Tim had been beyond his reach at the moment of the strike.

Alone with the boy for the first time since the accident, Greg found himself able to really look. With Phelps there it felt wrong for Greg to stare too long at the closed eyes, the strange burn on the head. Such looking was a father's prerogative. Tim was so slight, much smaller than he had ever appeared on the field. Greg had an impulse to scoop him up and remove him from there, as if it were being in the hospital that kept him from regaining consciousness. Maybe if he felt fresh air on his cheeks they would fill with color again.

He looked around, then bent low to speak in Tim's ear. He had read somewhere that people in comas could hear things.

"Hey, Tim. It's Coach Goodman." He felt foolish, and ashamed for feeling it.

"We're not going to run that play without you, Tim. So we need you back on your feet, okay? The guys are all pulling for you." The coaching words that came to him sounded brusque and inadequate compared to the feeling he had—that this boy needed to be held, to be rocked and whispered to until he was able to overcome the strange force that held him at a distance; that if he were encouraged steadily and gently he would find a way back to them.

Tim was still; only the machines stirred and whispered. Greg straightened up. Though he knew better, part of him had hoped that Tim was only waiting to hear his voice. Then, as on television, his eyelids would flutter and open dramatically. That was a stupid fantasy, of course, but after all, didn't the boy look up to him? Hadn't he picked Greg out as someone he could trust? One day, after hoeing a flower bed in Greg's backyard, Tim had mentioned that his mother had let him help pull weeds when he was little. He said he couldn't remember much about it—only that she wore a bright yellow outfit and the flowers she planted had been the same color. Greg was on the point of asking what had happened to her, but something held him in check. The boy said nothing more. At the time, Greg had thought he had done the right thing in not prying, giving Tim his privacy. Now he thought otherwise. The kid had wanted to open up to him, and all Greg would have had to do to let that happen was ask a simple question, then listen to the answer.

Phelps entered the room holding a paper cup. Some coffee sloshed onto his knuckles and probably burned, but he didn't react. Greg stepped away from the bed.

Phelps stared at him as if he were trying to decide something. He was unshaven and his eyes were bloodshot, making him look slightly crazy. His cheek twitched once. "You know, I'm not really in the mood to see you here."

"Sure, I don't want to intrude," Greg said quickly. "I care about him. That's all."

Phelps blinked rapidly. "You care," he mocked. "Oh yeah. Yeah, that's a great one."

"I didn't—" Greg began, then stopped. "Listen, I'm sorry if my being here upset you. I'm leaving."

Greg sidled out the door. He felt a sudden pressure building up behind his eyes. Earlier he had thought that if Phelps showed a little anger toward him it would be better, clear the air. But Greg hated being faulted. It was something he had spent his whole life avoiding. Now he felt Phelps's contempt for him as a black well, bottomless.

Without planning it, he turned into the chapel off the corridor. It was the most innocuous of rooms, with plush cranberry-colored carpet, matching cushioned pews, and lustrous maple woodwork; it reminded him of a first-class airport lounge. Alone, he let the door silently close behind him, and didn't bother to turn on any lights. A recessed spotlight glowed on the small brass cross fixed over the altar.

Settled on the pew, Greg tried to let go of Phelps's red-eyed accusation. He had never been one for praying; it always gave him the same self-conscious feeling he had just had when whispering in Tim's ear—as if some part of himself were looking on in ridicule, asking who in the heck he thought he was talking to. He was inexperienced when it came to religion. He had vague memories of going to Easter Sunday and Christmas Eve services when he was small, but his parents' efforts to take him to church had seemed halfhearted. He couldn't pinpoint when they stopped going altogether. He and Patty had been married in a park. A lot of people had done things like that then. The officiant had been some kind of minister Cass had rustled up, a man who hadn't troubled them too deeply with religious questions, and who had seemed pleased enough to preside over the happy occasion, and to drink champagne at the reception after.

Greg didn't know why he had steered himself into the chapel, or what he should do with himself once inside. It was cool and consoling to sit in the dim quiet. Ironically, he felt he was in a place where he could not be blamed for anything, as if his mere presence were evidence of good intentions. Whether there was a God Greg didn't pretend to know. It seemed not, judging from the randomness of things like lightning and where a fifteen-year-old boy could happen to be standing at the time when it struck. Then Phelps's words forced him to remember that Tim's position at that moment was part of a plan, Coach Goodman's plan. Maybe there was a God and he was using

Tim to punish Greg. But punish for what? What had Greg ever done that was so terrible? He couldn't think of anything specific, not anything worth God's hurting Tim over. But he did feel as though he were being made to suffer for something. Maybe if he sat here long enough his sin would take shape in the dark, coalesce into the shape of his failing. He had a hard time seeing his fault in Thursday's accident. The lightning had been so purely a *trick* of nature that in the whole episode he saw himself as much a victim as Tim. Well, not as much as Tim, of course. He wasn't lying comatose in a hospital bed right now hooked to machines. The neutral silence seemed to chide him. Comparing his trouble to Tim's was selfish; Greg tried to take back the thought. Maybe this was what prayer was like: allowing yourself to be held accountable even for your thoughts.

So *did* it come down to the moment of sending the boys back out on to the field?—his distraction or impatience that day, his focus on winning that got in the way of paying attention to the things that he should have? The obvious answer was yes. He had been in charge. He had been careless with the safety of other people's sons. His defense of himself had been that he couldn't imagine being blamed for something he hadn't meant to happen. But the thing had happened, regardless, and on his watch. The fullness of his responsibility began to slowly unfold within him, and once it began unfolding he could see that it would soon use up all the space, that there would be nothing left, no margin remaining for any other kind of knowledge.

Before he let this fact swallow everything, all other recognition, he saw one more thing—saw it in the simple, unexceptional glow coming from the recessed lights above the altar. He had had years and years to appreciate his life, to make something good of it, to be happy. He saw those years now the way you step close enough to see a picture dissolve into paint daubs—no form to it any longer, just color and swirls of energy from someone's hand. He saw that life abstractly—as a prism of haloed color through the tears he finally allowed to surface—because it was now on the other side of a divide he thought he would never cross again.

The chapel had produced a kind of peace in Greg, the kind that comes from being ready to shoulder consequences. He was prepared to suffer—to berate himself and allow others to do the same. The trouble was, the clarity he had achieved sitting quietly on his cushioned pew seemed to be evaporating as he drove home in the stark light of midday, past the jumble of car dealerships and the supermarkets vast as ocean liners. The reader board of the Baptist church moved him not at all with its message: *Repent and Jesus Will Forgive All.* By the time he reached his house he could remember the text but not the solace of his confessional thoughts. For some reason, wrestling with his guilt had felt almost like an exalted thing in the chapel, whereas by the time he pulled up into his driveway it had the physical characteristics of a hangover.

Patty was waiting for him. This was the night of their twentieth high school reunion dinner-dance, part of a weekend of reunion activities she had helped plan for two years. The approach of this milestone lacked the drama it might have held had he moved away, married someone from another town or state, and now been poised to return, to remember where he had begun. Greg lived where he had begun, a mile away from his mother. Aside from four years at college,

he had never even left Williamette High School. But Patty was excited about seeing old friends who were coming back. Not only had
she served on the reunion committee, but her personal preparations
had gone on for weeks. She had been to the salon and had had an interesting goldeny tint applied to her hair. She had spent many Sat-
urdays looking for the right dress, and had refused to show it to him
when she brought it home. He would have gladly skipped the dance,
but understood that Patty had long had her heart set on going.

Surprisingly, she brought it up first. How could they go now, with
Tim lying there in that unconscious state? What if something
changed with him when they were out at a party? Patty's distress was
genuine. Greg didn't admit it, but uppermost in his mind was how it
would look; Joy Scinterro had suddenly made him aware of a Public,
and he felt that every action gave him credits or debits on some in-
visible scoreboard.

But there was all Patty's work to think of, her position on the committee, her eagerness to see people; what good would it do Tim, or
Mr. Phelps, for them to stay home? It was Greg who suggested the
compromise of going for the dinner and leaving before the dance.

He showered and shaved, and applied the cologne one of his
daughters had given him for Christmas. It didn't smell like anything
he could put his finger on, not like the lime or leathery smells he was
used to wearing. This one tugged at him from different directions;
sometimes he thought he smelled spice, sometimes the deep part of
the woods where it was damp and mossy. He had one shoe in his
hand and was buffing it with a brush when the phone rang. Patty answered it in her bra and underwear; her pantyhose fluttered from her
free hand in the fan's breeze.

Patty's back was to him and she hunched over the receiver, listening. Finally she said, "Don't do anything now. We'll talk first
thing tomorrow. I'll meet you at Aldo's for breakfast, okay? Are you
going to be okay until then?"

Greg knew then it was Sandy; Aldo's was their favorite spot to
meet. He had about twenty seconds to prepare a neutral mask before
Patty hung up the phone and turned around.

"What's up?" he said.

"Sandy thinks Mitchell is having an affair."

"Oh, come on."

"Why 'Oh, come on'?"

"Mitch?"

"Why not Mitch?"

"He doesn't seem like the type. Besides, I would know about it if he was." This was a bold move, but he thought it best to take the offensive. Raise the issue before Patty started grilling him about what he knew. He hadn't exactly lied. Not in terms of the actual words he had said.

"Well, she found a receipt or note or something."

"What kind of note?"

"I don't know. She was sort of hysterical just now. I'll find out more tomorrow."

"Why is she calling you? Shouldn't she be talking to Mitch?"

"I don't know, Greg." Patty sounded impatient. "Maybe she needs to sort it out first. Anyway, he's out of town at some conference."

Greg felt a flash of primitive male loyalty. He wondered if he should track Mitch down, give him a heads-up about this. Then he came to his senses. He was implicated deeply enough already. In fact, he realized he had just had a perfect opportunity to come clean with Patty, and he had blown it. He could have apologized for keeping it from Patty, told her he felt confused and trapped by the knowledge, as well as angry at Mitch. Which was all true enough. Patty would have forgiven him on the spot. But instead he had obeyed the impulse to deepen the cover-up, as if it were he having the affair, not Mitch.

A double pall hung over them as they got dressed for the dance. Even when Patty stepped out to show him her dress, a sleeveless, silky little thing in hazy blue which set off her light tan and made her look about twenty, neither of them could summon much excitement for the evening.

The sun was still bright as they drove downtown. Greg kept smelling the unfamiliar cologne he had put on. Every time he noticed it he had a moment of wondering who else was in the car with them, then he remembered; it was he.

"Why didn't they hold this at the Benson, anyway?" he asked. It was where their prom had been.

"The Benson was booked. I didn't know you were so sentimental," Patty said, laying her hand to rest on his knee. He wondered if all wives rested their hands on that spot when their husbands drove. He had always liked it, and now it steadied him with its familiar comfort.

"It's just that this place wasn't even built when we were in high school," he said. "Kind of weird, is all."

"Does it feel like a long time ago to you? Or not? Sometimes, for me, it's like it all just happened, but then I remember the girls are as old as we were when we met."

He glanced sideways at her as they drove across the bridge. The light from the sun was melting into the river, making her skin glow. "You look the same as you did then," he said.

She looked at him, pleasure crinkling the corners of her eyes. "What a smooth talker I married."

"No, I mean it," he said. And he did. His wife hadn't seemed to age. When he saw an old picture of them, her long hair center-parted, his bushy waves over his ears and collar, he was surprised by the blank unwritten looks on their faces. Now she had the little lines around her eyes that came from paying bills and squinting at the lines on thermometers marking children's fevers. Her upper lip showed the faint stitches she used to hold back a retort to him or one of their daughters. The amused parentheses around her mouth were always there, ready to deepen when one of them made her laugh. He preferred this face to the one in mint condition; it was more her own. He supposed his own face bore evidence of what he had lived, too, or at least had dropped the startled expression of pure ignorance.

INSIDE THE hotel he started to rev up a little. It did make you feel different, really dressing up, as if you were a social class above yourself, someone with more money, a better job. They spent a few minutes searching the wall for their pictures blown up from the senior yearbook. They found Patty's first—she had had hers taken outdoors by a tree; it was the fashion then. Hers was captioned *Everyone's friend.* She grimaced. "Boring, huh?"

He gave her shoulders a squeeze. If she hadn't been so friendly, so ready to start a conversation and make him feel interesting and worthy, he probably never would have spoken to her. Unlike him, she had never minded the risk of talking to someone new. "Not boring, nice."

"Just as bad. Here's yours." She pointed to a pained-looking kid with unruly hair and plaid suit.

"Christ, I wouldn't buy a used car from him," Greg said, although his caption said *Loyal and dependable,* as if he were a golden retriever.

Just then Patty was waylaid by some woman Greg didn't remember, which gave him a few extra seconds to examine his portrait. Although he was smiling for the camera, there was an anxiety around the corners of his eyes that gave him a worried, too-eager-to-please expression. He looked nothing like Kiley's Will, who draped himself in amused ennui like a college professor, or Melissa's Jason, who reeked of smarmy confidence like a Hollywood actor. Those boys seemed way ahead of where Greg was in high school. He had never been free of a jumpy, worried feeling, had never been completely sure of himself, even when he had Patty around to steer him.

Patty was turning to him now, introducing Clarissa Jetty, her friend from when they both had parts in the school play. Clarissa now lived in Phoenix, where she sold ads for a cable network. She was deeply tanned and wore silver bracelets all the way up both arms to the elbow.

"Of course Greg doesn't remember me, Patty," Clarissa teased. "I don't think he saw another girl besides you all during high school, did you, Greg?"

"Well." There seemed no right way to answer this question, with both women looking at him. And in fact he didn't remember her. "It's just that you have this Southwestern look now. I didn't recognize you." Her gauze dress hinted at being sheer, if seen in the right light. Greg had the impression of a lot of skin—long bare arms and bare legs, shoulders, and a wide expanse of that space that isn't neck and isn't breast, but on Clarissa was tanned and ridged with bone. He suddenly wanted one of what she was holding in her hand—it looked like a gin and tonic sweating into the paper napkin she had wrapped around its base.

"I'll get us something to drink," he told Patty.

It took him a while to make his way. Hands were clapped on his back, and he was stopped by old friends and acquaintances whom at times he didn't even recognize. They had thickened, and, in some cases, grayed, and their skin looked loose and used. But people easily picked Greg out to hail him, as if he were unmistakably the same boy he always was, only now with a decent haircut, and better taste in suits.

He stayed free of conversational snares until he was able to edge back to Patty and present her with her drink. Whiskey sour; he hadn't needed to ask. She was still comparing notes with Clarissa, whose sun-toughened skin and heavy silver jewelry made Greg think of being on vacation. The hotel decor contributed to the effect—the ballroom dotted with palms and exotic tropical blooms, a complicated indoor landscaping that even included a little waterfall splashing over a rock. Greg took a sip of his drink and watched Patty talk; his wife was very much the beautiful accountant, all neat edges and wholesome diet and moisturized SPF 30 skin. She seemed twenty years younger than Clarissa, and also more contemporary, with her sleek dress and short hair. But Clarissa, vaguely hippyish, long dark hair, looked as if she tasted like salt.

Clarissa caught him staring and smiled. Greg excused himself and went to join a knot of guys he had played football with. A few of them he saw once in a while around town; like him they had never moved away. These guys had changed for him by gradual degrees. Greg had followed the births of their kids, and his girls had gone to school with some of those children. But some guys he hadn't seen in twenty years, and because in his mind's eye they had never aged past graduation, he had moments mistaking them for their fathers. One of these was Monty Reece.

"Hey, buddy, great to see you," Monty said, gripping his shoulder.

"Monty. Where do you live now?"

"Minneapolis. My wife is from there. You're still around here?"

Greg nodded. "What do you do in Minneapolis?"

"I run supermarkets, if you can believe it. My father-in-law put me in the business with him."

Greg could believe it; Monty looked like a man in charge. He wore a chunky gold ring and a watch with three small dial faces. His suit was made from a fabric so soft and buttery that Greg's season-less gabardine suddenly felt like burlap. Monty was taking out a card from a thin leather case and pressing it on Greg. It said *Fremont Reece, Chief Executive Officer, Daybright Markets, Incorporated.*

"I never knew your name was Fremont," Greg said, reading it.

"You'd expect me to tell you something like that in high school? Listen, I've been hearing the most incredible story about you—you got zapped into a coma by lightning or something."

"Not me. I mean, I was hit, but it was a kid who got it the worst. One of my players."

The circle of former teammates who had been standing and talking nearby gradually shifted and reformed around Greg. He heard himself telling almost word for word the narrative Joy Scinterro had drawn from him. He began to notice the sense of pleasure that came from the telling, a feeling of mastery over the event that made it seem as though it had happened to someone else, a character. When he tried to physically get back to the experience—that moment of feeling obliterated by a force so much greater than anything that could be described—he found he could not. He could talk about it now, but he could not feel it. He was safely back in the normal world.

Meanwhile, the circle had grown as people listened in. They peppered him with questions—did he lose consciousness? did it feel hot? did he have time to feel frightened?—and once again Greg became conscious of a Public, to whom this had not happened, would not happen, who looked to him for reassurance and also a kind of vicarious thrill. He said again how lucky he was, and how they all should be thinking of Tim, who was still hanging in the balance. He felt he was in supportive company here, with ballplayers who—no matter how many years had passed—could use the time they had played together as a touchstone, common ground to bring them together again. They wouldn't blame him for going ahead with practice. They knew that hanging tough to a practice schedule was a good thing.

He saw Patty over on the other side of the room, talking to a bunch of women. The thought of her hearing his monologue embarrassed him. She was right about his not talking so expansively to her. But then, she somehow didn't expect him to. She seemed to assume he wouldn't have much to say, and so he didn't. But these listeners were expectant—it had begun with Joy's sympathetic nodding. People were waiting for him to tell his story; he had lived through something of importance and they hungered to hear about it, in as much detail as he could remember.

He shifted and saw Clarissa at his elbow. She swirled the ice in her empty glass.

"Quite an experience," she observed.

He nodded, feeling like a fool. He didn't want to talk about lightning anymore. He glanced up again and saw Patty still far away, talking to the women, her back to him.

"Get me a drink?" Clarissa held up her glass.

Relieved to move away from her, yet glad to have an excuse to return, Greg headed for the bar farthest from Patty. He realized he hadn't asked Clarissa what her drink was—he thought gin and tonic. To be sure, he lifted the glass to his lips and drank the few drops that were left. As he tasted gin his lips brushed her fuchsia lipstick mark on the rim.

When he returned she took the drink and appraised him for a few seconds, sipping.

"You've changed a lot, you know," she said.

"I have?" He didn't think he had changed much.

"You're a lot surer of yourself, for one thing," she said.

"How do you know? We never even really knew each other." He wouldn't tell her that he still couldn't put a face on her in high school.

"I watched you then. I had kind of a crush on you. I kept thinking that if you and Patty ever split—" She stopped and smiled broadly behind him. Greg knew Patty must be coming their way.

Clarissa waited a beat, still smiling into what must have been Patty's face over his shoulder, and then, as his wife joined them, stepped back, making them a circle of three.

He couldn't say exactly how Clarissa rearranged her expression, but as she turned to Patty now her face was friendly yet somehow slack, whereas a second ago she had seemed all tensed energy to Greg.

"Greg was just telling us about getting struck by lightning," Clarissa said. "What an amazing thing."

"It was," Patty said. She turned to him. "It's all people have been asking me about. Everyone saw your television interview, or heard about it. You're famous."

His wife's face was open, a little softened by drink, her eyes bright. She was having a good time. Inwardly Greg let out the breath he was holding. A band started playing "Stairway to Heaven."

"Let's dance," he said to Patty.

She smiled over her shoulder at Clarissa as he led her away.

"That was a little bit rude to Clarissa," she scolded, as she snuggled against him. Her voice was happy.

He had a perfect view of Clarissa over Patty's head as they danced. Instead of turning away, seeking someone else to talk to as soon as she had been abandoned, she continued to look after them, smiling. Her eyes were now directed at his, but he kept his half closed so she wouldn't be able to tell if he was seeing her. She was an odd girl— or woman, he meant. This night had him thinking of them all as seventeen again. He and Patty slow-danced the way they used to in school, standing mostly in one place, but kind of rocking back and forth, every now and then taking a half-step in a new direction. It was a form of dancing invented by teenagers who weren't really thinking about dancing, but about holding tight to someone in the dark.

THEY GOT drunk; he was sure afterward that this played the major role in what happened next. The buffet dinner was slow in coming, and as the cocktail hour stretched on, he and Patty must have had four drinks each on empty stomachs. Then, as they seated themselves at one of the round tables for eight—Patty and Greg; Monty and his wife, Julie; Alice Farmer, who was Patty's best friend in high school, and her husband, Jim—Clarissa came from out of nowhere and seated herself on the other side of Greg. A spare seat was on the other side of Clarissa; apparently she hadn't brought an escort. Greg glanced down to see if she wore a wedding ring. But she wore at least six rings on various fingers, and it was impossible to tell.

Patty was chatting to Alice on her left, and Monty was talking across the table to Greg about the coach at his son's high school who demanded year-round workouts of the varsity players, and who had taken the team to four state championships in a row. As he talked, Greg was acutely conscious of Clarissa's presence on his right, and how she had inadvertently leaned her crossed legs under the table toward his own. Their legs were touching so lightly that, depending on how you breathed, they could at some moments be said not to be touching at all. Then he'd feel the slightest pressure again. He momentarily lost the thread of what Monty was saying, thinking about Clarissa's leg. Experimentally, he shifted his own leg an inch away, and to his astonishment, felt her move hers, too. He glanced at her, and she smiled back at him. They were drinking wine with dinner and he was beginning to feel his vision fuzz slightly, but he couldn't tell if Clarissa had had too much to drink or not. She looked completely composed.

After dessert, the band started playing again. They had said they would leave the party after dinner, but now he didn't see the point of rushing away. Leaving would be meaningless to Tim, and no one else seemed to be shocked at their presence here tonight. They could stay for a few dances at least. Monty asked his wife to dance, and Jim asked Alice, but she said she was feeling too light-headed, so he asked Patty instead. With Patty and Jim dancing, Alice rose and said she was going to the ladies' room. That left Greg and Clarissa. Greg watched Patty on the dance floor and felt for a moment that she was someone else's wife. He admired her with a distant feeling that included no sense of possessiveness. If she was going to dance with other people, then he guessed he had a right to, too. He turned to Clarissa with an invitation on his lips, but before he even spoke she said with mock irritation, "Well, finally," and stood up. "I was beginning to think that you were going to moon after Patty the whole song," she said.

He guided her to a spot on the floor over by Patty and Jim, who gave them a little wave. Greg liked fast dancing, but he never knew quite what to do, so he settled for a kind of bobbing up and down to the beat. It was what most guys did, he had noticed. The real reason for this kind of dancing was to watch women move their bodies, and from his vantage point he could watch both Patty and Clarissa. Patty had perfect rhythm and some reliable moves that she never varied. Her body was lithe and pretty, and as he watched, she became familiar to him again. He could count the moles on her shoulder, and say where her scar from the oven rack began on the inside of her forearm.

Clarissa, on the other hand, moved sinuously, unpredictably, and he watched the gauze swish in between her legs. She had thin, muscular arms, and she used them when she danced, sometimes raising them both straight up when she wanted to make her whole body a kind of exclamation point. The song the band was trying so hard to be the Stones at was "Brown Sugar," and to see Clarissa's ecstatic face and closed eyes, you'd think it was Mick and the boys themselves prancing up there on the hotel's collapsible stage. The song ended suddenly, just a minute after they had started, and Clarissa opened her eyes and cried, "Oh, not yet!" She leaned over to Patty and looped her arm around her neck and said, "I'm keeping him for one more, okay?"

Patty laughed and said, "Be my guest." To Jim she said, "I'm going to go see if Alice is feeling okay."

That left Greg and Clarissa again. The band fumbled around on-stage before the next song, and Clarissa hummed and danced in place impatiently. She seemed to have forgotten Greg, and he stood awkwardly, waiting for the music to give him something to do. When the band started again, they were playing a slow dance, and Clarissa stepped forward into his arms without hesitation. Greg wished they could sit down. It wasn't just that it was a slow dance, it was the way Clarissa wanted to slow-dance, melting into him, leaving no space. He didn't dislike it, exactly. But he was afraid everyone would think the flagrant contact was his idea. He smelled her hair, which was a mix of tobacco smoke and perfume. He couldn't avoid touching the skin of her back, because of how low-cut her dress was. She was taller than Patty, so he didn't have to stoop over so much. Clarissa hummed in his ear, causing a little tickle, and he felt her breath warm on his neck. Then he got an erection. Panicked, he tried to put distance between them. She leaned her head back and said, "Well. Not as immune as I thought."

He was embarrassed, wanted to look away, but she kept her head cocked back so she could see him. A minute before, he had been waiting for the song to end; now he was praying it would last another five minutes to give him a chance to collect himself. He started running football plays in his mind, shutting out all thoughts of Clarissa. He willed the nerves in his hands to be numb so he wouldn't feel her skin. He stared into the space alongside her right ear and separated himself from her enough so they were no longer touching with their bodies, though she was still in place as his shield. He was going through the split-drive play when the song ended.

"One more?" Clarissa asked impishly, her eyes merry.

"That's it for me," Greg said roughly, putting an arm's length between them. She was still grinning.

"Relax, Greg. I count it as a compliment, nothing more. Makes me feel young again."

Suddenly he grinned too. "Oh, you're young," he said.

"Well, if you mean I still behave like a kid, you're right there."

He was beginning to remember her from high school—halter tops,

same long hair, kind of a loner, even then. He couldn't put her with
any particular pack or group, except maybe the drama students. She
said she had had a crush on him. It was a pleasant kind of thing to
find out after all this time, an unexpected gift that could make him
feel better about that plaid-suited kid with the shifty eyes. In return
he didn't want to leave her with the impression that he had disdained
her then or found her unattractive now. As they pressed through the
crowd of dancers, he allowed his hand to rest lightly on the small of
her back. Before they emerged into the open he leaned toward her
and said, "It *was* a compliment, you know."

Then they were walking back to the table. As they neared the
back of Patty's chair, Clarissa whispered in his ear, "Room 653, all
weekend, if you want to pay me any more."

THE NUMBER blazed in his mind as he danced with Patty, then Monty's
wife, then Alice, who was feeling better. He didn't talk to Clarissa the
rest of the evening; she was mingling with other groups, and dancing a lot. He watched her whenever he thought he safely could; once
over Patty's shoulder during a slow dance. He saw the number when
they drove home, using it as a kind of beacon to steady his driving.
It was the last thing he saw when he and Patty fell into bed at two-
thirty in the morning, exhausted.

When the alarm went off at eight so Greg could get up for the
men's golf tournament, he panicked momentarily when he couldn't
think of the number: 536? 635? Then it clicked back into his consciousness, and he was able to get out of bed to stand in the shower,
to go down freshly shaved for breakfast, even read the morning paper
while the number danced safely in the margins of the articles.

He had no thought of driving to the hotel instead of out to the golf
course. The number had been something to amuse himself with,
nothing more, something that made him feel his life was full of possibility, that every move he made was a conscious choice. As he
backed out of the driveway and drove slowly down his residential
street with its row of identically designed split-level houses, he felt
that he was *choosing* to drive to the golf course, that he could do any-

thing at all with his morning, and that as an utterly free person, he had made the choice to play golf with his high school buddies. Then, just before the freeway entrance that would take him toward the golf course, he received a clear mental image of his clubs sitting in the garage, where he had left them.

HE DIDN'T see anyone he knew in the lobby of the hotel as he hurried to the elevator. He had not called first from the house phone, so he didn't know if she would be in the room. In fact, he expected that she would not be, and that he would simply get back in his car, head to the golf course, rent some clubs, and play in the tournament.

She opened the door wide, standing there mussed and sleepy in a silky-looking robe.

"You're not on the women's hike," he said stupidly.

She gave a hoarse bark of laughter and turned back into her room, leaving the door open behind her for him to enter.

He stepped in quickly, just to get out of the hall, and shut the door. He wondered if she had looked out the peephole first, to see who it was. It bothered him that she wouldn't have—did she open her door for anyone, wearing just her robe?

Clarissa lit herself a cigarette and plopped on the bed, sitting cross-legged on top of the covers. She squinted at him though a veil of smoke. "You're an early bird," she said.

"Golfing," he explained.

She raised her eyebrows and nodded. Took another drag of her cigarette. The room was strewn with clothes and open bags.

"I'm parched," she yawned. "How about some orange juice?"

Greg was still standing uncertainly. He nodded. Orange juice would be good. Suddenly he had a tremendous thirst.

Clarissa punched the room service number and ordered a pitcher of orange juice. "And a bottle of champagne," she added, winking at Greg.

While they waited for the room service delivery he stood at her window.

"You have a nice view of the mountain," he said. Off to the right somewhere in the dim panorama was the golf course. He pictured himself there now, teeing off with his assigned foursome, the guys making jokes about each other's shots.

When the knock came, he jumped slightly, then mumbled something about using the bathroom. When he emerged the waiter was gone. Clarissa was pouring them each a mimosa.

The drink was incredibly soothing to his dry throat. He perched on an ottoman, and she had hopped back onto the bed, leaning back against the headboard, her bare legs stretched out in front of her where the robe had parted. He realized he knew nothing about her.

"Are you married?" he asked.

"Was," she said.

"What happened?"

She shrugged. "What ever happens? It ends, that's all."

"Kids?"

"Nope." She wasn't going to help him out. She drank her mimosa and smoked, and watched him with her sleepy, amused expression.

"Do you like Phoenix?"

"Love it. Do you like Portland?"

It was Greg's turn to shrug. It was where he lived; he had never thought much about it.

He had no more conversational gambits to offer, and neither did she. He suddenly wanted more than anything to be golfing. He stood up and put the glass on the table. He had opened his mouth to tell her he had to be going, that his coming here had been a mistake, that he was sorry if he had caused any confusion, when she stretched and her robe fell open the rest of the way, exposing her small tanned breasts and long thin waist. She was wearing a minuscule pair of flowered panties. He stared.

She said, "You're a little overdressed, aren't you?"

He was surprised that such a moment should present itself without fanfare, that it should simply present itself. There was no planning, no buildup, no pent-up desire for this woman or anyone else besides his wife. He thought of the long-ago running with Jane, the kink she got in a calf muscle one day, his offer to massage it out. How his fingers had searched deep for the knot as she trusted him with the full weight of her bare leg across his lap. How he had lain awake for weeks after that, getting as far as fucking her in his sleep, one night jolting awake from a dream about her to find himself coming into his hand. How he had lived with thoughts of Jane all summer until she came back from vacation talking about a new boyfriend. And even then.

But desire now came upon him without warning and with no fantasy life attached to it; it announced itself sudden and whole. What had never taken the shape of a decision in his mind—not even when he was downstairs keeping his back to the lobby as he waited for the elevator—was now even less so. At no point when pulling off his shirt, stepping out of his shoes, or unzipping and dropping his trousers to the floor was he deciding to do this. It was more like being pulled with a tide; he had thought he was swimming parallel to the shore, when all the time he was being tugged seaward. That's what he thought of as he stood undressed and erect before Clarissa: of the sea, of her salt, of drowning in her. He wanted to drown. There was no separating this sudden exhilaration from a kind of flailing panic. Or the flailing from his need. Or need from the pure drifting pleasure of abandoning himself—which meant turning his back on all of it: Tim in his hospital bed, the school with its scorched field, his big house on Fircrest Drive that held his family, tiny and faceless at this moment.

He moved toward the bed and then was on the bed, over her on his hands and knees. She was smiling up at him, but he had never felt less like smiling. She maneuvered to put out her cigarette, and she was still reaching for the nightstand, grinding it out in the plastic ashtray, when Greg lowered himself onto her, his hands telling him with every new inch of skin that the woman was a perfect stranger to him.

II

P atty watched Sandy cry. They were in a rear booth, which muffled the normal din of Aldo's a little and afforded them some privacy. She fished out a pack of tissues and watched Sandy use them one after another until none remained. Her friend's face was pink and bloated. Patty wanted to shield her; she ordered for them both so Sandy wouldn't have to speak. When they were alone again, Sandy's eyes filled anew.

"The Stardust Motel," Sandy said bitterly. "Dated the same night he was supposed to be at a business meeting. I put it back in the pocket where I found it and waited. Then a week later he said he was going to a basketball game with a client. I said, 'Why not take the boys?' He got all irritated with me for asking that—said business was business, even if it was a game."

Patty could imagine Mitch taking that tone with his wife, over the very lie he was using to cheat on her. She had heard him insinuate that Sandy was too heavy, that she was dumb, that her customer service job at the telephone company was nothing compared to his brilliant work with computers. She had always wanted Sandy to call him on it, but had never seen her do it.

Sandy pulled a napkin from the aluminum dispenser and blew her nose. "So the night of his 'game' I left the house before he did and went to the motel."

"To confront him?" Patty asked.

"No, I only wanted to see him there with my own eyes. I parked in the back behind some trees. I was afraid he'd notice my car, but when he arrived he never even looked my way. Seeing him there . . ." Sandy's voice wavered and broke. She rubbed the tears from her eyes roughly. "He went into a room. Five minutes later, a woman pulled up in her own car and went to the same room."

"No one you know?"

"No, thank God. I mean, what if it had been you? Who could I have called then?"

*"Me?"* Patty said, backing her face away from the table, shocked. Then she saw Sandy trying to smile through swollen eyes.

"Oh. Joke." But she still felt the slight racing of her pulse from entertaining the thought, first, that she would ever take a lover, and second, that she had been linked, even in a sentence, to Mitchell Brown, a wiry, glib man who, she realized with unexpected emphasis, was about as far from her sexual type as she could imagine getting. Not that she had devoted a lot of time to thinking of her sexual type; Greg was it by default.

"Of course, she was thin," Sandy said. She sounded as if this fact made her the angriest of all.

The waiter appeared, wanting to know if there was anything else they wanted. They shook their heads and allowed him to top off their coffees and take away the snowy mound of tissues Sandy had stacked on her untouched plate of pancakes.

What could Patty tell her? That Mitchell was a shit was too obvious, too empty a statement.

Sandy sighed and sat back. "I shouldn't be bothering you with all this. After what you and Greg have been going through the past two days. I'm selfish."

Patty reached over and touched her arm. She couldn't think of anything more horrible than being Sandy in that motel parking lot, keeping her head low as if she were the guilty one.

"Of course you're not selfish. There's nothing we can do for Tim right now. We can't just stop living while we wait. I'm glad you called."

"That poor father. It's funny," Sandy mused. "I can imagine losing Mitch. But I could never imagine losing D. K. or John." She tugged on an auburn curl. "Children are different, aren't they? Even if they were to grow up and do something really horrible, you'd always take them back. No question."

"So you're not going to, with Mitch. . . ." It wasn't for her to say it, although she didn't see how Sandy could live with a man who had been to bed with someone else. It almost reassured her that Mitch seemed like the type: cocky, salesman-slick. Greg frustrated her in dozens of ways, but she had always known down to her bones that infidelity was never one of his offenses.

"Not going to take him back? Is that what I said?" Sandy's mouth pulled up in a self-mocking smile.

"*Are* you?" Patty shook her head at the thought.

Sandy's lip began to tremble again.

"I just don't like to see you treated badly, Sandy."

"You're so lucky," Sandy sniffed. "Greg is so completely honest with you."

"He doesn't lie," Patty conceded. "But he's certainly not perfect."

"Nobody's asking for perfection," Sandy said. "Just a little respect."

WHEN SHE got home, Greg was still at his golf tournament, and the girls were out. Patty automatically picked up a stray sock as she crossed the kitchen. Over the years she had trained herself never to walk through a room without picking up an object that was out of place and needed to be returned to a room in the direction she was heading. She did it so unconsciously that she would find herself answering the phone and beginning a conversation, only to look down minutes later surprised to see Greg's sneakers in her hands, or a red-marked geometry quiz.

She threw the sock in the hamper upstairs and lay down on the bed. She should get up and go for a run. Everything was catching up with her—the crisis Thursday, her drinking from last night, and now Sandy's troubles. Poor Sandy. Patty knew she wouldn't kick Mitch out. But even after he begged her forgiveness, she'd never be able to trust him again, never know if working late was really working late. It didn't matter; Sandy would rather live like that than risk being alone. Patty had listened to years of Sandy's hurt feelings and anger over Mitch; there had always been some dramatic blowup to relate in detail. And every time she concluded by saying how lucky Patty was to have Greg. It always felt like an invitation to reciprocate with the details, if any, of Patty's own marital disappointments. Patty had them, of course, but they weren't the type that were easy to narrate. Over the years the problems had seemed to grow both more pronounced and more ephemeral—the way Greg was so closed up, the way he'd go inside himself when she needed him most, the accumulated loneliness of that. These weren't the kind of complaints that would impress Sandy. Mitchell's crimes were so much more palpable—cutting remarks, shouted insults, and now adultery.

The doorbell woke her from a dream about the reunion dance that scattered as soon as she opened her eyes. She remembered only the dream's color: twilight blue, the color of granular shadows.

With effort she roused herself to answer the door. It was their retired neighbor Stan, asking to borrow their mower. Patty led him out to the garage.

"Greg off-duty today?" he asked.

She hated Stan's little quips, which always sprang from the premise that wives ruled the roost and husbands merely took orders and tried to stay out of trouble.

"He's golfing," she said. Patty hoisted up the garage door—Greg had been promising to put in an automatic opener for two summers now—and rolled out the lawn mower. She remembered that the last person to use it had been Tim Phelps. Patty had liked that boy—*did* like that boy, she meant. The coma made it seem as if he wasn't with them any longer, but she wouldn't allow herself to think that. Tim didn't yet have the veneer of sophistication that her girls and their boyfriends had. Instead he had called her Mrs. Goodman with a politeness that verged on reverence. She had always made it a point to bring him some lemonade and cookies midway through his yard work, and he was so embarrassed and pleased by this kindness that sometimes she had thought he was going to cry.

"Greg's going to have a hard time golfing without his clubs," Stan said, pointing to the bag leaning against the wall.

Patty looked at the clubs with surprise. "He must have forgotten them," she said. "I'm sure he can rent. He's playing in a high school reunion tournament."

"Well, just so he's back under lock and key by suppertime, eh?"

Patty watched Stan roll the mower down the sidewalk and tried not to despise him. You had to make allowances for old men. What Patty couldn't figure was how Betty, his wife, seemed to take the jests as some kind of compliment, a tribute to the moral superiority of the fair sex.

WHEN THE doorbell rang next, it was a stranger in khakis and a sport shirt.

"Is Gregory Goodman here?"

"No, he's not. May I help you?"

"Mrs. Goodman?"

"Yes."

The man put a thick envelope into her hands. "This is a summons for him to answer a civil complaint." Then he turned and was gone before Patty could say a word. Patty put the envelope on the kitchen table and sat down to stare at it. It had to be about the lightning. Greg had told her that Mr. Phelps had been approached by lawyers, but neither of them had really believed that anything would come of it. Still, the thought that Mr. Phelps might be planning to sue had stopped her from writing a note to him after the accident. She had never met Tim's father, but her impulse had been to write down all the small things she had noticed about Tim: his care with her plants, the way he'd lift them gently to one side when he was pulling weeds around them, how he wouldn't rest until he had completely finished a job, and how he straightened up after himself like no teenager she had ever seen. She would have praised Tim's character to his father, but wouldn't have said how these things, coupled with his almost ineffable sweetness, had made her just a little sad, even as they had moved her. He didn't have to be as good as all that for her to like him.

When Greg drove up, Patty was prepared to help him. Greg's way of dealing with this would be to read the summons and toss it aside. He wouldn't want to think about what kind of trouble he might be in. Even Patty had a hard time focusing on the matter of Greg's guilt or negligence in this; she much preferred to think of ways they could mobilize themselves. She had called her mother and gotten the name of a lawyer. The number was waiting right beside the phone. They would open the summons together, call the lawyer, then put the legal issue out of their minds for now. She couldn't believe that Greg would be held liable for what had happened. It was a tragedy, but there was no sense in trying to blame a person for what comes down out of the sky.

Patty opened the door to welcome him into the house and heard the roar of their lawn mower coming from Stan's backyard.

"Who won the tournament?" she said, bracing the screen door open.

Greg raised his head from examining anthills ranged on the cracks in the walk. "Monty," he said.

"Was it fun?"

"Sure."

"I saw you forgot your clubs. Were you able to rent?"

"Yeah," he said. Greg looked ashen. He was even more tired than she. Maybe she shouldn't show him the summons just yet. But he sat down heavily at the kitchen table.

"What's this?" he asked.

"I haven't opened it. A process server brought it for you. I don't think it's good."

He looked at her apprehensively. Then he reached for the envelope and opened it.

"It's Phelps," he said almost casually.

She nodded. "That's what I thought. I got the name of a lawyer from my mother if you want to call him right away."

"Negligence and reckless endangerment," he said. "That's the charge." His voice was almost lighthearted.

Patty went over and wrapped her arms around his shoulders. He stiffened slightly.

"It's going to be okay," she said. She sniffed his clothes. "Who's been smoking?"

"Some of the guys. We had a drink afterward in the clubhouse."

She laid her cheek on the top of his head. His hair smelled good, though his shirt smelled smoky. Maybe he had used one of the girls' herbal shampoos this morning.

"You want to go upstairs?" Patty said in his ear. For some reason, the cigarette smoke made her feel sexy. Greg felt so solid in her arms. Sandy was right; she was lucky.

Greg looked down at the kitchen table in front of him and patted her hand. "I'm wiped out," he said.

Patty sat down beside him and sighed. "Me, too. I'm glad these reunions only come once in twenty years."

Greg bumped his chair back from the table and said, "I'm going to take a shower."

PATTY WAS making a salad for the potluck that night. She had always enjoyed doing methodical things in the kitchen like chopping vegetables. When she had several neat piles all different colors, she began measuring out the ingredients for the dressing. Patty always followed recipes exactly. The few times she had departed from them, things always went wrong.

Greg was still damp when he came downstairs. He had changed into clean Bermuda shorts and a peach-colored polo shirt. He grabbed a slice of red pepper.

"What's for lunch?"

"Whatever you want to make," she said. "This is for the potluck tonight."

He dropped his hands to his sides. "Do we have to go to that?"

Patty was trying to level off a quarter-teaspoon of tarragon. "Don't you want to?"

"Not really. Last night was enough reuniting for me."

"Well, you got to go to the tournament this morning, too. I had to miss the hike because of Sandy's crisis."

"Oh. Right. How'd that go?" He asked her in the tone of voice he used when he really didn't want an answer.

"She's okay." Patty wasn't in the mood to talk about it yet; maybe tonight. The whole scene with Sandy had left her drained. She knew Greg wouldn't press her. He preferred to let emotionally ticklish topics slide by without inspection when he could. For once it suited her to let him do so.

"I really don't want to go out again," Greg said. "Especially now that I'm being sued."

"Greg, the lawsuit is going to go on for months. You can't stay in the house the whole time because of it."

"I think I'll stay home tonight."

Patty looked at him, her hands on her hips. "That'll be a lot of fun for me," she said. "You know I hate going to things like that alone."

Greg didn't answer her, getting a bottle of beer from the refrigerator and twisting off the cap. He went out the back door, and Patty saw him through the kitchen window, sitting on the patio. Suddenly she felt sorry for him. He did look miserable. She tossed the vegetables with the dressing and set the salad aside. They would have it tonight with a cook-out, at home.

WHEN THE phone rang, Patty was still facing Greg, watching his profile as he sipped beer. If Greg had turned to look at her he would have seen her smile fade as she talked. He would have seen her eyes fixed on him as she sat down at the kitchen table with the phone to her ear. He would have seen her hang up and still be sitting there, so that the two of them, one inside the house, the other out, resembled statues in their remarkable immobility.

T hough she felt herself moving through the kitchen, putting salad ingredients away, and though she exchanged words with the girls before they went into the den to watch a video, her own movements seemed an illusion to her. In this stillness, Patty tried to see around the things she knew for sure to the thing she didn't. Greg hadn't golfed, but had said he had. When supposedly golfing (but not: Stan's finger pointing out the clubs, Julie Reece's surprised little laugh—"Monty won the tournament? Doesn't he wish!"), Greg had been at the hotel. Did that have to mean he had gone there to find her? Was there really only one way to string these hard beads of fact together?

Patty saw them dancing together again: the heavy silver bracelets that slipped all the way up her arms when she raised them above her head, Greg's hand touching her bare skin. Had she had a misgiving when Clarissa had announced she was "keeping" Greg for one more dance? She didn't think so. Maybe the tiniest prick of surprise—not at Greg's standing there lamely, allowing himself to be "kept," but at Clarissa's assertiveness. No, that didn't surprise her, either. Clarissa had always been confident, sure she would get the part in the play if she decided it was hers.

She made herself a cup of black coffee and sat at the kitchen table, waiting for Greg to come in the house. He remained outside a long time, as if he felt himself already banished. Patty heard a curious rushing sound in her head, like the sound you hear when your ear is pressed to a shell. The hollowness went straight through her; she was composed of space. She was glad to let the noise of the girls' movie drown her out, fill the kitchen. Confront him now? Or just hold the knowledge to her, making sure she wasn't jumping to a wild conclusion? If she kept it to herself for a few days, she could watch him, judge his actions. Then she thought of Sandy and her stakeout at the motel, the degrading position of having to spy and suspect.

When Greg finally came in, he gave her a perfunctory half-smile, the kind he used as a substitute for communication when he wanted to be left alone. He got another beer from the refrigerator. The fact that he would turn himself off now, as he had done so many times in the past when she needed a connection to him, suddenly enraged her.

"Julie Reece called to check on the time for the potluck," Patty said.

"Oh?" Greg's voice was detached.

"She said Monty missed you at the tournament this morning. He didn't win it, by the way."

Greg turned to her, his face expressionless, the unopened bottle of beer in his hand.

"She also said she caught sight of you at the hotel this morning."

"Well, Julie Reece certainly had a lot to report," he said sarcastically.

"Why did you lie, Greg?"

"It's no big deal. On my way to the tournament I realized I'd forgotten my clubs, and thought I'd drop by the hotel to see a football buddy. We got to talking, and I never made it to the tournament." Greg was looking past her to the microwave.

"Clarissa played football, too? Wow. What a girl." Patty intended to smile with mock amazement but felt herself grimace instead.

Now he was looking at her, panic in his eyes. "What are you talking about?"

"Oh, Greg." The look on his face was as good as a confession. Patty shook her head, tears filling her eyes. *"Why?* Just because she was all over you last night? Someone you claimed to not even remember? Have you been doing this kind of thing for years and I've just been too stupid to see?"

"Patty. No." He crossed the room to her and tried to put his hand on her shoulder. She jerked it away.

"Patty. Please."

"Please what, Greg?" Patty felt her voice rise shrilly, lowered it because of the girls. She needn't have; the sounds of a chase scene roared from the den. "Please *what?*"

"I love you."

"You *love* me?" she said.

He nodded, tried to touch her arm. She drew back as if she had been scalded.

"Don't touch me. Ever again."

He sat still, looking past her. Then his face caved with grief in a way she had seen it look only once before, when Kiley had gotten pneumonia at the age of two, and they had walked into the hospital room to see her tiny body encased in an oxygen tent.

"Patty, I made a huge mistake. I've never done anything like this before, and I never would again. I don't know what made me do it now. Please, Patty." He stared straight at her as she said this, his eyes wet with tears. He looked so scared. She wanted to believe him, wanted to forgive everything, even—God, the irony—wanted to comfort him. But he had just admitted it: he had lied to her, had driven from their house—the house where they were raising their daughters together—and gone purposefully, single-mindedly, to Clarissa Jetty's hotel room. They must have arranged it last night, in between Greg's dances with his wife.

"I want you out of this house tonight," she said.

"What?" His face was incredulous.

"I'm not spending another night under the same roof with you."

"Then you leave," he said. "This is my house, too."

"Half of it is yours, and you'll get it in a settlement. But you're not staying here."

"Patty, for God's sake—"

Melissa came into the kitchen, heading for the cupboard where they kept the chips.

"Hi, Dad," she said. "Want to watch a movie with us? Eddie Murphy."

"Your father's leaving," Patty said.

"Where are you going?" Melissa said, pouring corn chips in a bowl. "Mom, do we have any salsa?"

"He's moving out."

Melissa's hand froze. She suddenly looked ten. "This is a joke, right?"

Patty felt Greg's eyes on her. She had the power to spare her daughters, to spare them all. She felt like a crone, like one of the sisters of Fate with a string and a knife in her hand. All she had to do was speak, laugh it off, release them from this moment before fracture, before everything they depended on broke into a thousand pieces. Melissa would say, "Very funny, Mom," then turn around and go back to the den to watch the movie. Greg would come over and put his arms around her, grateful beyond words. She would be like a saint in his eyes. Then she remembered how her husband had kissed her goodbye, just as on any other day, before driving straight to Clarissa Jetty's room. She didn't want to be a saint.

Melissa's lip was trembling. "What are you guys *talking* about?" she said.

Greg stood up and went to hug her. "It's only temporary, sweetheart. I did something stupid and your mom doesn't want to see me around for a while. We're going to work it out."

Melissa looked at her, her face accusing. "He doesn't have to leave, Mom. What could be so bad that he has to leave?"

Kiley wandered into the kitchen, and stopped, looking from one stricken face to another. "What's wrong with everyone?" she said.

PATTY DIDN'T watch as Greg's car backed out of the driveway. She heard the girls follow him out, heard voices murmuring out front, heard his car engine start up and then its diminishing sound as he moved down their street, away from them.

She heard the girls climb the stairs and heard Melissa sniffling. She heard them both go into Kiley's bedroom and shut the door. She wondered if they were lying on the bed curled together the way they did when they were little and wouldn't sleep without each other. She wished she could go be with them, feel their arms around her, too, but she knew they wouldn't speak to her now. Patty had put on sweats and drawn herself up into a ball underneath the quilt. She was still shivering. She had taken aspirin, and then on second thought had taken a Valium from a small prescription bottle that was two years out of date. She couldn't remember what it had been prescribed for originally, couldn't imagine herself ever having had a reason for needing it as she did this moment.

When she woke it was dark, and her throat was dry. Her head hurt when she moved her eyes. She went downstairs, hoping to find the girls in the den, watching TV. They weren't in the backyard or in the kitchen. She went back upstairs and found both their bedrooms empty. At nine she heated herself some soup and made tea. She wrapped a blanket around herself and sipped tea in the den, the TV off, a blank gray-green eye. She tried to remember if the girls had told her about their plans tonight, and what she might have given permission for. She couldn't remember a thing.

She felt as if she had the flu; the shivering was growing worse. Her anxiety over the girls intensified. She had been wrong to withdraw from them before they had discussed things; she saw that now. She should have put them first, tried to give them something to hold on to. She was glad now that Greg had told them the separation was only temporary, though that was not true. But the girls would need to get used to this a little at a time, and if they needed to have some hope at the beginning, so be it.

At ten they came in together. They quit talking when they saw her. Patty struggled up from the couch. "Where were you girls?"

They avoided her eyes. "We went to get a pizza," Kiley said.

"Do you want to have some tea with me and talk about what happened today?"

They shook their heads. In unison. And went upstairs, without even saying good night.

On Tuesday the girls started school. Patty was grateful for the brief flurry of activity Monday night as they traded phone calls with their friends, trying to determine if everyone would be wearing shorts, jeans, or skirts on the first day. It would have been Greg's first day back, too, had the principal not called on Monday to deliver the message that the school district was also being sued by Mr. Phelps, and that the school board had suspended Greg with pay, pending an investigation into the lightning accident. Patty didn't know where to deliver this message until Greg called later that day to let her know he was staying at his mother's house, in case she wanted to reach him. She told him what the principal had said, and into his silence felt how strange it was for her to stand back and let him flounder, how the automatic gesture of reassurance she might have made was suffocated by this new, pervasive anger.

Patty had thought about taking a sick day from work, but as soon as she was at her desk she was glad she hadn't. She had an audit report due Thursday, and when she plunged into its long columns of blessedly neutral, wonderfully truthful numbers, she began for the first time in almost forty-eight hours to feel like herself. She loved her job, loved how she took reams of pure data and converted it into slim reports in which everything was tabulated and made perfectly clear.

Work had saved her life when she was a young mother just coming back from two years at home with the babies. As much as she was devoted to them, would walk through fire for them, and had practically fainted with pleasure at the grassy scent of their toddler skin, she had been going mad at home. Other mothers advised her to go easier on herself, let the house get messy, let the children finish the day wearing rompers that had been stained at lunch. But Patty couldn't stand to be around disorder, and when she stayed at home found herself doing two loads of laundry a day, and picking up every toy as soon as the children had played with it. She knew such obsessiveness wasn't good for her or for the girls. But it was only when she was back at work, pouring her perfectionism into balancing numbers, that she was able to let a little healthy chaos into her home.

Now, her house was in perfect order. Having Greg out of it just one day showed her how much she was in the habit of picking up behind him, and how absolutely neat things would stay with him missing.

At noon she called Sandy, who worked a couple of blocks away. They arranged to meet at Kizer's deli. On the walk over, Patty couldn't decide if she was up to telling Sandy about Greg. The hurt was so personal, so embarrassing and stinging. Yet she thought she almost owed it to Sandy, to confide in her friend at her lowest moment, put them on an equal footing.

There were no tables, so they settled for places at the counter, the lunchtime crowd pressed against their backs. Unbelievably, Sandy looked radiant.

"I know you're going to be mad at me," she said happily to Patty, taking a large bite of her sandwich, "but Mitch and I worked things out."

"You forgave him?" Patty asked, shocked.

"Patty, you should have seen him. He was so guilty and so sorry and so sad. I had to. He practically didn't even give me a chance to yell at him because he was so busy telling me what a louse he'd been. He totally broke down."

"What about the other woman?"

"Oh, that's over. Mitch said he isn't even going to finish the software job he was working on for her company. He's going to subcontract it out. He gave me his solemn word that this would never happen again."

"His word."

Sandy looked at her, annoyed. "Yes, Patty. I'd appreciate it if you wouldn't sound so sarcastic. Mitch and I are going to start completely over. We're going to Hawaii at Thanksgiving, and we're leaving the boys with my parents. Kind of a second honeymoon."

She found herself gripped by an unreasonable anger toward Sandy—she suddenly hated her springy curls, her childish freckles, the crumb of French bread on her complacent lips.

"Don't you think you're being naive?" Patty inquired coolly. She was gratified to see the irritating mouth open a little in surprise.

Sandy looked at her uncertainly. Then she jutted her chin. "No, I don't. That's pretty judgmental, don't you think?"

"The man makes a fool of you and you take him back with open arms. I'm supposed to congratulate you?"

Tears sprang to Sandy's eyes. "Let's just forget it, okay?" she said curtly, gathering up her sandwich wrapper and cup. "I don't expect you to understand. You've never had to deal with something like this before. You're the one with the perfect marriage."

"*Dammit,* will you please stop telling me what kind of a marriage I have? You have no idea what you're talking about." Patty's voice cracked.

A man who was trying to shoulder past them to a vacant stool glanced quickly at them and then away.

"I've got to get back," she muttered. Sandy followed her out onto the sidewalk.

"Patty, what's wrong with you?" Sandy asked. Her forehead was creased with puzzlement. "What's happened?"

Patty stared at her helplessly. If she couldn't say it now she would never be able to. She would be admitting that the friendship was a sham, just like her marriage.

"Greg cheated," she finally blurted. The words made something in her shrivel. They sounded so banal. She suddenly realized why Sandy retailed every painful detail of her marriage. It transformed the pain into something you could hold at arm's distance—it turned the pain into a story about pain. But Patty wasn't ready to do that yet. She needed to feel it to understand it, if understanding was possible.

"I don't believe it." Sandy shook her head. She put her hand on Patty's forearm. "Tell me," she demanded.

Patty looked at Sandy's concerned expression, the curiosity that animated her eyes.

"I can't talk right now," Patty said. "I'll call you."

"If you don't," Sandy called after her, "I'm calling you. I'm not letting you do this alone."

Patty waved.

PATTY COULDN'T forget Sandy's glowing skin, her happiness over her reconciliation. Was she right, after all? Were you supposed to deal with an unfaithful husband by screaming and crying and then accepting his remorse, his fresh promises? Maybe that was possible if you could believe that the infidelity was a symptom of absolutely nothing, that it existed without a context and in a vacuum. It would be like saying Greg gave in to a moment of sexual hunger the way he sometimes gave in to a craving for a bacon cheeseburger, though he knew it was bad for him. Ridiculous to think that believing that offered any consolation. If the matter was that trivial, then such a lapse was bound to happen again. Or had already happened before. Patty wasn't Sandy; she wouldn't live her life in a way that accommodated a pattern like that.

If Greg's act wasn't trivial, then that meant it was large; it was important. It might have been one act (was it?), but it rendered a kind of diagnosis for the whole marriage.

There was a strange thing happening with Greg out of the house.

Every resentment Patty had buried throughout the years was surfacing, as whole and fresh as the day on which it had been conceived. Without her husband's actual body around, a kind of hologram of him was popping up in every room, inviting Patty to stage old fights with him free of the boundaries of time and space. The grievances were so established that she hadn't even bothered to fight about them in recent years: the way he could sit in an armchair watching a football game on television while she spent two hours picking up the house around him. How he never even *saw* that. The way he made her do the emotional work of their marriage, always forcing her to air their differences. Then when she'd bring something up, he'd stare at her as if he didn't know what she was talking about, until even she felt the whole thing was her problem.

The trouble with Greg was that he couldn't face emotions, his own or anyone else's. Patty had scored him once in a marital personality quiz she had seen in *McCall's* magazine, and found him to be a perfect passive-aggressive. To all the world, Greg Goodman looked like a perfectly calm, friendly kind of guy. Which he was, most of the time. But because he couldn't get at any of his deep feelings, he showed his hostility to Patty in little undermining ways. Like tuning her out when she talked about her day. Or never doing any of the heavy lifting when it had come to disciplining the girls.

Greg occasionally blew up to vent his irritations, but he never looked very far into their causes. Patty even believed him when he told her he had no idea why he had been unfaithful to her with Clarissa Jetty. How like him not to know. But not knowing didn't change things. The fact was that he had hurt her in the one way she could never quite get over. He had to realize it, too; she had cried for weeks in college when they had broken up, and he had immediately begun going out with someone else. She had always resented how easy he had made that look, and it had almost kept her from taking him back. Like his attitude then, his attitude now made this adultery look offhand. And to be so offhand he must, on some level, really not like her.

Did she like him? It hadn't been necessary to consider it for the longest time. The most important relationship in the house for years had been between them and the kids, with Patty and Greg automatically united by that demand. Their family patterns worked as smoothly as a watch, and the watch itself was the household—its ticking the filling of the cupboards, the feeding and sheltering and schooling of the girls, the mounting of seasonal defenses against disorder, against fallen leaves and growing grass and clogged gutters. These things didn't need thinking about, just as rolling into the crook of Greg's arm night after night didn't need thinking about, or brushing her teeth didn't need thinking about. Now that the mechanism had been smashed, ground into fragments by a heel, Patty was trying to see what had driven those predictable sweeps of its minute hand. What was there about Greg and Patty's marriage that made it inevitable, or inviolable, or permanent? If you swung a stick at a wasp's nest, that thing that looked so substantial, so voluminous and crafted, turned out only to be papery shreds. After the confused, angry swarming of the wasps, there was nothing.

Who knew, at the age of sixteen, why you were attracted to another person? Patty knew she had been drawn to Greg's looks, his physical presence, his silence that to her signaled depth. The fact that Greg had been reserved as a teenager had seemed like the sign of a thoughtful and complicated person to Patty. She had also liked the feeling of being in charge of their conversations, of knowing that Greg was somehow—for all his bulk and muscle—verbally dependent on her. It was only after they had been married for several years that she had begun to realize what a burden it was, feeling your own feelings and guessing at someone else's, and living on the basis of what you imagined to be true.

PATTY DIDN'T know what to do about the girls. They were avoiding her at every turn, and she knew this not talking about things was going to make it worse for them in the end. Not that Patty wanted to humiliate herself by talking about it. She didn't want to share this with them, though she hungered for the consolation of their company, their near flesh to make her feel less alone. But it was she who should be consoling them for the absence of their father. How to explain that absence to them? It didn't seem possible to tell her daughters that their father had been to bed with another woman. What good would that do fifteen-year-old girls who were having their summers of first boyfriends? Patty wanted them to know the truth so they would understand, but she didn't want the price of knowing such a truth to be a lasting bitterness, like an aspirin dissolved too soon on the tongue, spoiling the taste of everything that came after. She supposed they might have guessed it already, although perhaps not—the urge to protect themselves would be strong. Even guessing it, they would probably want their mother to forgive their father.

Patty had so far turned to no one in her family, not her own mother, who would urge reconciliation, not her father, who would be embarrassed and not want to go into it, and not her sister, who was on her third husband and seemed to treat divorce and remarriage as matter-of-factly as if she were letting an old lease expire and signing a new one. And the girls, whom she longed to hold, to cuddle, into whose hair she wished she could cry—the girls went stiff and angular whenever Patty entered the room.

THE FIRST time it happened, Patty was in the parking lot of Thriftway's. She had bought frozen fish sticks, frozen pizza, frozen waffles, frozen ravioli, and frozen burritos. She discovered when she went to pay that her wallet was missing one of the two twenties she was sure she had in it. The total came to $24.79, and after holding up the line while she rummaged through her coin purse for some singles and quarters, she finally gave up and charged the whole thing on her ViSA, an act she associated with poor and desperate people. The entire episode took only two minutes longer than it might have if she had not wasted time searching for the money, but it was six P.M. on a weekday, and everyone behind her was hungry and impatient, standing in wrinkled work clothes, and she heard a muttered comment behind her about disorganized people. Then when Patty returned to her car, which in fifteen minutes had heated up to about a hundred degrees, she had the sudden insight that one of her daughters had stolen the twenty-dollar bill from her. That's when she couldn't seem to catch her breath, and when the parked cars around her own swam and melted together. She couldn't even command her own hand to start the car engine and turn on the air-conditioning, or press the button to lower the windows and open the sunroof. Instead she sat there, gasping for air that wouldn't come, knowing that her groceries were thawing, that people had thought badly of her in line, that her daughters hated her and were deceiving her, and that her husband had cared so little for her that he didn't even bother to be careful when he drove off to have his affair, but walked in broad daylight past all the people they had known in high school, to the bedroom of a woman who was not even attractive, who dressed in a ridiculous way, and who was obviously—Patty knew no other way to say it—a tramp.

It took several minutes for Patty's breathing to return to normal. During this time she had been able to get some air circulating through the car, and to turn the radio on to the news. She let the sound of the announcer's voice soothe her, his words wash over her as he reported a recent Supreme Court decision regarding prisoners' rights, that the NASDAQ was up thirteen points in mixed trading, that Congress was discussing a bill to limit federal assistance to state fisheries programs, and that, in a look at local news, high school football player Timothy Phelps had now been unconscious for seven days after having been struck by lightning during practice, and that the school board was looking into charges that the Willamette High junior varsity coach, now suspended, had been guilty of reckless endangerment of his team on the playing field that day.

Patty turned off the radio with the same indignation as if they had been talking about her, then remembered; they weren't. They were talking about Greg, a totally separate person.

When she got home, Greg's car was at the curb. What an odd feeling it was to see the car positioned just as it had been on a thousand other days, but to know that everything it signified now was different. He was a visitor.

He was sitting on the patio. Neither of the girls appeared to be home, although it was six-thirty.

She took her time putting the groceries in the freezer, then opened the sliding glass door and went outside. She took the seat opposite his, noticing how the vinyl cushions had collected a film of dust; she would have to come out here with a sponge after he left.

He tried to smile at her. He looked good, shaved and clean. She didn't know what she'd expected, but the fact that the past three days hadn't taken a physical toll on him irritated her.

"Patty, this is ridiculous. I want to come home. I have a right to be at home."

"I think you gave up some rights Sunday morning, Greg."

He looked away and drummed his fingers on the Plexiglas table beside him.

"It's not fair to keep me away from my own daughters."

"No one's keeping you away. Just arrange to see them."

"You know how hard that's going to be. I'm lucky if I run into them fifteen minutes a day when we live in the same house. When is the last time I got one of them to go out to a movie or dinner? They're not into that kind of thing anymore."

Patty shrugged. "You might be surprised. They've never been in this situation before. Anyway, they seem to be totally on your side. They haven't talked to me since you left."

Greg looked at her. "You haven't told them?"

She shook her head.

"I appreciate that." He cleared his throat.

Patty was silent a minute. "I don't want to, but at some point I might have to. They're furious with me. I think they think I threw you out because you didn't take out the garbage or something."

"You can be pretty tough about that."

Patty didn't smile.

"I miss you, Patty. I'm as sorry as I've ever been about anything in my life. Isn't there any way you could forgive one mistake?"

"How do I know it's one mistake?"

"Because it is. I swear it."

"Oh."

Patty remembered what Sandy had said about Mitch's tears, his beating up on himself, his sworn reform. Weak Sandy, for buying into that.

"Look, we can go to counseling or something, if you want," he said.

"Greg, I really don't feel like paying to tell some third party that my husband went off to screw the first woman who made herself available to him."

"It's not like I was waiting for the chance," Greg said, his voice low. "It just happened. I don't know why."

That his defense was ignorance only enraged her. That he was so willfully unaware of himself that he wouldn't even stop to see what might have gone into it—whether it was something about Clarissa or something about Patty, or even the pressure he was under because of the accident. It didn't matter. He did it, and was trying to play dumb as a way of not taking responsibility.

"You keep saying that," Patty said, her voice rising. "As if that makes it somehow more bearable—that you didn't know why. Don't you think you should try to figure it out before you come back here, asking me to pretend it never happened? Have you, for one second"—she was shouting at him now—"imagined if things were the other way around? How it would make you feel?" Stan and Betty could probably hear her through their open windows. Her nails were hurting her palms from her clenched fists.

"I'd take you back, if you were sorry."

"Oh—so you take the whole thing so lightly that it wouldn't even matter. Well, thank you. That's good to keep in mind."

"That's not what I meant." He exhaled and shook his head. "It's clear I'm not going to be able to say anything here that will be the right thing."

"That's right," Patty said. She heard the petulance in her voice, but couldn't do anything about it. She didn't want to.

"Patty, be reasonable. I don't want to lose you. I don't want to lose the girls."

The front screen door banged, and a minute later Melissa poked her head out the back door. She had the first smile on her face Patty had seen since Sunday.

"Hi, Daddy, are you home?"

"For a chat. And I was hoping to see you girls. You want to go grab a bite?"

"I just had McDonald's with Sarah."

"Well, you want to come and watch me eat something? You can have dessert."

"Jason's coming over. We're going to a movie."

"Do you have homework?" Patty asked.

"Not really," Melissa said, talking to the table.

"What does 'not really' mean? Do you have homework or not?" Patty's voice was sharper than she intended.

"It means I have to read a chapter for social studies, but I can do it later, *okay? Jeez.*" Melissa banged the door shut and disappeared.

Maybe Patty had gone about things wrong kicking Greg out. Maybe she should leave instead. Let him live here and deal with the girls.

After a silence Greg said, "Where's Kiley?"

"Who knows?"

"Patty." Greg paused. "We were barely on top of things with the girls with both of us here. What's going to happen now?"

"That's a good question." Her hands, still in fists, longed to pound against him, startle the expression of fatherly concern off his face. Instead she banged the door behind her as loudly as her teenager had.

PATTY WATCHED Greg's car pull away from her window upstairs in the bedroom. Again, she felt her chest close up and the room go airless. She sat down on the bed, and her fingers clutched at the spread, making little bunches out of the cloth. Objects around her grew bright with color and then twisted like taffy while she fought to get air. Then, just as suddenly, the things in her room were themselves, and Patty drew a large breath.

Overnight she had lost control of the girls. The moment Greg left the house Sunday, it was as if they had counted themselves free of all normal boundaries. Their anger had translated into not talking to her, which meant that there was no one to ask permission of, since their father was not around. Not asking permission had turned into not needing permission, and not needing permission from anyone rendered Patty meaningless to them.

Patty went down the hall and knocked on Melissa's door. Then she knocked louder, to be heard over the music. She opened the door a few inches and saw Melissa sitting on her unmade bed painting her toenails a pale lavender.

"Melissa, do you know anything about a twenty-dollar bill that was missing from my wallet?"

"Ky and I needed lunch money," Melissa said dismissively.

"And you didn't feel it necessary to ask me before getting money out of my purse?"

"You were in the shower. We had to get going. We were getting a ride."

Patty didn't know what to say. It almost sounded reasonable, the way Melissa put it. If the girls weren't being this rude to her, she might not feel so betrayed.

"Don't take money again without asking first."

Melissa shrugged. "Okay."

"And I don't want you to go out tonight. It's a school night, and you said you have some reading to do."

Melissa looked up, panicked. At last she was making eye contact. "Mom, it's only twelve pages! I can do it when I wake up tomorrow. And the movie gets out before ten."

Again Patty felt stymied. If she didn't feel she was losing control in general she would probably allow this. But she had to assert herself.

"If you had asked me beforehand, I might have said okay. Especially if you had been home for dinner and done your reading then. But now I'm saying no."

"Mom, that's so unfair!"

"Tell me what's unfair about it."

"How did I know I should be home for dinner? It's not like we've had any regular meals the last two days. How am I supposed to know anything about what's going on around here, anyway? You and Daddy just do what you want and don't bother to tell us what's going on. Then you blame us for doing the same thing."

Doing what she wanted. Was that what Patty was doing?

"We're adults, and we have a problem right now, and I'm sorry things aren't normal. They probably won't feel normal for a while. You, on the other hand, are not yet an adult, and now, especially, I need to know I can count on you to follow some rules."

Melissa stared sullenly at her, and then put the cap on her polish. She had inserted a cotton ball between each toe, which made her look as if she had strange paws instead of feet.

"When is Daddy coming back?" Melissa was using a fingernail to scrape some errant polish from the skin of her big toe.

"I don't know."

Melissa silently studied her pedicure, then began plucking the cotton puffs from between her toes.

"You must know! You're the one who sent him away. He didn't want to go, he said so." She clutched her bouquet of white balls. "Mom, we don't *care* what he did, okay? Even if it was really, really big."

Patty knew then that she knew. Or knew as much as she was able to let herself. Patty was on the point of telling Melissa that the offense wasn't *against* her, therefore it wasn't hers to forgive, but stopped herself. Of course it belonged to her. It belonged to them all. Sadness filled her for her daughters, even more, in this particular moment, than for herself. She reached over and petted Melissa's hair, which was no longer as innocently soft as a child's. She put something sticky in it now, some mousse or other product unnecessary in any-one's eyes but her own.

"Mom, can I please go to the movie? Jason's already on his way over. I'll ask you first from now on, okay? And I'll read my social studies tomorrow morning. Please?"

Patty considered. Perhaps she had made her point. Certainly she was encouraged by the fact that she and Melissa were talking at all.

"All right, but don't go anywhere after. I want you in bed by eleven."

"Sure."

"Where's your sister, anyway?"

Melissa shrugged. "Probably at Will's house."

AFTER MELISSA left, Patty dialed Will's number. His mother answered, and told Patty that she hadn't seen Kiley all day and that Will was at a band rehearsal. Kiley came in at ten, and tried to skirt the liv-ing room where Patty was reading and head directly upstairs. Patty was right behind her.

"Kiley, I'd like to know where you've been all evening."

"With Will."

"His mother said he had a band rehearsal."

"Oh, great. Call my friends' mothers and make me look like a jerk."

Kiley had not turned around, and Patty was talking to her moving back as she walked upstairs.

"I'd like an answer. Where were you?"

"I told you, with Will. I hung out at their rehearsal." Now she was in her bedroom and turned to shut the door, ducking her head so she wouldn't have to look at her mother. Patty moved into the doorway. Her daughter's eyes were bloodshot, and clinging to her jeans and T-shirt was the unmistakable smell of marijuana.

"You've been smoking pot, Kiley."

"Oh, *please.*" Kiley turned and plopped facedown on the bed. She reached up to her nightstand and turned on the radio. Some kind of noise that Patty wouldn't even call music poured out of the speakers at top volume. Patty went over and turned it off.

"Don't lie to me. I can smell it all over you."

"One of the guys in the band may have smoked a joint. I don't do that stuff."

"Kiley, you are grounded for three weeks. You will not see Will, you will not baby-sit, you will not go out with your sister or your other friends. You will go to school and come home. Period."

"The hell I will," Kiley yelled, springing up to a sitting position. Her eyes were puffy as well as red, and her hair had straggled out of its clip.

"Four weeks."

"Who's going to make me stay home?" Kiley screamed in her mother's face.

"Your father and I will make you," Patty said, before she thought. Even after she remembered that Greg didn't live with them, she didn't take it back. Greg didn't have a job right now. He could pick Kiley up after school and see that she stayed home until Patty got off work.

"You can't make me, and he can't. He's not even here. The only way you can make me is if you put me in chains, which you'd probably love to do."

Patty said, "Five weeks."

Kiley said "Fuck you," and before Patty even knew what she did her hand darted out and slapped her daughter's face. Then she turned as calmly as she could and left the room. Kiley got up and slammed the door behind her so hard it made the pictures in the hall rattle. "Fuck you, fuck you, fuck you," she screamed from inside her room.

Patty went in and sat on the edge of her bed. She was trembling. She had never hit either girl in her life. Once or twice she had threatened a spanking, but that was all. Greg had been dead set against using any physical punishment, even a swat on the hand, because of his father. Now she had slapped Kiley, and far from giving her back a sense of authority, she felt in that moment that Kiley was entirely lost to her, and that she had just proved it. She was afraid of her own daughter, afraid that she couldn't enforce the grounding. What leverage did she have? What protection did she have against rage like that? When the twins were toddlers, they had both had tantrums when they didn't get their way. But you could hold Melissa through hers, and the pressure of your arms and the sound of your voice would get through to her, and little by little her screaming and crying would relax into sniffles until finally she was your own child again, the one you knew, snuggling in your arms. But you couldn't contain Kiley during hers; she'd go limp and slide out of your arms like butter, or turn her arms and legs into a windmill of kicks and blows. You had to let her get through it herself on the floor, screaming and writhing and sometimes pounding her head on the floor. It was hard for Patty to watch, but afterward Kiley, too, would climb into her lap for a hug. It was like a storm passing through her, pure and cleansing. There was no malice in a baby, as there was in her fifteen-year-old daughter, a person who, Patty discovered, could stare at her mother with pure hatred.

On Wednesday her boss, Andrew Nichols, called her into his office, which was on the corner of the sixteenth floor and had two walls of glass. One faced east across the Willamette to Mount Hood, and the other faced south with a view of the river traffic and the bridges. Andy was a pleasant middle-aged man with thinning hair and expensive suits. His features seemed somehow too generous for his face, the bulbous nose and wide mouth giving him a deceptively comic appearance. The benign face had been a business asset; people never quite realized how serious Andy could be about the bottom line until he had gotten the better of them in a negotiation. But he had always been a friend to Patty, letting her work at home when the girls were sick, giving her flextime when she needed to attend a school pageant or be a room mother on a field trip.

"Patty, you've been doing great work. You're my most consistent accounts manager."

"Thanks, Andy."

"You know about the Sunlink expansion project."

Patty nodded.

"I want to pull you off your regular accounts and give you sole responsibility for Sunlink. It will mean some traveling back and forth to San Francisco. Are the girls old enough to do without you for short stretches?"

For some reason she heard herself saying travel would be no problem, that she could handle the overtime, that she welcomed the responsibility—all the answers she had never let herself give because of the family. They were the right answers, as far as her job was concerned. Andy said it was high time she put herself on the partner track; if she performed as well as he expected on Sunlink there was no telling where she might go with the company.

She took the elevator back down to her small, windowless office on the fourteenth floor and shut the door behind her. She surveyed the pictures on her desk. The most recent family portrait was three years old. The twins still had braces on and were dressed alike for the photo, something they had stopped doing shortly after the time that picture had been taken. Patty had her hair a few inches longer then, but Greg looked about the same. They all faced forward, parents in back, girls in front, smiling for the camera. She could still remember the patter the photographer had used to get them to loosen up: "Patty, get that frown off your face, that little one parked between your eyebrows; Greg, you look about as relaxed as a frog on a freeway. Now you girls, just keep it up, you ravishing beauties. What are we going to do about these parents of yours? Okay, okay, here it comes—I see Patty beginning to uncurl, there's a teensy smile on Greg . . . we're almost there, think Tahiti, think Yucatan, Pago Pago, Bora Bora, Walla Walla . . . okay! We got it."

And he did get it. The family looked totally united in their natural, full smiles, as if just coming together to sit side by side were pleasure enough in this world.

What had she just promised Andy? The words leapt out of her mouth with no forethought. Of course travel would be a huge problem. The girls couldn't be alone, not now.

WHEN SHE asked Greg to come back to the house, she was chagrined at the relief in his voice. She corrected the mistaken impression immediately.

"I mean just for a couple of days, Greg. I've got to go to San Francisco on business. You need to be here for the girls."

"Well, it's a start, right?"

After supper on Sunday, Patty wrote the address and phone number of her San Francisco hotel and pinned it to the refrigerator with a Willamette High Cougars magnet. She stepped around Greg's duffel bags in the front hall and found him in the garage, filling the mower with gas. As she saw him bent over the funnel, holding the gallon can in a steady, patient manner, she felt an unexpected surge of tenderness. She stood still, remembering what love felt like—a warmth that moved along your nerves, an exquisitely live feeling. She saw herself running from the bus stop home to their campus apartment with its five square feet of patio that they were so proud of. The urgency to reach him. The almost physical addiction of his smell, how she'd wear his flannel shirt as a jacket in order to have that scent wrapped around her all the time. Patty both envied that young woman her passion and saw her as heedless—unaware and unconcerned. Rushing toward some future she had no understanding of.

"Okay, Greg. I left my number inside. Call me if anything is up with the girls."

As the cab pulled away from the curb she felt how strange this departure was: she was estranged from everyone in the house; no one except Melissa had even wished her a good trip.

Patty only had breathing attacks on the way to her house, or in her house. Never at work, never on her way to work. And now, with every tenth of a mile the taxi meter measured between Patty and her family, her breaths seemed to grow freer and fuller until she was not aware of them at all.

WHEN THE flight attendant announced their descent, she ran a brush through her hair and freshened her lipstick. Morgan would be waiting to pick her up at the gate. Patty had told him she would take a taxi to the hotel, but this was her first trip to San Francisco for Sunlink, and he'd said he wanted to welcome her. The expansion was Morgan Hale's project. If everything went through, he would go from being vice president of operations to chief operating officer. Tomorrow Patty was presenting a preliminary brief on the tax profile of the expansion, and tonight Morgan wanted to meet with her to be prepped.

She saw him before he saw her. She had met Morgan on one of his trips to Portland when Andy was wooing him for the account, and was conscious of finding him attractive. No doubt her girls would find him homely next to Greg. He was, in fact, everything Greg was not. Greg was fit and lean and still wore the same size Levi's he had in college. Morgan was bulky under his custom tailoring. His face was jowly and pink. Greg did his best never to wear anything more formal than a corduroy jacket; Morgan was the kind of man who seemed born for business wear. Her father had favored sport coats and slacks, bought off the rack, for his job selling insurance. His ties had always been a little off center, and despite her mother's interventions, he liked sporting vinyl pen holders printed with the company logo in his breast pocket. Patty had always admired the men she worked with who dressed in a more conservative—and, in her mind, more powerful—corporate style.

He took her wheeled suitcase from her. "Nothing checked? Are you this efficient in every area of your life?" Patty smiled at him when he rested his hand lightly on her shoulder in greeting.

He lifted her suitcase into the trunk and opened the car door for her. It was some expensive womblike sedan. Patty settled back in the cushioned leather seat and let the city slide by as he wove through the streets to her hotel.

"I haven't been here in years," she said.

"No? What a shame. It's truly a great city, one of a kind. Tomorrow I'll show you around. After your presentation we could do a couple of things in the afternoon, have some dinner."

"I'm sure you've got a family to attend to," Patty said. It was more a question than a statement.

"They're used to my business hours," he said.

He pulled the car under the hotel awning and handed his keys to the valet.

"Let's give your bag to the bellman and go into the bar to talk about the meeting," he said. Patty checked in and followed him into the darkened lounge; a jazz trio was playing from the corner. The place was jammed with people, and the only open table was next to the musicians.

"How about if we talk in the room?" Patty suggested. "There's no light here anyway to look at the charts I have." As soon as she said it, she wondered if the suggestion was improper. She had so little experience with business travel. In her self-consciousness the details of the marble lobby seemed extraordinarily vivid to her as they waited for the elevator—she stared down at the ashtray and wondered who ever dared muss the fine white sand imprinted with the hotel's seal. Inside the elevator they were reflected in the brass doors—two well-dressed people heading up to a hotel room at night. It took her several tries to get her key card to work right, but he tactfully did not try to assist her.

"Nice," he said, as she went around the room turning on lamps. Her king-sized bed dominated the space. Someone had already turned down the spread and left a boxed candy on the pillow, along with a card to fill out for room-service breakfast. Patty tried not to look at it as she arranged the two chairs by the desk and spread out her papers.

"Should I phone for something to eat? Some coffee?" she asked.

"No, not for me. How about cracking open the safe, though?" He gestured toward the mini-bar with its plastic seal.

Patty crouched before the refrigerator and inspected its rows of miniature liquor bottles. "We seem to have everything," she said.

"Bourbon, straight up." Morgan stood by the window, surveying the view of downtown. Patty handed him his drink and popped the tab of her diet Coke. He nodded toward her soda. "I'm disappointed. You're not joining me?"

"I've got to keep a clear head for tomorrow."

"You'll do fine. You know, I was delighted when Andy said it was you who was going to be assigned to the project."

Patty tried to conceal her pleasure. "Well, let's work on selling your board on the deal. I've got some very attractive tax options to show them."

It was close to midnight when he left, but they were well rehearsed for the meeting. They were both exhausted when she saw him to the door.

"Breakfast tomorrow?" he asked.

She had been looking forward to ordering something in her room, but Morgan's suggestion had the power of statement for her, as if he were merely voicing what had already been decided. It wasn't something she minded. In fact she liked releasing control to someone else for once.

After seeing him out she changed into the terry hotel robe and began her ritual of removing makeup and rubbing night cream into her skin. Then she patted a few drops of a special gel around her eyes that was supposed to eliminate lines. The gel came in a tiny jar and cost sixty dollars. Patty had just bought it, and every night she peered into the mirror to see if she looked younger. Tonight she thought she did, but maybe that was only because of the hotel's expensive soft light and the fact that from here she could not see herself in contrast to her daughters with their perfect skin. Maybe she was enjoying this trip too much, she thought ruefully—like a wicked stepmother abandoning the beautiful daughters to go to the ball herself. But it wasn't like that at all. The beauties were safe at home in the castle where they belonged. And Patty wasn't here to please herself; she was just doing her job.

S un flooded the conference room and lit up the sheen on the mahogany table. China coffee cups were scattered here and there. No one had touched the tray of pastries in the middle of the table.

"Excellent presentation," one of the vice presidents was saying, tapping his copy of the report.

"We should steal her away to Sunlink, don't you think?" Morgan asked, clapping his associate on the back.

"Wonderful idea. Has Morgan seen that you have everything you need?"

"Oh, yes. He's been extremely helpful."

"Fine, then." The man gathered up his papers and shook her hand in parting.

Patty turned to Morgan when they were alone. "So you think it went well?"

"I think it went very well. I have a feeling we're going to move ahead on this. That means I'll be coming up to Portland and Seattle in the next few months to open up the new offices." He propelled her to the elevators by touching her elbow. "Are you still up for some sights?"

"Sure, if you're free. I've got plenty to keep me busy if you're not." She lifted her stack of Sunlink annual reports.

"I'll be tied up here until two. Then how about I swing by your hotel and we head to North Beach? Ever been there?"

"Not for ages." Not since, Patty thought, she and Greg had taken a weekend trip to San Francisco just before the girls were born. They were poor and had no money for a vacation but were desperate to get away. They drove the twelve hours down I-5, and stayed in a modest motel on the waterfront.

"We'll start there for some coffee. Then for dinner I know a great place where we can get oysters."

Morgan sent her back to her hotel in a company car, and she worked out in the health club while she waited for him. She jogged two miles up a simulated hill on the treadmill, giving herself steeper and steeper inclines until she thought her lungs would burst. To finish runs she often invented little superstitions for herself. This time she told herself that if she finished the course in under seventeen minutes she would somehow find her link to the girls again: they would talk to her; they would not despise her. She pounded the treadmill, her pace machine-brisk. But the imaginary hills were too much; her breathing started tearing at her lungs and her feet were falling farther and farther back on the belt. She was forced to make the last half mile downhill all the way, coasting across some imaginary finish line just as the magical seventeen minutes elapsed. But she had cheated the hills, so she wasn't sure if the spell would count.

When her room phone rang, Patty was ready, wearing a pair of gray wool trousers and a soft paisley jacket. Morgan had changed from his suit into a sport coat. He looked every one of his years, which Patty guessed to be somewhere in his late forties. But on him the age looked good, a prosperous air of confidence. He was standing outside his car—in the daylight she saw it was a Mercedes—waiting to open her door. The damp fog of the morning had burned off into hazy sunshine with a cool breeze. The air tasted of salt.

He gave her a circuitous tour of downtown, then drove to North

Beach, parking in a pay lot although a spot on the street had opened up right in front of him. They paused to watch coffee beans being roasted in the window, then went into the coffeehouse, where people lounged on the benches or sat at the small marble tables with newspapers or laptops or notebooks they were scribbling in. A fat man with long silver hair and a beard to his chest was spouting philosophical jargon to two scraggly young men. A girl with dyed black hair, nose rings, and short black nails was sipping mineral water and leafing through a magazine. Patty and Morgan ordered cappuccino and found a table. The air was pungent with the smell of ground coffee.

"All of a sudden I feel like I'm on vacation," Patty said.

"I like getting out of the financial district and coming here. Makes me feel simultaneously young again and like an old fart."

"You're younger than the silver-haired professor over there."

"Ah, but I don't have the same—what would you call it?"

"A certain Peter Pan quality, maybe. I don't think he's met up with a barber since the Summer of Love."

"While I, on the other hand, bow meekly to convention and get the standard business trim every two weeks, whether I need it or not."

Patty shook her head. "Hopeless old fart."

"You're not supposed to agree. You're supposed to protest that I'm one of the Young Turks. A mover and a shaker."

"Oh, you're that. You were very impressive, you know, the way you maneuvered the discussion today. Did you always know that you wanted to be an executive type?"

"I always wanted to make money. My father worked long hours and made good money, and I grew up thinking that was what a man does."

"Is he still alive?"

"Alive and well and playing golf in Palm Springs, just the way he planned it."

"And your mother?"

"Tanning in Palm Springs."

"Sounds like they're content."

Morgan shrugged. "They're not unhappy. What about your folks? They in Portland?"

"In the suburbs. My dad is getting ready to retire from the insurance business. I think he plans on getting one of those motor homes and taking trips six months out of the year. My mom's not too keen."

"Doesn't like to travel?"

"More like she doesn't want to clean fish for my father in the woods when she could be home shopping with her friends and changing the wallpaper in the house." She sipped her coffee. "Tell me about your kids," she said.

"There's William, at Stanford. Then at home there's Kate and Thomas, both in high school."

"Does William want to go into business?"

"He doesn't know. He's an English major, which I suppose I don't mind. He can always get serious in graduate school. They're all good kids. None of them has a nose ring, thank God" he said, nodding at the black-haired girl. "Sorry—do your daughters wear those things?"

"No, why?"

"You winced when I said that."

"Oh. No. Just thinking, I guess, about how they'll do what they want at this age no matter what. And how scary it all is, because you try to warn them about consequences, and they refuse to believe it."

"They're supposed to refuse to believe it. It's the definition of being young. It makes them invincible."

"That's the trouble, it doesn't."

They finished their coffee and wandered around some shops; then Morgan suggested they get tickets for a cruise around Alcatraz.

"It sounds hokey, I know," he said. "But it's great to get out on the water on a day like this. Does wonders for the soul."

On the boat they leaned against the rail, letting the wind blow in their faces. Seagulls dipped after the boat's wake.

"I like how you let your hair get messed up in the wind," Morgan said. "That's so important in a woman."

Patty laughed.

"I'm serious. It's test of character."

She filled her lungs with the salt air. Today all the cells of her body felt full of oxygen; she pictured them looking like vibrant little rings of light.

When the boat docked, Patty said, "That was a great idea."

"I'm taking you to do all my favorite things. It's a selfish way to run a tour."

"Don't be silly. What's the next favorite thing?"

"We've got some time before dinner," he said, looking at her. "Did you know your hair's all messed up?"

His gaze made her nervous. "I thought you said it was a virtue."

"I wasn't complaining."

A short silence fell.

"How about a walk through the park?" he asked.

"Perfect."

At dinner they talked business. "I wasn't just joking, you know, about recruiting you after this project. We'll be expanding all departments. Are you interested?"

Patty looked down at her plate, a giant white platter with a confetti of herbs sprinkled over a tiny piece of seared tuna. "Well, I'd be interested in hearing what you would offer. Why not? But my boss at Dobson Brothers has been making nice noises about a promotion to partner soon."

"Oh ho—already playing hardball. I'd be disappointed if you didn't. We'd put together something attractive."

"Are you talking about here or in the new Portland office?"

"Let's see how things play out."

A white-jacketed waiter silently appeared and refilled their wineglasses. Another one glided up to replace Patty's knife, which had disappeared with the appetizer plates.

They drank decaf espresso out of tiny silver demitasses that seemed the size of thimbles. Some magic should result from drinking from those cups, Patty thought, as if she were Alice underground. Then they walked out into the night, which had again turned damp.

Before he returned her to her hotel they walked along the pier with its sharp smells of tar and fish. Since it was a Monday night, few tourists were roaming the waterfront. She had an odd feeling of belonging, and for a moment she did imagine living here. The vision contained only herself—in this daydream Greg and the girls must have been at home in Portland. That way Patty had both a strange new life as well as her old one preserved for her as if under glass, like one of those scenic globes you could shake and shake with nothing coming loose except the momentary turbulence of snow.

THE NEXT day after another round of morning meetings he put her in a company car for the airport.

"Thanks for making everything so easy," she said at the curb. "And the sightseeing yesterday was wonderful."

"It was my pleasure. Really. I'll see you soon." He hovered over her, bearish and endearingly eager to be helpful with her bag.

She shook his hand, which somehow struck her as too deflating, too brisk. But you couldn't hug a business colleague goodbye. Funny how instantaneous their rapport had been. And how at home she felt out in the world with her one suitcase on wheels. Last night before bed she had called Greg and the girls. Called Greg, that is—the girls hadn't wanted to get on the line. He had sounded relaxed and happy. He'd said the girls were fine, upstairs doing their homework. Was it really fair to make him move back to his mother's for a week and then come back over when she was due to fly down here again? These trips would go on for at least two months.

An idea began to take shape in Patty's mind, one she realized had been floating there in a hazy background since the episode with Kiley. What if Greg moved into the house and she moved out? Where was it written that the woman and the house went together like a turtle and a shell? Greg was miserable at his mother's, and he had nothing to do but meet with his lawyer and watch football on TV. The girls needed someone around more, and Greg was already spending afternoons at the house with Kiley, making sure she obeyed the grounding. Wouldn't it be simpler if he just moved in and she took a studio apartment downtown? Andy had said she could expect a big bonus and probably a promotion. That would offset the expense of the studio and then some. It could be a temporary arrangement, just while she had to do so much traveling. Maybe if she gained some distance from her daughters she could better see their behavior for what it was—an acting-out of their confusion and pain rather than a complete rejection of her, which was what it felt like. The girls could come over to her new place; instead of fighting all the time they'd do things, have fun. They'd have the talks they never did at home. Greg would be the parent forced to keep order, nag about homework and curfews; Patty would get to be the one they missed, the one whose car they eagerly waited for when she drove over to pick them up.

All the way to the airport she veered back and forth between thinking the plan was completely absurd and completely sensible—inevitable, even. Maybe somehow without knowing it, she had been headed for this path the minute Greg's unfaithfulness had been exposed. And yet, in an odd sense, Greg's specific crime had ceased to be the point. Something that was happening inside Patty was now the point. Dispassionately she saw her house, it's absolute testimony to family life and creature comfort, and her husband, young and good-looking in a way that a lot of women her age would kill for. She craved none of it. All her yard work, the curtains she had put up, the bedrooms she had painted—none of it had any hold on her whatsoever. She felt it slipping off her shoulders the way you shed a heavy winter wool coat, amazed to return to the lightness of your own limbs.

They were already calling her flight to Portland—a place she suddenly felt she was coming to for the first time, a hometown that had paradoxically assumed the proportions of an unknown city. At the security gate she fed her suitcase and then her handbag to the X-ray machine, which broadcast ghostly gray images of her comb, her coins, all her hard metallic parts.

There was no reason to head straight back to the house; the girls were still in school, Greg was home waiting for them. It was flawless September weather, sunny and warm with no burning edges to the heat. Patty took a taxi downtown and stashed her suitcase at her office. Then she went for a walk. People sat in the Park blocks eating their lunches on benches, and a nursery school walked its children in a hand-holding procession. Brick apartment houses built in the twenties and thirties lined the leafy avenue up toward Portland State. One building had a vacancy sign she almost missed, its entrance set back in a small courtyard guarded by two stone fonts filled with chrysanthemums. A green-and-black-striped awning shaded the leaded-glass door. The manager's bell was answered by a plump woman around fifty. Patty told her she was looking for a studio.

"Well, dear, you're in luck. That's what's vacant now. Most people want a one-bedroom, and there's a waiting list for those. You want to take a look?"

Patty nodded and followed her through the red-carpeted lobby. The faded wallpaper was a print of horses and carriages that must have dated back to the forties. "It's a quiet building; we don't take students. A nice mix of folks, some older, and some young like yourself who are working."

"I work downtown," Patty said.

The woman nodded. "Well, you'd find this convenient, that's for sure." She pulled open a black iron gate and motioned Patty into the tiny elevator. "This unit's only on the second floor, so I imagine someone fit like you would want to take the stairs. But I've got a bum knee, so this is quicker for me."

The elevator started with a lurch and bumped into place on the second floor. Patty followed the manager into a dim hall lit by amber glass fixtures. An intimate smell of must and cooking odors hung in the air, but it wasn't exactly unpleasant.

The woman unlocked the door numbered 28. "Here we are," she said. "Go right on in."

Patty felt a sensation like dreaming as she entered the tiny white room she might choose to live in. She told herself she was here on a lark. Still, she couldn't help seeing the room furnished with images of herself sleeping here, waking up here—and then what? She had never lived alone in her life. After living with her parents she had moved into a dorm and had a roommate. Halfway through college she'd married Greg and they'd lived in married student housing. Then she and Greg had graduated and had the twins and bought a house. That had been Patty's life.

The woman was chattering, pulling up shades and opening closet doors. "You can see it's just been painted. The shades are new, and the carpet's been shampooed. Your heat's included. It's steam heat from that radiator there." She opened a sliding wood door to a tiny kitchen. "It's just an efficiency kitchen, but most people living alone don't want much more than that," she said. To the left was a lunch-box-sized aluminum sink below two white-painted shelves, and a small counter covered in pink-and-gold linoleum. Directly in front as you faced the kitchen was the smallest gas range and oven Patty had ever seen. To the right hung a glass-fronted cupboard with a couple feet of counter beneath and a half-refrigerator below. It wasn't possible to actually enter the kitchen, beyond the initial step. You stood and turned left, front, or right, depending on what you wanted to do. Patty liked the sound of "efficiency kitchen"; it sounded as if there were no work to having it, no endless washing up of someone else's cups and dishes.

"Your closet's over here," the woman continued, crossing the room in three strides and gesturing up a couple of steps to a walk-in closet that had a set of built-in drawers and two rods for clothing, with a shelf above. "These stairs here open up for storing shoes and such," the woman said, backing down off the steps to demonstrate how each had a hinged lid.

"And here's the bed," she announced, pulling a handle Patty hadn't even noticed and lowering a bed from the wall.

"A Murphy bed!" Patty said. "I've never seen one of those outside of the movies."

"Some people don't like to use 'em," the woman said. "It's not the best mattress in the world, but it saves you some space. Bathroom's there," she pointed, "opposite the door." Patty peeked in and saw a small claw-footed tub with a hand spray attached, a tankless toilet, and a doll-sized sink with a mirror cabinet. She went in, ostensibly to try the faucets, but really to see herself in that mirror. What did she look like here? She saw a woman who looked startlingly young and smooth; she decided it must be the rosy cast of the pale pink fixture.

When Patty emerged from the bathroom the woman shrugged. "That's about it," she said. "Rent's four seventy-five a month, plus a ten-dollar key deposit and a three-hundred-dollar security deposit, and last month's rent in advance. Month-by-month lease, but you've got to give thirty days notice."

Patty cast another look around. The apartment was as snug as a berth in a ship, with everything ingeniously fitted inside everything else. There wasn't an inch that was wasted, and this pleased her. "I'll take it," Patty said, her heart pounding. "I could write you a check now."

"You don't have any pets, do you?"

Patty shook her head.

"Good relations with your last landlord?"

"I've never rented. My husband and I own a home, but we're separating."

"More and more of that these days, isn't there." The woman clucked and shook her head. "You'll meet my husband another time. He's out picking up some tiles now. He keeps things fixed pretty well around here, so if you ever need a drain unplugged or anything, just give a holler. Gus would rather do it himself than see you pour some of that Drano down. These old pipes are kind of delicate, and he babies 'em. By the way, I'm Muriel Rheinhardt."

"I'm Patty Goodman. How early could I move in?"

"Place is yours if your credit checks out, which I'm sure it will, you having a job and a house and all. Move in anytime."

"Tonight, then," Patty said.

Muriel raised her eyebrows. "Well," she said slowly, studying Patty. "I suppose we could get that credit information this afternoon and give you a call."

"I'm sorry to rush you," Patty said. "But I need to move out as soon as possible." She felt slightly fraudulent, watching Muriel's expression soften toward her. She didn't mean to portray herself as desperate. It was just that she thought that if she went home to sleep tonight she would not be able to leave. The house would take her back. She would look at her daughters and come to her senses. Already her resolve was weakening. *It's an experiment,* she told herself. *Just for two months to see what happens. You're not leaving them.*

Patty followed Muriel into the elevator, and they entered her apartment on the ground floor, which was several times as big as Patty's studio and decorated with an extensive collection of commemorative plates and spoons. Doilies covered the arms and backrests of all the chairs and couches, and provided a base for Muriel's assortment of dog and cat figurines. A small furry dog yipped and circled Patty's ankles.

"Now Bo-Bo, you calm down. This is Patty." Bo-Bo pranced and squeaked the whole time Patty was filling out the application in her neat printing. She couldn't imagine Bo-Bo calming down. She guessed when you were the manager you were exempt from the no-pet rule, even though it was true that Bo-Bo took up no more space than a teacup.

Her credit information would prove solid, she being the married, property-owning citizen she was. All of the accounts Patty listed were under Greg Goodman first, then Patty Goodman. Patty didn't know why she had set things up that way, seeing as how she was the one to open the accounts and keep track of them. But it was a gesture to Greg; he could be titular head of the house. She wrote Muriel four separate checks: one for the prorated first month's rent, one for the last month's rent, one for the security deposit, and one for the key deposit. On each memo line she registered the purpose of the check. Patty kept immaculate records; if someone wanted a copy of a canceled check she had written five years ago, she could retrieve it in two minutes flat.

Out on the sidewalk, she glanced at her watch to time the walk to the office. It turned out to be eight minutes. Had she really gone out and in an hour's time rented herself an apartment? It appeared that she had. She was going to have a new life. She would have nothing to clean, nothing to cook, nothing to pick up. She would have no laundry, except one load a week that she could do in the basement machines Muriel told her about. She would have no forty-five-minute commute in the mornings and evenings. She would have no teenagers to argue with—but at this, her heart began pounding again. She couldn't leave the girls. This had all been a kind of temporary insanity. She'd go back, ask Muriel to tear up the checks. Patty started to retrace her steps, but got only halfway. She paused to sit down on a stone bench.

Could she really do this, live by herself? Patty sat frozen in the mellow autumn sunlight, half expecting this new aloneness to sit on her chest and squeeze away the oxygen. But nothing happened. She enjoyed the air.

"SO THIS is all about your anger," Greg said accusingly. All of their talks now took place on the patio, as if the atmosphere inside the house were too combustible.

"The funny thing is, I don't feel angry anymore. But I don't feel married to you, either."

"Patty, we took vows," he said.

"That's right, we did," she replied. "And you're a funny one to be reminding me of that."

"I can't believe this!" he exploded, kicking the patio chair. Patty watched it topple over without commenting. The chair had fallen against a table holding a glass. Seeing the glass shatter on the cement made things easier for her.

She packed only her favorite clothes. Patty wasn't going to take anything to her studio that she didn't like to have around her. She considered bringing some kitchen things with her and rejected the idea. It would be easy to buy whatever she needed, and the girls didn't need to notice a missing this or that when they were making breakfast. The thought of them sitting down in the morning at the round table, her place empty, momentarily stopped her short. Then she remembered how no one ever sat down together anymore. The girls slept in as long as they could, then straggled out the door, grabbing a cold Pop Tart as they went.

She had barely been able to get their attention to tell them she was moving out. Melissa had looked at her for a moment with wide eyes, then ducked her head and mumbled, "Yeah, okay." When Patty tried to hug her, she turned her head and wouldn't respond. Kiley had not looked at her at all. After making her announcement, Patty had stood in her daughter's bedroom door a moment, awaiting a response. Hearing nothing, she walked away. The last words Kiley had said to her were a week ago. They were "Fuck you, fuck you, fuck you."

At the door Greg stared as if he didn't know her. "Just like that," he said.

"No, nothing's 'just like that,' " she said. "Greg, what I said about not feeling married—"

"Yeah, I get the picture," he said tersely.

"I didn't mean that I was going to *act* like I wasn't married. I'm married until I'm not married. What I meant was, I don't feel the emotional connection right now."

He said nothing.

"Okay, well, bye," she said.

She was turning to go when he stopped her by grabbing an elbow. "Patty, I never felt more married to you than I did that Sunday morning. It was a mistake. I knew that the whole time."

"I believe you."

He held her arm, waiting for more. When it became clear she had nothing to offer, he dropped his hands to his sides and walked away from her.

Patty's joints felt unexpectedly resistant as she walked to her car. Her children were in that house. She pictured them young and trapped in their bedrooms as if by fire, imagined hearing their cries for her.

It was the angry stiffness of Greg's neck that kept her from turning around and going back in. She had set her course. Nothing terrible would result from it; the girls would be fine. He was their father and he loved them—of that, at least, she was certain. They were safe with him until she came back, one way or another, to claim them.

III

The first thing he had done when he came back was mow.

The yard hadn't been touched in almost three weeks—not since Tim did it the last time. Greg had driven by the Phelps house a number of times when Mr. Phelps was at work and seen how unkempt his lawn had become, too. He had been tempted to go around back and start up the mower that Tim used and mow Phelps's yard for him, front and back. The whole job would take forty minutes. But he drove on, worried that people were beginning to notice his car.

Greg's own house had begun to look shabby and unloved because of the long grass, sprouting clover, and dandelions, which grew in a messy fringe over the edges of the cement driveway. Greg had cut only two swaths the length of the backyard when the grass-catcher sagged with its load and he had to turn off the engine to empty it. He reattached the bag and began again. Cutting the grass was a good way to relax. The noise of the engine covered everything, even the voices swirling around in his head.

There were a lot of voices to keep at bay. There was the voice of Larry Wang, the Willamette High School principal, talking to him in a placating way about how this thing would blow over and meanwhile

Greg should just enjoy the rest, since he was getting paid during the suspension anyway. There was the voice of his lawyer telling him not to worry, that there were a lot of witnesses on his side, and that especially if Tim woke up and recovered fully, there wouldn't be much sentiment to find a scapegoat. But the thing was, Tim wasn't recovering. Greg was scared, and no longer for himself. The fact was large and unmistakable: the kid was not waking up, though no one, according to Wilson Perry, who was closer to the official word than Greg, had given up hope yet.

At his mother's house, Greg had felt twelve again, the voice of his father yelling at him even though his father was supposed to be dead now. After supper—his mother's creamed tuna and noodles, or fried ham steaks that settled like stones in his stomach—Greg sat in his dad's old lounge chair to watch television, and had the nightmarish sensation that he had become his father, since no one else had ever used that armchair. After the sitcoms, when his mother changed to the home shopping channels, Greg would excuse himself and retreat down the short hallway of the house to his old bedroom. His football posters were gone, though he could see by the spray of thumbtack holes on the wall where they had hung. He'd lie on the sagging twin bed and try to read the newspaper while he heard the voices of the shopping hosts describe an indispensable new poly pantsuit that came in six colors including the luscious melon that the model was wearing. Sometimes he'd put his paper down and close his eyes, carried along by the encouraging voice of the salesperson—"Just look at that detailing around the pockets. Ladies, you're not going to find workmanship this special in the department stores!" After a while of listening to the announcers describe the rare qualities of each new item with their mesmerizing zeal, Greg almost began to believe that it was possible to start a life over by simply picking up the phone and ordering a one-carat tanzanite ring with diamond pavé accents, or a bisque porcelain doll wearing an Empire satin robe trimmed in genuine ermine.

Beyond the sheer misery of being there, his mother had been start-

ing to depend on his presence in an overwhelming way. Greg had always stopped over once a week to mow or replace a lightbulb or
change the storms to screens. But now she was asking him to take her
everywhere, though she was still perfectly capable of driving herself.
Greg found himself sitting in the Clip 'n Curl, waiting for her to get
her shampoo and set, and feeling, as he watched her doughy face that
looked strangely massive and powerful above the plastic drape, her
thin hair combed in wet stands across her scalp, that he was going
insane. He could actually imagine himself throttling his childish, irritating mother, and in the chilling clarity of this vision he saw the
loose white wattles of her neck shake, and her watery blue eyes
bulge.

He knew that his mother wasn't the problem. But her implacable,
chattering presence along with his exile in his childhood twin bed
was the symbol of all that had precipitately gone wrong, of an adulthood that had dissolved around him in a matter of days. The voices
hounding him were numberless. There was Tim's voice the day Greg
had met him, shy and dogged at the same time, importuning Greg to
call his father and get him to sign the permission form. There was Mr.
Phelps's low, flat voice from their first wary meeting. Greg never ran
into him anymore at the hospital; he went in the mornings, when
Phelps was at work. Funny how the tables had turned on them: it
used to be Phelps who was the out-of-work bum; now it was himself.

Of course there was Patty's voice, which had changed during the
two weeks that had passed. First her tone was of raw hurt, which is
what had prompted him to try to explain how stupid he had been, to
ask her to forgive him. Now he wished he had been able to control
that impulse. Maybe she would have doubted her suspicion, maybe
she was hoping he would deny it so she could think she'd imagined
everything. But he had been unable to let the accusation stand that
he had been unfaithful before this; so like a dope, he'd admitted to
the single mistake to defend his overall innocence. He didn't know
how Patty had managed to move beyond that hurt so quickly, to a
kind of deadness in her voice when she talked to him. What scared

him now was that no feeling seemed to be there at all anymore, as if the anger had burned everything, including itself, to ash.

It was funny, but Clarissa's was one voice Greg couldn't hear. Clarissa was a phantom. She had appeared, excited him, been available to him, then disappeared into thin air. Like the strike of lightning, about which he remembered less and less, it was as if Clarissa had been sent to him for the purpose of a single moment, and that purpose was to finish undoing him, until nothing of Greg remained by which he knew himself.

so HE had been overjoyed to have his lawn to mow. He knew he was only back in the house for the length of Patty's business trip, but moving his bags in the front door had seemed like progress to him. Even though it had been almost dusk when the cab took her away, Greg finished the front yard and emptied the grass-catcher one last time, shaking the clippings onto Patty's compost pile in the back corner of the yard. He didn't know if he was supposed to do anything with the pile or just keep putting new stuff on top of it. He decided to leave it alone. The idea was that it would all rot together, right? He went into the kitchen and found a beer in the refrigerator. Clarissa had asked him to get in touch with her if he was ever in Phoenix, he remembered that much from her parting words. There were days, trapped in his mother's house, when he had considered pointing his car toward the desert and disappearing for a while. What did he have to stay for? Not a job, not a wife who wanted him. He supposed two facts, equally compelling, held him in place. The first was his daughters. The other fact was that, after the exhilaration of driving on the open road for a day and a half, what would be waiting for him in Phoenix? Someone he didn't know, a woman he had no particular liking for, who had her own life and would be surprised and probably irritated that he had actually showed up. No, Clarissa didn't really exist. There was nothing to drive toward.

Greg had sat on his front porch steps enjoying the view of his neatly trimmed grass. His skin pleasantly itched from the grass dust.

In the distance he heard the faint booming of the bass drum from the high school marching band at practice. His team's first game had been a week ago, and they had gone ahead and played it. Greg had spent a tortured couple of days trying to figure whether or not to go. If he showed up, it would be a sign of confidence in himself and a signal that he was not cowed by the lawsuit against him. But finally he hadn't gone. The thought that he would be sitting in the stands as an outsider, seeing the gap caused by Tim's absence, and very possibly making the boys feel uncomfortable or confused on their first game day, was finally all too much for him. He didn't even call Perry for the score afterward, but waited for the neighborhood paper to print it. Greg's team lost, twenty-nine to seven.

WHEN HE had last talked to Mitch, he wasn't surprised to learn that Sandy had found him out and then taken him back. He was a little surprised that Mitch had given up the affair so easily.

"Hey, it's like I said from the beginning. I didn't want to put my marriage out of business. I'm back in the fold."

"For a while, anyway, right, Mitch?"

"I don't plan these things, Greg. I just take them as they come. But *you*, my *God*. You didn't think a single thing through—not a good time to go meet this woman, not an alibi. And then you go and admit everything to Patty without making sure of what she knew first. Talk about going down in flames."

Now he was back in the house, and it turned out not to be temporary after all. It was again his lawn to mow, his domicile to guard. The pleasure of that mitigated a little the anger he felt as he clattered the plates into the dishwasher. By the time he had sponged down the counters the anger had given way to pure bewilderment. She couldn't possibly mean it. The house was theirs together; it was the magnetic center of things—it would surely be only a matter of time before Patty succumbed to its pull and rejoined them. Look how lightly she had packed. That wasn't the car of someone who was planning to begin a new life.

Greg was at the hospital, in the cranberry-colored chapel. He had been spending most of his time here on his visits. He felt self-conscious lingering too long in Tim's room, and there wasn't anything to say or do there to make a difference. If a nurse or doctor walked in when Greg was sitting by Tim's bedside, Greg jumped, feeling as if he were going to have to defend his presence, explain who he was. No one ever asked him, though. He wondered if they knew, if they whispered it to each other in the halls and at the nurses' station.

But in the chapel, which no one but him seemed to use, he could sit as long as he liked. In the dimmed light Greg allowed his mind to rest like a flat horizon. If there was a God, then He would know everything about Greg anyway, so there was no need to go into detail. If there wasn't a God, then there was no point in wasting breath. Time in the chapel was the only part of his day when he felt the way he used to—unremarkable, that he was just living a life like anyone else. Since the lightning, Greg had felt himself marked out, targeted. He doubted that the episode with Clarissa Jetty would have happened if his life had not already been swerving out of control. Going to bed with Clarissa had been his way of grabbing the wheel and overcorrecting for a skid: he hadn't thought at the moment when he turned the wheel that it was the wrong way to save himself; he'd just followed the impulse of his adrenaline and done it.

Every day Tim looked less like himself, as if the coma were slowly transforming him from an wiry teenager to a wax doll. His muscles were losing their definition, his eye sockets were becoming shadowed and sunken. Everything about him was receding. Greg thought of Tim's sleep as a kind of short circuit; something that should be simple to fix, except no one knew anything about the wiring.

He had always disliked hospitals, but this time he was grateful for the neutral ground. Medicine was impartial; you could feel it in the swift, uninterested glances that the white-jacketed personnel swept over you if you happened in their path. Tim was critically ill; therefore the doctors and nurses were passionately committed to the care and investigation of his body. Greg was healthy, so his presence was of no significance to anyone. He could walk the halls, sit in the lobby or the cafeteria, or even visit Tim's room, and go completely unnoticed. There was a freedom in that invisibility, like the freedom Greg felt in the chapel, where he ceased to be a person at fault.

The benign atmosphere of the hospital was different from when he had visited it seven years ago when his father was dying from colon cancer. Then the old man had cast the force of his personality over everything. If Greg sat in his father's room he offended because of the glare of his youth and health; if he sat in the cafeteria then the fact of his appetite was a betrayal and an affront; if he sat in the lobby watching the news on TV then his callous indifference to his father's pain deserved rebuke. As usual, there was no winning with his father, no escape from guilt, even when Greg had done nothing wrong at all. Even picking out the casket he had not been free. He knew his father's voice so well that every choice he looked at elicited the familiar contemptuous tone: *Whaddya think I am, a goddamn Rockefeller?* Or if Greg looked at the low-end models, he heard his father say, *Oh sure, save your pennies so there'll be that much more for you to spend when I'm in the ground.* Of course, there was nothing to spend after his father's burial, anyway. His parents had just barely gotten by on social security and his father's pension, and the union's death-benefit check extended only as far as the headstone.

Greg had often wondered if his childhood would have been different had he had a brother or a sister, someone to exchange a wordless look with when their father was out of control, a defensive line. But there was no one to grant him this outside perspective until he discovered the rough, friendly discipline of coaches. Pleasing them was straightforward work: do your part to win the game, or at least try. Minimally, follow directions and keep a good attitude. When you screwed up, the punishment was running laps or dropping down for push-ups. Anger, humiliation, fear, rebelliousness—it could all be channeled into making yourself stronger and more skilled. All the roiling energy of emotions could be wired directly to the muscles, so that the edgier you were to begin with, the harder you worked your body, and the harder a body you became. Harder in this case was better: you could take more, and you could also dish more out if that was what was required. Tim had absorbed this principle immediately, and begun to put it to use.

THE RIDDLE of Tim's mother had begun to bother him. Was she dead? If not, why wasn't she around, visiting the hospital? Maybe hers was the one voice Tim was waiting to hear before he would consent to return to them. Greg called Wilson Perry at school and asked him to look at Tim's file and find out anything he could.

"Don't you think you'd better stay out of things until the legal business is through?" Perry asked.

"I'm curious. Just find out if she's dead. If she's not, see if there's an address for her."

Perry called him up that night to report.

"She doesn't sound dead from the file. Last name's different: Morrison. Lorraine Morrison." He read Greg an address and phone number. "I don't think you should make any use of this information," he warned.

"Don't worry about it. Thanks, buddy. Your name won't ever come up."

"Uh, how's it going, anyway?"

"Fine."

Perry paused. "You're back in the house?"

Greg took a breath. "Just me and the girls. Patty took a place of her own for a while."

"Jesus."

Greg felt he needed to reassure him. "This is probably a kind of phase for us, you know? We've been married over eighteen years. Wait until you get married, then you'll see. You go through phases." Greg had not told Perry about Clarissa Jetty. The only person he had told was Mitchell.

"Sounds like a pretty drastic phase to me. I'm not sure marriage is in the cards for me, anyway. I mean, Rachel and I get along fine with our separate places. What's the point in rocking the boat?"

Greg tried to imagine himself unmarried throughout his twenties like Perry, keeping his own apartment any way he liked, the mess on the floor consisting of his own dirty socks and the sports pages rather than baby toys and smashed Cheerios. But he couldn't unwish the children he had made. More than anything, his children made his life his own; from the moment they'd entered it he couldn't imagine a different version of events. You couldn't tell that to childless people, though. They would either eventually find out for themselves, or they wouldn't, and continue leading lives that could change direction according to a whim.

That was what made the question of Tim's mother so perplexing to Greg. Divorce or separation he could understand. But having a kid and never even seeing him? Not knowing or caring that he was lying in the hospital in critical condition for three weeks? He dialed the phone number, and a recording told him that it was disconnected. He looked up Lorraine Morrison in the phone book and found no listing. He glanced at his watch. Eight o'clock on a Wednesday night. Not too late to take a drive by the address Perry had given him, which was in the direction of downtown.

Melissa had done her homework and was over at Sarah's house watching a video. Kiley was watching TV in the den, still serving her time. Greg had considered lifting the grounding, but so far couldn't bring himself to reverse Patty's decree. But he might set her free this weekend. After all, it wasn't as if he and Patty had never smoked a joint in high school.

He poked his head in. "How're you doing?"

"Okay." Kiley had adopted an attitude of polite indifference to him.

"I was thinking we could end the grounding this Saturday."

"Whatever."

If she wasn't going to be grateful, Greg felt like putting the extra weeks back on. But now he had offered.

"You know how your mother and I feel about drugs. We take this seriously."

"The united front," Kiley said dryly.

"When it comes to you girls, we are," he said, feeling guilty now that he had been tempted into leniency.

"I told you, I wasn't smoking. Other people were."

"Well, if that's the case, joints get passed around. It's hard to say no when you hang out with people who use. Does Will smoke marijuana?"

"Why, do you want to ground him, too?"

Greg held his voice in check with difficulty. "No, Kiley. Obviously I have no control over what Will does. But I do still have some say over what you do, and who you see. If he uses drugs, then you can't see him anymore."

"He doesn't use drugs." Her voice was so low that Greg could barely make out the words. He decided to take them at face value.

"Okay, well, you can go out this Saturday if your attitude improves between now and then. We'll take it a day at a time."

" 'Just say no,' 'a day at a time'—gee, Dad, I really feel I've grown from our little talk. Kind of like being in my own personal rehab center."

Greg's fury rose. No wonder Patty had had to get away from this.

He turned and stalked out of the room and went upstairs to put on a clean shirt. When he came back down, he was able to speak in a normal tone.

"We'll forget about lifting the grounding until your tone changes. I'm going out on an errand for about an hour."

Kiley was staring at the television screen when he left. He had no idea how his daughter had become such an unpleasant person in the course of a summer. Didn't she have everything she wanted? Good looks, friends, a boyfriend, a nice home, and—even if they were having some problems—two parents who cared about her? Look how nice a kid Tim had remained despite the odds he had battled, and Greg had a feeling they were formidable, though he didn't quite know their extent.

That was his project: find out what he could about Lorraine Morrison. Her address turned out to be a cheaply constructed two-story apartment house in a neighborhood near the river that was residential verging on industrial.

Greg rang the manager's bell and waited. Inside he heard the raucous sound of a TV turned up loud. He rang again, then knocked. Finally he pounded. An overweight young woman in tight cutoffs and an Olympia Beer T-shirt answered the door. Her long hair hung in straggles, and she regarded Greg with a dull, unfriendly expression.

"We're not renting," she said.

"I'm hoping you can tell me which unit one of your tenants lives in. Lorraine Morrison?"

"Don't know her."

"Have you been manager long?"

"Six months. No Lorraine."

"Can you tell me which tenants may have lived here longer than a year? Maybe they would remember her."

"I don't want you disturbin' no tenants. You a bill collector?" She squinted at him knowingly.

"No. I'm a high school teacher. I'm looking for Lorraine to tell her that her son is in the hospital. He was my student."

The woman stared at him through her small mascara-fringed eyes. Clearly she didn't believe him.

"I think she ought to know about her son, and I'm not sure the father's gotten in touch. The kid's very sick. He might even die." Greg said this for dramatic effect; he had not seriously allowed himself to think it before now. But once said, it had the sickening sound of truth.

From inside the apartment Greg heard a crash and then a child's wail. The manager looked over her shoulder. "Stop it!" she screamed. She looked at Greg impatiently. "Ask Frank in number seventeen if he knew her. He's been here the longest." Then she shut the door.

Greg also heard the mumble of the TV from behind the door of apartment 17. He was on the point of ringing again when he heard a faint call from inside. "Hold your horses, it takes me a while to get there."

Frank was a frail old guy wearing a stained white T-shirt and brown trousers. He leaned on a cane and stood in house slippers.

"And who might you be?" he demanded. His wispy gray hair was darkened from grease and combed straight back from his forehead.

"Name's Greg Goodman. The manager said you've lived here awhile and might remember a former tenant named Lorraine Morrison."

"Why would you be looking for her?"

Greg explained his mission. "I'd hate for the mother never to know, if—you know, if things turn out for the worst."

"I knew a Lori, but I never asked her her last name. Might be her. She never said nothing about a kid, though."

"Well, like I said, she may not have been in touch with him."

"What's your Lorraine look like?"

Greg said he didn't know.

"Well, Lori was real pretty, and nice, too. Only she lived with a sonofabitch of a boyfriend. Mean fellow, one of them kind that rides motorcycles in a gang. But Lori always had a kind word for me. Once during a rainstorm she stopped in to see if I needed anything from the grocery store, since she was headed that way. I didn't, because my niece always stocks me up real good with frozen dinners and Coca-Cola once a week, but I thought it was friendly of her to ask."

"Do you know where she moved to?"

Frank shook his head. "One day she was up'n gone. Didn't say goodbye."

"When was this?"

"Well, let's see. It would have been before Christmas."

"Did you know where she worked?"

Frank rubbed his grizzled jaw. "I b'lieve she waited on tables at some place right around here. I know she used to walk to work. She left in the evening and didn't come back until late. That no-account boyfriend of hers didn't bother to pick her up, even if it was after two o'clock in the morning. Can you imagine that? A young girl coming home by herself on the streets at that hour?"

"Did you say a young girl?" Greg felt his disappointment rise, keener now that he had thought he was on to something.

"Sure. Just a kid—like you."

GREG CRUISED slowly around the neighborhood. If Lorraine got off work at two, then she probably worked in a bar, not a restaurant. There were at least six she might have walked to from her apartment, but it would take a couple of hours to go to them all. Greg had been gone almost an hour, and he was concerned about leaving the girls alone too long. Anyway, what was he doing, playing detective? If he could make a simple phone call or visit and tell the woman her son was ill, that was one thing. But there was no need for him to go hunting for her. Hadn't Tim's name and picture been all over the news a couple weeks ago? Surely Lorraine would have seen it, and if she cared about her son, she could have visited him. Suddenly it occurred to Greg that she might have done just that. How did he know she hadn't? This was a ridiculous quest he was on.

If he drove just five minutes over the bridge and into downtown, he could be at Patty's apartment, ring the bell. It wasn't a serious thought. He pulled into a parking lot to reverse directions and head home, and wondered what she would be doing now. Getting ready for bed, probably. It had only been a day. Did she have any furniture? When she made her sudden announcement no one had felt like asking her for a description of her new place. Now he felt unnerved by not being able to picture her, as if without a mental image of her surroundings she didn't exist.

As he drove into the garage he noted that only Melissa's bedroom light was on. He had the sudden dread of not finding Kiley home, the misgiving that she had left the house on purpose to punish him, that she would be back outrageously late or not at all. He sprinted up the stairs and heard the voices of both girls talking in Melissa's room behind her closed door. He paused outside the door and waited for his breath to regulate.

"Good night, girls."

"Night, Daddy." That was Melissa's voice. There was a pause.

"Night." That was Kiley's lower, more grudging tone. But at least she was home.

Greg turned in the wide bed, trying to find a comfortable position. Tomorrow he had a meeting with his lawyer to prepare for the school board hearing. The board could decide to vote for reinstatement immediately, or they could take the issue under advisement and sit on it for as long as they wanted. Greg didn't know what he wanted to happen. He had started to grow used to the idea of himself as someone who didn't teach, who didn't have to return to school ever again. He had discovered that he didn't miss it—not the roll calls, not the crookedly Xeroxed memos, not the study questions at the ends of chapters, not the videos he showed of Martin Luther King's speeches or the Cuban Missile Crisis, and not his study hall duties pacing among the students like a prison guard, confiscating gum and notes.

These past few days he hadn't even minded rattling around the house by himself because he felt so lucky to be home, to have a home. When Patty was on her trip, he had found the energy to start building new shelves in the basement for the yard tools. The precision of measuring and drilling holes soothed him. After the shelves he intended to repair the part of the backyard fence that was leaning. The shutters on the house could use sanding and painting before winter. Once he started thinking about it, there was an endless amount of care his home needed—caulking the windows alone could keep him busy for days. He liked the thought of patiently circling the house's perimeter with a ladder, sealing every gap with his caulking gun, even the fine cracks the eye could barely see.

I t was only ten o'clock, and he had four hours before he was due downtown at his lawyer's. He could stop at the hardware store, but that would take only twenty minutes. He would have liked to invite Patty to meet him for lunch, but he knew she wouldn't, not unless he had something specific to discuss regarding the girls.

He considered picking up the house, but he was clean and dressed, and anyway he didn't know where to begin. When he had arrived on Sunday and the house was still under Patty's influence, everything was smooth—tables were clear, floors were bare. He didn't think he or the girls were particularly sloppy, but nothing now was where it should be: clothing from upstairs was strewn about downstairs, and dishes and newspapers and junk mail from downstairs littered the upstairs. He clearly needed to get the girls to do their part, but he hadn't noticed what was happening to the house until he was tripping over shoes and kicking aside dirty laundry and wet towels. Tomorrow he would work on things, and get the girls to help sort out the jumble.

Now he had half a day—plenty of time to check out those bars around Lorraine's old apartment. The search was only to satisfy his curiosity, and the route was right on his way to his lawyer's office.

The first place on his list was a square concrete cube with the windows painted black: the Golden Spur. Its only adornment was a neon boot and spur above the door that he heard sputtering and fizzing overhead as he walked in. Two figures sat apart at the bar; in the dimness to which his eyes had not yet adjusted Greg saw them only as shadows. The air was heavy with old cigarette smoke and the smell of sour beer. A battered pool table whose felt had been taped in several places occupied one side of the room.

Neither of the patrons looked up as Greg went to stand between them at the counter. A lean middle-aged man with a pencil-thin mustache and a bar towel draped over his shoulder was leaning against the bar watching a Three Stooges movie on the television mounted on the wall.

"Help you?" he said, not taking his eyes off the screen. Curly was being beaten over the head with a baseball bat, slumping to the floor as the sound of birds twittered in his head.

"Yeah. Can you tell me if a woman named Lorraine Morrison works here?"

"Nope."

Greg took this as meaning that she didn't work at the bar, not that the man could not tell him.

"Did she ever, that you know?"

"Nope."

"Okay, thanks." The man didn't look at him. Curly rose from the floor with a dazed grin, only to be felled by Moe swinging by on a chandelier.

Next Greg tried Mom's Place and the Mandarin. He struck out there and at Hatfield's. When he got to Della's, he saw the city papers taped to the door, temporarily closing the place because of health code violations. That left only the Top Hat, a place that advertised Girls! Girls! Girls! on a new plastic sign that had been added underneath the fifties-style electric marquee depicting a top hat in flashing bulbs. Unlike the other places that had sported three or fewer customers each, the Top Hat had cars in the parking lot and at least ten customers scattered around the small tables inside. It turned out that the Girls! were topless waitresses, wearing little gold skirts like half the uniform the cheerleaders at his high school wore. Greg didn't know whether to wish he'd find Lorraine here or not. It would be embarrassing to talk about Tim while staring at his mother's breasts. In fact, it was pretty embarrassing to be here at all. Right now there was some music playing by Bonnie Raitt. Patty loved Bonnie Raitt. Thinking of her while he was here made his stomach feel watery.

He decided to bypass the beefy bartender with tattooed arms and ponytail and took a seat at one of the tables. It wouldn't do to inadvertently meet Lorraine's biker boyfriend before he found her. After a couple of minutes a waitress with blond pigtails came over to his table. Greg immediately looked down, studying the menu.

"Welcome to the Top Hat," she said.

Greg raised his eyes, making sure to focus on her face. She was too old for pigtails. There were little crow's-feet around her eyes, and she had a slight double chin.

"Are you serving lunch yet?"

"Yes, we are."

"Cheeseburger and fries, diet Coke."

"Is this your first time at the Top Hat?"

"Yeah." He wondered if he looked sweaty and shifty, the way he felt.

"We have a Virgin's Special that might interest you. Free pitcher of beer with any food order."

"Diet Coke will be fine, thanks."

When she turned to walk away he could watch her. She had a trim little ass and nice legs. From the back she could be twenty-one. The girl working the other side of the room probably was that young, with short dark hair and a thin build. She had huge breasts, strangely out of proportion to the rest of her. Silicone? He didn't know if you could tell, except by feeling, or even then. Greg looked around at the other customers as he waited for his food. It wasn't the kind of place where you could bring a newspaper to read as you sat. He felt it would somehow be rude to the waitresses.

What if someone from the school board found out that he was here? But for that to happen that someone would have to be here himself. And Greg didn't think anyone was. He saw a couple of guys in jeans and billed caps, a few old duffers that looked like Frank from the apartment house, and a sprinkling of guys in suits who looked like salesmen.

The waitress returned with his food and a plastic pitcher of soda and ice.

"I figured you could still have the special, even if it wasn't beer you wanted," she said, plunking it down.

"Thanks."

"Anything else right now?"

"Well, I'm hoping you might know if a woman named Lorraine Morrison works here. Might be the night shift."

The waitress eyed him. "I don't know everybody on the night shift, but I don't think I know a Lorraine."

"Lori, maybe?"

"You a friend of this Lorraine's?"

"I'm a friend of her son's. He's in the hospital, and I just wanted her to know. I teach at the kid's high school. The boy lives with his dad, and I'm not sure he would have tried to find her to tell her about the accident."

"Why not just call her at home?"

"The last address we had for the mother isn't current. But a former neighbor said he thought she worked here. I'm just giving it a shot. Maybe she used to work here and doesn't anymore."

The waitress left, and Greg began eating his cheeseburger. The food was good. That probably gave the salesmen the excuse they needed to stop in every now and then. Out of the corner of his eye he watched his waitress go over and talk to the dark-haired waitress. They both glanced back at him over their shoulders. He was glad he was wearing a tie and jacket.

She came back with a pad and pen.

"I asked around, and nobody knows for sure about this Lorraine. But how about if you put your name and phone number down, and if she works here she'll get the note. We'll make sure."

"I appreciate that." Greg thought that the woman was just playing it safe, and that Lorraine—Lori—must work here and one or both of the waitresses must know her. He didn't mind that they didn't trust him. After all, it was easy to make up a heart-wrenching story about some poor kid. Everyone in this neighborhood must assume that if you were a stranger interested in somebody's business, you were some kind of predator.

Greg wrote: "Please call Greg Goodman, 577-3970, regarding your son Tim. I am a teacher at his school. *It's important,*" and signed his name. He folded the paper over once and printed Lorraine's name on the outside. When his waitress returned to pick up his empty plates, he presented her with the note and asked for his check.

"But you didn't even make a dent in that pitcher of Coke," she said. "And the dancing is going to begin soon." She tilted her head toward a small black stage in the middle of the room.

Greg was beginning to get used to his waitress's bare breasts. They looked soft and inviting, and sagged just enough to convince Greg they were the real thing. Under different circumstances, he might have sat back and seen what the dancing was like. What was the harm, as long as he was already here? But he was conscious of making a favorable impression on his waitress, in case she might be reporting to Lorraine. He was here as a teacher, and people expected teachers to behave in certain ways.

"Thanks, but I've got to be going."

"Okay, then. We'll ask around for Lorraine, and see that she gets the note."

It was as good as saying they knew she worked here. Greg added

a forty percent tip to his total and left the Top Hat with some regret.
He had been to a topless bar just once before, in the company of his
college roommate and some buddies. They had been drunk then,
and Greg remembered only a lot of noise and hollering. The Top Hat
at noon was quiet and cozy, with the waitresses strolling around as
casually as if they were in their own apartments, and the men sitting
quietly, almost docilely, as if grateful to receive any slight attention.
The experience had been just arousing enough to make him feel
awake and interested in the day.

He drove slowly by the address Patty had given him, as if studying her apartment's facade could yield him some clue to her new life.
Living downtown in one of these stone buildings was such a foreign
thing for her to do. It was completely outside either of their experience. He would like to see the inside of the building, wished he
could call her and get her to walk over on her lunch break and invite him in. Greg still felt pleasantly charged up from the Top Hat.
He would rub her neck the way she liked, kiss her long and slow, the
way he used to before they were married, and she would pull him
down with her onto her bed. It would be like visiting a girlfriend,
making love to your wife in her own apartment.

Instead he drove down Park to Burnside, and circled the block a
few times looking for a parking spot. Patty had found him this lawyer,
had had the name waiting for him when he came home from the
morning with Clarissa. She had been ready to stand beside him then.
She had even, Greg remembered, tried to get him to go upstairs that
day, and he had resisted, feeling that his body must have traces of
Clarissa on it, despite the shower he had taken in her hotel room. Besides, Clarissa had emptied him; at that moment there had been
nothing left for his wife.

His lawyer's office was reassuring; Greg enjoyed visiting it. The
door to the office had a frosted-glass window with "Derby, Richards,
and Cruz, Attorneys at Law" painted on in old-fashioned black-and-
gold letters. Inside, the furniture was heavy and leather-covered,
and the magazine table looked to be solid mahogany. Greg had hired

Daniel Derby, the founding partner and oldest lawyer in the firm. Patty's mother knew of him from a friend who had successfully sued some doctor. Greg was nervous about the fees, but so far he hadn't seen a bill. Derby told him he didn't think the case would require too many hours of legal work. He would take a few affidavits, represent Greg at the school board hearing and at a civil trial, if it ever came to that. Derby doubted it would; he was sure the case would be dropped or settled. If they did go to trial, there might be medical and meteorological experts to hire for the witness stand, but since the school district was being sued as well as Greg, Derby expected that they would put on the main defense. Meanwhile Greg had no choice but to go along with his lawyer's advice and chalk up a bill.

Derby had mentioned that they might countersue Phelps for defamation, but Greg didn't see the point. He didn't have the stomach for a countersuit. What were they going to do, make the guy sell his house and his pickup to pay damages for Greg's emotional distress? No thanks. When Tim woke up, Greg wanted to be able to look him in the eye.

The receptionist, an older woman with half-glasses perched on the end of her nose, nodded that he could go in. His lawyer rose from behind the large file-strewn desk and shook his hand. Though gray and thick around the middle, Derby still had the look of the college football player he once had been; he even had a picture of himself in uniform hung among his diplomas and other mementos. Greg got along fine with him. From the beginning Derby had spoken of the suit as frivolous and of the school board's action as cowardly.

"Greg, good to see you, sit down." He gestured to one of the comfortable armchairs and took the other himself, opening a file as he sat. "Everything okay?"

"Sure, except for all this."

Derby waved his hand in the air as if shooing away a fly. "Nothing to worry about. Tomorrow's going to be a breeze. I'll just take you through your story as you've told it to me, and we'll concentrate on the main point—that you did not, in fact, lead those boys out into the middle of a lightning storm. I've got statements from your assistant coach and the team captain, and we'll simply stand on the facts: that it was a tragic but fluky accident."

Greg drew in a breath. "That's what it was."

"The only way the school board is going to see things differently is if they're a bunch of complete imbeciles. After all, they've got to stand beside you or they look liable in the civil suit. I just want to warn you not to get your hopes up for too quick a decision about reinstatement. They could be lily-livered about it, and sit on the thing until they know which way the political winds are blowing. But you're still drawing your paycheck, so—hey." Derby shrugged. "Enjoy the time off. Back to the grind soon enough, eh?"

They went through the points they wanted to make before the school board, then Derby swept his papers back into the file. They shook hands again, and Greg didn't tell him that he didn't care much whether the school board took him back or not. Derby was set on winning this thing, and Greg didn't want to deprive him of his chance to go into the game fighting.

TIMOTHY PHELPS died that night. Greg got a call from Wilson Perry at five A.M. Friday. Their had been no warning; the boy's condition had not been in decline. The official cause of death was heart failure: Tim suffered a sudden arrhythmia followed by a massive heart attack. Perry told him the news, then coughed uncomfortably into Greg's silence. "So, I guess I'll see you at the funeral," he said.

After hanging up, Greg sat in bed with the phone still in his hand. Grainy daylight filtered in through a crack in the curtains. His piles of clothing on the floor looked like the bodies of sleeping animals.

He lay in bed listening to the sound of his own heart pumping. It was incredibly regular and audible, and he wondered why he couldn't hear it all the time, why it didn't interrupt the ordinary operations of his day, calling attention to itself when he was making a sandwich or tying his shoelaces. Now his heart seemed to be working too well; it was oddly insistent. Greg began to feel irritated at the noise, the thudding sensation, the fact that his heart seemed to be forcing itself on him when he wished for a moment of quiet to understand what had just happened. Tim was dead. Before now, he had been injured, he had been recuperating. Now there was nothing left that Greg could hope for, no way to save things.

When the alarm went off at six, Greg was still in the same position, still feeling the distraction of his heart, wondering what kept it plodding forward. The clock radio had come on with some news about a bomb going off in London. Greg wasn't listening to the details, although the mention of several dead, several wounded, momentarily captured his attention. More people dead today of unnatural causes. Some might say Tim's death could be classified as natural because lightning itself was from nature. *Tim died a natural death.* Greg tried to determine if it sounded right. It didn't. He reached over and pushed the button that extinguished the newscaster's voice. The girls wouldn't be stirring until after seven. Greg had planned to be up early today to make coffee and read the paper and spend an hour at the breakfast table by himself, trying to get back into the feeling that he was an employed person. The appointment with the school board was at nine A.M., and he had wanted to look confident and disciplined, as if he rose early every morning and showered and shaved just like normal.

He wondered if they knew. They must, if Perry knew. He hadn't thought to ask Perry who had called him. Surely not Phelps. Perhaps Perry was on some list the hospital kept of people who were important in Tim's life, and Perry was named as the liaison with the high school. Greg resented that. Though officially ostracized, he was, after all, the most central figure for Tim recently besides his father. Maybe even more central than the father. Who had made sure his father allowed him to play? Who had coached him after regular practice ended to help the boy overcome some deficits in his training? And who had shared Tim's last moment of consciousness, their lives bound in the path of electricity that traveled the ground between them?

Greg called Derby, who said he would call the president of the school board and get back to him. Derby wanted the hearing put off until at least a month after the funeral.

"If we meet today they'll crucify you," he said.

Greg agreed to the postponement, saying little else. He could have saved Derby the trouble of representing him before the school board. He wasn't going back to his job.

GREG TOLD the girls about Tim's death before they left for school so they wouldn't be surprised with news of it in the halls. Melissa came up and put her arms around him, then stood back and brushed the back of her hand against her eyes and sniffed. "He was so nice," she said, her voice quavering. Greg didn't remind her that when Tim had been working in their yard, she had thought he was geeky. Even Kiley seemed affected by the news, mumbling something about being sorry before she slipped out of the kitchen door. He didn't bother to tell her to come right home after school. At the moment his daughters seemed almost like strangers to him, and Tim like his own relation, the son he had lost.

It might, after all, have been a boy that he and Patty had aborted their senior year. They never spoke about it afterward, hardly even at the time. He had worked extra shifts loading boxes at his warehouse job to pay for it. They were charged in advance of the procedure, and Greg remembered he had put several fifties together in his pocket for this purpose. They were the first fifty-dollar bills he had ever carried, and he didn't have possession of them for long. Patty had asked the nurse if Greg could stay with her throughout it, and they had told her no. He had sat in the waiting room, feeling guilty and relieved at the same time that the extent of his job was to pay and then wait, reading old magazines. Patty came out an hour and a half later, looking pale but otherwise normal. It was easy for Greg to pretend that she had been to the dentist having a root canal. They had stopped for doughnuts afterward and she had gotten upset because the powdered sugar was getting all over her mother's car. Then he took her home and the next night they had gone to the movies and everything was the same as it had always been, except they couldn't have sex for six weeks, and when they did, they were more careful.

Twice he picked up the phone to call Patty at work and tell her about Tim, and didn't. Finally he decided to take a drive. It was sunny and warm, the kind of day that students would be out skipping classes. First he found himself cruising by Phelps's house, slowly at first, then speeding up when he saw a figure pass in front of the living-room window. The figure looked like a woman's. He wondered if it was Lorraine Morrison. Phelps's truck wasn't in the drive; he must be out making arrangements. There would be a death notice for the newspaper, a coffin to buy, music and readings to choose. Phelps would need to pick out something for Tim to wear. Greg had done all these things for his father. To do them for a child was unthinkable.

He decided Phelps was not home, so he parked opposite the house and waited for the figure to reappear in the window. The grass was so long in the yard it was beginning to bow over from its own weight. In a few minutes the woman passed the window again, and Greg saw that she was older, maybe an aunt or grandmother. The woman had a thick torso, curled gray hair, and glasses. This was not Tim's mother.

Greg drove away feeling oddly relieved. He wished Lorraine Morrison would call him. He felt they had something in common, an exiled distance from Tim's last days. He headed his car toward the Top Hat.

As he stepped into the dark of the bar, the sight of the waitresses with their soft white breasts comforted him. He wanted to be fed again by the woman with the childish pigtails and the aging eyes. He waited a few minutes to see if she was working, so he might sit at one of her tables. She came out carrying a tray of beer glasses and a pitcher and smiled slightly when she caught sight of him waiting with his menu.

"You don't qualify for the Virgin Special anymore," she said, pulling out her pad to take his order.

"That's okay. Cheeseburger and diet Coke," he said. He handed her the menu. "Did you happen to find out if Lorraine Morrison worked the night shift?"

"She doesn't. Sorry. Thought I might know of her, but I was mistaken." she reached for his menu.

"Her son died last night."

The waitress stopped and looked at him, as if trying to decide if he was telling the truth. "I'm real sorry about that," she said softly. "I've got a son myself. I wish I could help you."

Greg watched her disappear into the kitchen. He didn't quite believe her, but he no longer trusted his own instincts. He had been picturing Lorraine as a kindhearted woman estranged from her son, just waiting for some messenger like Greg to reunite them. But he knew nothing about the situation, nothing at all. Large elevated speakers began thudding with the bass notes of recorded dance music. Lights came up over the stage and a dancer strutted out wearing a thong bikini bottom and stiletto heels. Greg sat where he was, watching hungrily, wanting to feel himself rocked by physical sensation, by bodies—the dancer's and his own—that were responsive and alive.

No one talked at breakfast. Greg wondered if the twins even talked to each other anymore. He remembered mornings just a few months ago when he would be comfortably ensconced behind his newspaper, Patty would be rushing around the kitchen organizing them all for their days, and the twins would be chattering to each other about classes or school gossip. He had taken it for granted then, that atmosphere of lightness and comfort.

After the girls left for school, Greg vacuumed the whole house and scrubbed the bathroom. He gingerly put aside the little tubes and brushes his daughters used on their faces. They didn't look like they needed to primp; they did it in such a way that it wasn't obvious. But here was all their paraphernalia, the glosses, the pencils, the mysterious hair tools. The bathroom smelled like fruit whenever they finished with it. Greg had a sudden, sharp memory of Patty's smells, the almond and citrusy ones that came from stuff she put on herself, and the deeper, indescribable one of her chemistry that he associated with sleep. But her scent was wearing off the bed. He was afraid he was losing her—afraid that if the quilts and the pillows ever completely released her smell, she would have vanished from his life for good.

He didn't enter the girls' rooms, but hung up the clothes in his own. He made the bed. By the time he was done the house looked passable. Not as absolutely tidy as Patty used to get it, but you could see the shapes of the furniture again. Greg was sweating from the exertion. It had seemed terribly important to have the house clean before he left it today. He showered and shaved and stood in front of his closet. The last time he had worn the dark suit was at the reunion dance.

THE PLACE was packed. He caught sight of one of the team members going in, a skinny second-string player whose name Greg couldn't remember. It was astonishing; in two weeks the faces of the boys he had coached had slipped away. It was because he hadn't played a game with them. During the first practices of the season all but a few of the players seemed generic to him; it was only after seeing what they were made of on the field week after week that they became completely real.

A few of the players were sitting together in the front row. Greg saw them turn and steal looks at him. He should have gone to their first game. It was wrong to stay away like someone guilty. Now he didn't even feel he had the right to speak to them. When Wilson Perry came in and took a seat by his side, Greg was seized with gratitude.

"How are the guys taking it?" Greg asked him.

Perry shrugged. "They don't say much, but you can tell they're shell-shocked. No one expected this."

The minister stood up then and began spouting general-sounding things about Tim's fine character. The whole thing felt false. You couldn't sum up a boy of fifteen with words like "courageous" and "generous." He hadn't even begun to be whatever it was he would be. Tim might have turned out all wrong, just the opposite of the minister's sugary praise. But the main thing was, he hadn't had time to be wrong yet; he hadn't made mistakes and he couldn't be said to have done any damage. He was blameless, and he was full of hopefulness about his life; that was about all you had the right to say.

After the service Greg hung back, waiting for an opportunity to offer condolences to Mr. Phelps. First the team members shuffled by Tim's father, shaking his hand with lowered heads. Then some parents and school officials clustered around him. Larry Wang, the principal, saw Greg and nodded. He looked as if he were about to cross the room to say something, then changed his mind. Fuck him. Greg kept trying to spot anyone who might be Tim's mother. He had decided the stout older woman was Tim's grandmother, Mr. Phelps's mother. They had the same bulldoggish look. No one else who acted like family seemed to be present. Just as Mr. Phelps seemed to be on the verge of leaving the chapel, Greg approached him.

"I hope you know how sorry I am," he said.

Phelps looked off to the side, his razor-pink cheeks flushing a deeper shade. He looked like a different man with his hair combed back and slicked into place. Greg was struck by the dignity of his suffering, the shadows bruising his eyes and the sharpened lines of his cheekbones and jaw.

"It was a horrible tragedy," Greg continued. He detested the lawsuit that muzzled him, that would seize upon any words he might utter and throw them back at him in the shape of an ugly and distorting cross-examination.

"It shouldn't have happened," Phelps said, biting the words.

"No, it shouldn't have," Greg replied. This would be Greg's last chance to offer anything, however meager. To hell with the lawsuit. He needed to say something simple and true about this. Something real enough to have said to Tim.

"Mr. Phelps, I would give anything to go back to the day of the accident. I should have called off the practice at the first sign of lightning. I will never, ever be free of that. I don't want to be free of it, because it would mean slighting Tim's memory."

For the first time since the accident, Phelps looked directly in his eyes. Just for a moment. Then he nodded, ever so slightly, and turned away.

Greg gave him a minute's lead time before he followed him to the door. As he emerged into the bright day he saw the Channel Nine news truck parked by the curb of the funeral home. Joy Scinterro, wearing a charcoal suit with a navy scarf at her throat, was trying to get Mr. Phelps to stop and talk to her. He brushed her away and entered the waiting black sedan. Greg didn't think Joy had spotted him. He ducked back inside the funeral home and found a side exit. His days of television interviews were over.

There wasn't much point in going to the grave site. He had paid his public respects, and he couldn't face any more people today. He slid into his sun-warmed car and sat fingering the steering wheel. His industry earlier in the day mocked him. He was a man with nothing to do. He was beginning to develop a craving for the Top Hat, not out of sexual appetite but because the atmosphere made him feel safe and anonymous. It was the same feeling he'd experienced at the hospital chapel.

Greg saw a woman in a raincoat, scarf, and dark glasses leave the funeral home from the same side exit he had used. She crossed the street and walked quickly away from the milling crowd and news trucks without looking to the left or right. He sat up. He had made a point of scanning all the pews in the chapel, but he hadn't seen this woman. She must have come in late and stayed out of sight somewhere. She was about the right age. And she was alone.

Greg got out of his car and walked after her. The woman was moving at a good pace. He glanced over his shoulder and saw Joy Scinterro holding her microphone and talking directly to the camera in front of her. Wilson Perry was still engaged in conversation with some of the boys and their parents. Greg sprinted half a block to catch up, then slowed to a walk again. He must not scare her. He knew there was no real point to finding Lorraine Morrison anymore; what did he have to tell her? Especially if she was coming herself from the funeral. But he was driven by the momentum of his earlier search, by curiosity, and by something else, too—the vague feeling that meeting her would help him put Tim's death to rest, that she was, like him, an illegitimate mourner.

The woman stopped at a bus kiosk a block and a half away from the funeral home. She sat down on the bench inside the shelter and stared straight ahead. Greg had only a few more steps to decide what to do. Sit beside her and try to strike up a conversation? Pretend he was taking the bus? No, that wouldn't work. What woman coming from her son's funeral would be in the mood to make small talk with a stranger? Furthermore, if she did turn out to be Tim's mother, how could he undo his deception?

He approached the bus shelter slowly, and, he hoped, nonthreateningly. He stopped at a distance of a few feet from her.

"You wouldn't possibly be Lorraine Morrison, would you?" he asked.

She looked at him, seeming to shrink into the bench. Her dark glasses obscured her eyes, but Greg was betting that the thin face, the fine bones of the nose and chin, were related to Tim.

"Sorry," she said. Then she stood up. Greg heard the bus rumbling behind him.

He had to detain her long enough to find out. Either that, or he had to jump on the bus and follow her. If she wasn't Tim's mother, she wouldn't have paused like that. She wouldn't have reacted as though the question he asked were some kind of assault. He had been seized with such a sense of hope a few seconds ago, and now felt such a corresponding rush of loss, that he had to try again.

The brakes squealed as the bus came to a stop.

"Please!" he said over the noise. "If you are Tim's mother, just give me five minutes."

The doors of the bus folded open in front of her.

"I need to talk to you," Greg said to her. She didn't move.

"Getting on?" the driver called down.

"I can give you a ride wherever you're going. Or I could get on the bus with you. Would that be better?" He took a step forward.

She shook her head to the driver. The doors closed and the bus roared away from the curb.

"Look." She turned to him. "I don't know what you want. But I'm not the person you need."

"Are you Timothy Phelps's mother?"

"What if I am?"

"Then you're the person I need."

THEY DIDN'T speak again until they were in Greg's car, safe from the stragglers remaining in front of the funeral home.

"I'm Greg Goodman. I was Tim's—"

"I know who you are," she said. She unwound the scarf from her hair, which was an unnaturally vivid shade of red cut in long, layered waves. She had a tiny, compressed face that, when tilted down, almost disappeared behind a curtain of hair. "You're the guy on TV."

"A mistake," he said.

She shrugged.

"Do you have time for lunch?"

"I thought you said you were driving me home."

"Sure I will, if you don't have time."

"Oh, I have time," she said. "I'm just trying to get clear on what we're doing here."

"Talking? Over lunch?"

She shrugged again. "All right."

Greg drove in silence, sneaking a look at her when he could. She caught him when they were stopped at a light, and removed her dark glasses for him to see.

"Satisfied?"

"It's just that you've been on my mind for a while," he said.

GREG CHOSE a steak house with dark lighting he hoped would relax her. She lit up a cigarette before opening the menu. When she smoked, she lost the innocent look she had. Tiny lines arrayed themselves around her eyes as she squinted against the smoke; she drew deeply and purposefully. In five or six drags she had smoked down to the filter. She stubbed it out and regarded Greg silently as he scanned the menu. Her gaze made him nervous. He closed the menu. It didn't really matter what he ate today.

"Whatever you're having," she told Greg when the waitress stood ready to take their order.

"Two small top sirloins, medium; baked potatoes; salads with house dressing," he said. "Iced tea for me."

"Scotch and water," Lorraine Morrison ordered.

"Forget the iced tea," Greg said. "I'll have one of those, too."

"Don't let me be a bad influence," Lorraine said, smiling slightly. When she opened her mouth, Greg saw how her top teeth overlapped crookedly.

"Thank you for sitting down with me," he said after the waitress left. "I know I must have seemed pretty weird just popping up like that. I saw you leave the funeral home and I took a chance. I've been trying to track you down."

"I got the note," she said, fingering the pack of cigarettes.

He hadn't been crazy. The woman in the Top Hat did know her.

"Jackie—the waitress you gave the note to—said you wanted to tell me about my kid getting hurt. Well, I already knew. So there was no point in calling you."

He nodded. "Do you still work there?" If she did, that meant she was a dancer or a topless waitress. He had seen no fully clothed women in the place.

"Not anymore. It was a good gig while it lasted, nice tips. How'd you know about it, anyway?" She seemed unembarrassed about the Top Hat.

"Frank. He says hello."

She looked at him blankly.

"Frank? The old guy at the apartment house?"

"Him? Oh, jeez."

"I tried to find you at those apartments first. It was the address Tim had put in the school file."

At the mention of Tim, she looked away. Then she picked up her glass of scotch and took a drink.

"Well, you found me. I still don't understand why you wanted to."

"I'm not sure either, to tell you the truth."

She waited. The waitress delivered their salads and bread.

"Everyone thinks I'm to blame for the accident," Greg began. "Even I do, in a way, though I swear I didn't think I was being reckless keeping the kids outside. Everything seemed fine. The sky was clearing."

Her glass was empty. She seemed to be looking for the waitress.

"I'm sorry if I'm boring you," Greg said peevishly.

Her eyes bore down on him, narrowed now. "Hey, who the fuck do you think you are? You invade my privacy, bring me here, and want me to sit here and *comfort* you? You need forgiveness? Okay, I forgive you. Are we finished now?" She shifted in the booth; he was going to lose her.

"No, please, relax. I'm sorry. I'm not looking for you to comfort me. I thought—it sounds presumptuous, I know—that somehow we could do each other some good. I mean, obviously I don't know your situation at all. I just know that Tim lived with his dad and that somehow you've been out of the picture. I admit I've been curious about that."

She had lit another cigarette and smoked it silently, looking away. "That's not your business," she said.

"No, it's not. But Tim talked about you once, a memory he had of you from when he was little. It sounded like he loved you a lot."

At this her eyes filled. "You bastard," she said. She sat and smoked. Greg felt they were in kind of a standoff.

Finally she turned to him. "What did he say about me?"

"He said he remembered helping you with a flower garden in the mornings when it was cool. You showed him which were the weeds and which were the flowers. The flowers were yellow, like your shorts. That's how he remembered he shouldn't pull them." It didn't seem enough to offer, after what he had dangled in front of her. "It was the way he said it, you know? The tone."

The waitress appeared with their steaks. She looked down at their untouched salads. "You want to keep these?" she asked. They shook their heads.

"Another scotch, please," Lorraine ordered. The waitress removed their salad plates and reappeared a minute later with a fresh drink.

She took a sip. "He loved that garden. I gave him his own spot to dig. He was only three years old, but he did a real good job being careful with the flowers." She fidgeted with her napkin. "He say anything else?"

Greg shook his head slowly. "He would have, though, if I'd given him half a chance. I wish I had."

"Yeah, well, we all wish," she said flatly. "You get over it."

"Maybe I'm not supposed to. Maybe I'm supposed to keep thinking about what I should have done, and what I shouldn't have."

"So go ahead and think. But I don't see why you have to involve strangers in your little therapy sessions." There was no malice in her voice as she said this. Greg realized she was teasing him.

They fell silent. She seemed unaware of the lunch in front of her. Greg, on the other hand, was suddenly starving.

"Aren't you going to eat anything?" he asked.

She shrugged. "You start." She watched him cut a bite of steak and chew. After a moment, he ceased to feel self-conscious. There was nothing accusing about her gaze. She was simply watching him. He ate, and she sipped, and for a long while neither spoke.

"I saw you at the hospital," she said finally. "You were in his room. I waited until you left."

Greg nodded, hoping she would continue.

"He'd grown so much," she said. "Even though I knew all these years had passed, in my mind he was still a little kid. I guess I thought he was going to just *stay there*, you know? So that it would never be final, my going away. I planned on seeing him sometime. It was just never the right time."

The waitress came to clear their plates. "Is something wrong with your lunch?" she asked Lorraine.

"It's fine," Lorraine said. "I'm not hungry. Someone back there must have a dog, right?" She gestured at the kitchen.

"Sure, if you don't want it," the waitress agreed.

Greg ordered coffee, and Lorraine asked for another scotch. He was trying not to jump to conclusions about her drinking. After all, the woman had just buried a son. She was entitled to drink as much scotch as she wanted. On the other hand, she held it very well. As if she were tossing back Cokes.

She was silent, and Greg wondered how to get her talking again.

"So Phelps called you to tell you he was in the hospital?" he asked.

She snorted. "Not exactly. We weren't what you'd call close. I heard it on the news. Actually—this is kind of funny—I heard it from you. I happened to turn on the TV when you were talking to that reporter."

Greg was taken aback; the television interview suddenly seemed as though it had been fated to happen. He was glad now that Joy Scinterro had made him say so much. When Lorraine had heard the news she had gotten the real version.

"It must have been a shock," he said.

She didn't respond. Was she tired of him already? Greg tried a little bait to raise her.

"I'm glad you knew, however you heard. I was worried Phelps hadn't gotten in touch with you. He seemed a little on the vindictive side to me."

This wasn't exactly true. Phelps had been an enigma to him. He hadn't, after all, barred Greg from visiting Tim's hospital room, though Greg was sure he could have. The lawsuit itself Greg didn't hold against him. He even understood it, in a way. A man couldn't let a son die without reacting somehow.

Lorraine frowned slightly. "He kept a grudge," she allowed. "But"—she shook her head—"I gave him reason. I left him with a four-year-old to raise. He hated me. I don't blame him for that."

"Why'd you leave?"

"Let's just say I wasn't doing Tim much good being there," she said.

"Tim turned out to be a really nice kid. Whatever time you spent with him at the beginning had an effect."

She tilted her head, examining him. Her own face was a smooth mask. "You really do try to be sweet, don't you?" Then she straightened up, reaching for her cigarettes and lighter. "Hey, all this looking back on the good old days has been a lot of fun, but I need you to get me back now."

"Can we meet tomorrow? Another lunch?" Greg was just following his impulses. He still felt that Lorraine Morrison was somehow crucial to him, that they hadn't yet scratched the surface of whatever business it was he had with her.

She looked askew at him again, almost sympathetically this time. "Jesus, you are one hell of a mess," she said.

Greg waited at their usual spot. Lorraine wouldn't let him drive right to her apartment, even on the first day he had dropped her. She had made him pull alongside a Circle K mini-mart, next to a strip of weeds and a Dumpster.

"This is close enough," she had said. "We don't want you to have any misunderstandings with Rick."

Rick was her boyfriend, apparently the guy Frank from the old apartment had despised for his ungentlemanly ways. Lorraine had made it clear it was best that she not mention Greg to Rick, which was fine with Greg. That was how this half-hidden spot of concrete and broken glass had come to be their rendezvous point. As he waited for her there, he was keenly aware of how illicit their meetings seemed. This friendship could not be justified—not to Rick, not to Patty or the girls, not to Phelps, not even to someone like Mitch, who would assume all the wrong things about it. It occurred to him that Tim was the one person who might like it that Greg and Lorraine knew each other, and this pleased him.

He didn't know why she was giving him the time of day, though he was grateful that she was. Maybe beneath that impassive front she presented she was hurting over Tim, too. She had seemed to erase him from her life, discussing her son with no one. Then Greg had appeared at a bus stop, wanting to talk about nothing else. So maybe she indulged him because some part of her craved a connection to Tim. Or maybe she was just bored and he offered novelty. She turned out to have a lot of free time on her hands during the day, like him.

Greg had stopped trying to figure out his own need to see her. He wanted to see her and so he asked to. After their lunch at the steak house she had spoken only to tell him which way to drive. Finally, just before she got out of the car, she turned to him. "Okay, you win," she said, as if they had been arguing. "Pick me up here at noon tomorrow." Then she had disappeared down the street, and Greg understood he was not to follow. He sat there an extra five minutes, giving her time to get out of sight. He never doubted for an instant she would keep the appointment.

The next day had been sunny and warm, a perfect late-September afternoon. He had assembled a picnic for them, remembering to include two bottles of wine. She hadn't cared where they went. He drove out to Rooster Rock Park in the Columbia Gorge. There was something domestic about the way they had spread the blanket, unpacked the lunch. They had sat on the beach facing the expanse of the Columbia, which flowed placidly by, with no chop or little cat's paws of foam. The Washington shore seemed to float in the distance, green and mild. By contrast, the Oregon side rose at their back, a carved and dangerous wall of basalt studded with sharp precipices and waterfalls. Greg had eaten most of the lunch, and Lorraine had finished most of the wine. She had asked him some questions about his family. He filled in the picture of his home life for her, the way it used to be and the way it was now, with Patty gone. Lorraine was a good listener, soothingly blank and calm, like the river. She just sipped her wine and nodded, and it was easy to talk into the silence.

Yesterday she had not been available, and Greg had been forced to pace his house like a restless animal, waiting for this morning to arrive so he could see her again. Now he was parked in the space by the Dumpster, and she was late. Waiting made him anxious; he had no way to get in touch if she didn't choose to show.

Then she appeared at the passenger window out of nowhere. She had a quiet, catlike grace, which still surprised him; it was out of keeping with badly dyed hair and smoke-lined face. There were times, watching her move, that he wanted to call her beautiful.

She flashed him a smile, her crooked teeth marring her looks, but only for an instant. She didn't smile all that much; perhaps she had trained herself not to.

"Sorry I'm late. I had to wait for Rick to leave, and he took his time today."

Greg wondered if Rick had lingered to take her back to bed. He shook off the thought. Greg had no right going there, not even in his thoughts.

"How about a drive to Timberline?"

"Too far. I need to be home around two. You said we'd go back and stop at those waterfalls."

"Absolutely." He headed out to the gorge again, this time taking the old two-lane highway that rose at a steep pitch above the river, winding along the cliffs. When he was with her he felt as if they should be on some kind of expedition. A boy Tim's age would like these places; maybe he was with them somehow.

As they climbed she started drumming her fingers on the armrest.

"Not nervous about heights, are you?" he asked.

"Oh, no," she said. Still she shifted uncomfortably in her seat. His ashtray, never used before he met Lorraine, was brimming. He had the fan on to get rid of some of the smoke, and had cracked the window, too.

"I can stop at Crown Point. You look like you need a breath of air," he suggested.

"Okay, good."

The parking lot of the overlook was deserted. They were the only ones there to stand and survey the broad path the river carved between the two states, its massive banner of dark blue. Below them was a sheer face of stone.

Lorraine dragged deeply on her cigarette. Fresh air seemed to make her miss the smoke in her lungs even more.

"Ever wonder what it would be like to fall from a place like this?" she asked dreamily.

"No," Greg said truthfully. "You?"

"Oh, yeah. When I was little I used to think about falling all the time. If I walked across a bridge I'd have to stop and hold on to the rails with both hands because I never could be sure I wouldn't just jump over without planning to."

Statements like this would make him nervous coming from anyone else. But Lorraine was somehow beyond the pale for Greg; she could do or say nothing to shock him. The essential fact about her was that she had left her son when he was four. The essential fact about Greg was that he had placed Tim in the exact spot lightning would come for him. These actions put them together beyond the bounds of ordinary niceties.

Before they got in the car she tugged on his sleeve. "You brought some wine for us, didn't you?"

"Sure."

"Well, I want some."

Greg had made up his mind that Lorraine's drinking was her own business. There was nothing wrong with his bringing wine on a picnic. If she wanted some at ten o'clock in the morning, she could have it.

He poured the Chablis in a plastic cup and gave it to her. She reached out for the bottle as well and he handed it over.

They started winding along the road again. Just before they got to Multnomah Falls, a cruiser appeared in Greg's rearview mirror.

"Keep the wine out of sight, okay?" he asked her.

"Why, are we going to get busted?" she teased.

"Just keep it down low. There's a cop behind us."

"I can see the headline: 'Greg Goodman, Decent Citizen, Arrested for Driving with Open Container and Floozy.' Will you give an interview? Or is that just for when you kill kids?"

"Why don't you shut up?" he suggested tensely. He concentrated on driving precisely the speed limit, which was thirty. With luck, the cop would get impatient and pass.

Lorraine shook her head sorrowfully. "You know, Greg, I really have no idea why you insist on having these playdates with me. Look at you. You're sweating. You don't even look like you're having a good time." She lifted the bottle to pour herself more wine as if there were no police car within a mile of them.

"Goddammit, Lorraine, keep the wine out of sight!" He tried to grab her wrist but she twisted away from him, in the process spilling half a cup of wine on the carpet.

"Whoops!" she said gaily. She wrinkled her nose. "Now we're going to have to get one of those little deodorizer trees to hang on your mirror."

The cop was staying two car lengths behind, showing no intention of going around them. Greg tried not to keep checking his mirror; it would only make him seem guilty. He allowed himself to look once after every curve. The parking lot for the falls was coming up. Either stopping or continuing was a gamble. He signaled and turned off. The cop signaled and turned off right behind him.

"Shit." Greg chose a parking spot. The cruiser slowed down, glanced their way, and kept going, making a circuit of the lot.

"Cheers," Lorraine said, raising her glass to the back of the cop, who was not so far away from them that he couldn't have seen her in his rearview mirror. But the cop slowly finished his tour of the parking lot and turned back onto the highway.

Greg turned to her, furious. "Are you crazy?"

She downed the rest of her wine. Then she snuggled over to him. "I thought that's what you liked about me."

He drew back, disgusted.

She stretched elaborately. "Oh, relax. Don't you know that cops never stop guys with short haircuts driving shiny new Honda Accords?

It's right there in the cop manual. He couldn't have known you had some trailer trash in the car with you. He was dazzled by your Audubon sticker."

"Let's just get out," he said shortly. "Take a walk." For the first time, he began to wonder if he was losing it, going after this woman, trying to get to know her.

Lorraine hauled her bottle of Chablis out of the car with her, intending to carry it.

"I've got a backpack," Greg said shortly. She handed the bottle over and he stowed it away.

He didn't know how she could do it, hike and smoke at the same time. But she kept right up with him. In fact, when he stopped to get a look at the falls she brushed by him, and when he turned to follow he found that he had to scramble to keep up with her skinny legs. She wasn't even wearing sneakers, just some kind of platform sandals. She'd have trouble once the paved path ended at the bridge. Then they would have to turn back.

She tossed her cigarette butt behind her, and Greg stepped on it, grinding it out. After a few switchbacks they reached the stone bridge, where they stopped to look above them. She arched her back to offer her face to the misting spray. Greg couldn't help noticing that her nipples underneath her T-shirt were hard from the cold, just as he had not been able to keep his eyes away from the shape of her ass in those tight jeans as she hiked in front of him.

"I'm getting hypnotized," she said. "Try to watch just one drop at a time."

He looked up and saw what she meant, the way you could see the falls as a solid white column, or you could see it in atomized form. If you picked a single drop to watch you had to fall with it, all the way to the rocks below. He jerked his eyes up.

"Makes me dizzy," he said.

"And you didn't even have wine," she said, her voice teasing again. "Catch up," she said over her shoulder.

He was about to warn her about the rocky path, how she wouldn't be able to negotiate it with her shoes, but she was already starting up the trail, lightly stepping around tree roots and rocks.

She paused at a sort of natural cave, a hollow of rock under an overhang. "This is great," she said, backing in. "Come on in."

"I'm too big," he said, looking in.

"Try."

He squeezed in with her, and breathed the curious mixture of moss, earth, wine, and tobacco. They had never touched before. Now they were shoulder to shoulder, their backs against the cave wall. She fished the bottle of wine out of the pack.

"I'm sorry I was mean to you before," she said, taking a sip directly from the bottle.

"No big deal," he said. He didn't feel angry anymore.

"It's chemical, you know? I get mood swings really bad. Then I have to drink. And drinking doesn't really do it for me anymore. So I do other stuff sometimes. But it's all really unpredictable, and sometimes when I'm coming off shit I get mood swings even worse."

"Is that why you left?"

She didn't say, "Left who?" Every conversation they had led back to Tim. She knew that as well as he did.

"I wasn't good for him," she said sadly. "He had such a sweet little face and then I'd scream at him and he'd look at me pure terrified. I was going to ruin him if I stayed, take all that sweetness he was born with and turn it into something bad. Leonard wasn't the greatest dad in the world, but he had me beat by a mile. I knew Tim would come out okay with him." She laid her head on Greg's shoulder, as if tired. He stayed still, so she wouldn't move it.

"I don't believe you would have turned him into something bad," he said.

She lifted her head and spoke calmly. "I hate to break this to you, Greg, but what you believe or don't believe has no bearing on anything."

He said nothing, stung.

Finally she pushed up her cotton sleeve to reveal an arm scarred with angry red marks. "Do you get it now?"

He looked for a few seconds. "Yes," he said.

"No you don't. Don't fool yourself into thinking you get a fucking thing." She tugged her sleeve back down and folded her thin arms around her bottle. Somewhere in the trees a bird called. It almost sounded like human speech, like a word they'd be able to make out if they listened hard enough.

"Did you use when he was born?"

For a while she didn't answer, and he didn't think she was going to. Finally she spoke. "I was straight when I had Timmy," she said. "Leonard saw to that. He's the one who helped me get clean. He put a lot of effort into it. I was his project, kind of like a car he was restoring. When I got pregnant, Leonard was really happy. He thought that would seal it, that I'd never slip back again."

Greg tried out an image of a younger Phelps, a Leonard (maybe sometimes a Len or a Lenny?). A man who was looking forward to the birth of his child. An optimist.

"But you did slip back."

"Not at first." Lorraine paused. When she resumed, her voice was amused. "Leonard would come home from work with these stupid presents for me, shopping bags full of maternity dresses with big collars and bows."

Greg made a little laugh. "My wife had a few of those."

"But ridiculous on me, right?" Greg pictured her tiny face, lost above the snowy white collar. Her hair was probably a different color then.

"The whole idea was ridiculous," she said bitterly. "I should never have gone through with it." She drank some wine.

Greg was startled into imagining Tim never born, Greg's own life an unbroken calm, the lightning harmlessly grounding itself somewhere else.

"Don't say that," he said, surprised at his anger.

"Oh, come on. What difference did it make? He's gone. He was never meant to be." She answered in her tough, breezy voice, the one that felt like a put-on but maybe wasn't. Greg didn't know her well enough. Maybe she was that cold. Greg saw the kid's face, Tim's concentrated expression of effort and attention.

"You wouldn't say that if you had bothered to know him. He was a great kid—with or without you. He was—" Greg's throat closed up.

She glanced sideways at him. "Oh Jesus," she said. "Don't. Don't. If you do, you're going to make me." She touched a finger to his wet cheek and then leaned or fell into his arms, the two of them like that for a long time in their house of stone.

AFTER TAKING her back to her drop-off point he headed for home and a nap. Since the funeral his house's surfaces had been swallowed up again, engulfed in shucked-off clothes, newspapers, fast-food wrappers. His check from the school district arrived in the mail in its window envelope, printed on rainbow-colored paper with the superintendent's signature etched in black. He stared at the check as if he had never seen one before. All the artifacts of his old life—golf clubs, coaching sweatshirt, nylon zippered briefcase—were similarly strange and unfamiliar to him. Even talking with his daughters was an effort since Greg had become obsessed with Lorraine.

The phone rang just as Greg was getting his shoes off.

"Mr. Goodman? This is Ronald Parks, head of security at Nordstrom's department store downtown. Is your daughter Kiley Goodman?"

Greg froze. "Yes."

"Well, Mr. Goodman, I'm sorry to have to tell you this, but our house detective stopped your daughter from leaving the store with some items in her backpack she hadn't paid for. She was shoplifting."

"Shoplifting?" Greg's stomach flipped. The light from the hall window hurt his eyes.

"Yes, sir. Our first action in a situation like this is to call the parents if the offender is a minor. But your daughter was stealing, and we are justified in pressing criminal charges if we so desire."

"Please. Let me come down there. I'll pay for the things. I'm sure we can straighten this out. Let me be there before you do anything."

"We'll be waiting for you."

"Can I talk to her?" Greg felt the slickness of his sweat against the receiver as he waited. He heard a chair scrape the floor on the other end.

"Daddy?" Kiley's voice was young. It was on the edge of tears.

"Kiley, I'll be right there, okay?" He resisted the temptation to ask her what in the hell she had been doing. Time later for that. Right now she was alone, she was in trouble, and he had to make his way to her.

IV

Patty received the call as she was putting the final touches on her notes for tomorrow's meeting. She was just about to go downstairs to be picked up by the airport limousine. But after getting off the phone with Greg she called the travel secretary in a panic and told her to reschedule the flight. Then she paged the driver of the car to tell him she wouldn't be needing a ride. Patty zipped her laptop computer in its case and rushed out the door. Halfway down on the elevator she realized that her notes were still sitting in the printer's tray in her office. She waited for another elevator to go back and get them.

Greg and Kiley were waiting for her in a booth at the Wagon Wheel Café, a place where she and Greg had eaten cheeseburgers when they were still dating. She bumped through the after-work crowd, awkward with her computer and purse hanging from one shoulder and her small suitcase on wheels behind her. She slid into the seat opposite them.

"Another trip?" Greg asked, staring at the suitcase.

"You caught me just before I left. I was able to delay things by a couple of hours."

"I guess we should thank you."

Patty ignored him. She looked at Kiley, whose face was blotchy and pale. Her daughter smiled weakly at her.

"What's going on?" Patty asked.

Kiley started to say something, and then her lip trembled and she bit it to keep from crying.

"Greg? What's happened?"

"Kiley was stopped in Nordstrom's today by the store detective. They called me and I went down there. She had some stuff in her bag that she forgot to pay for. It's all taken care of."

"Taken care of?" Patty echoed. "What do you mean?" She looked at her daughter, who was turning her soda glass in her hand and avoiding Patty's gaze. "Kiley, how do you 'forget' to pay for something?"

"I just did." Kiley's voice was almost a whisper.

"Everything's paid for now," Greg said. "Kiley said it was a mistake. She had put the stuff in her pack while she tried to decide between some things, and then she just forgot all about it."

"And you believe that," Patty said flatly. She was staring at Kiley, who wouldn't look at her. "Kiley, what's wrong with you?"

"It was a simple mistake, Patty," Greg said.

"Would you please stop telling me that everything is a simple mistake, Greg? Maybe you don't know how to take responsibility for your actions, but Kiley is going to learn."

"And you're going to teach her about responsibility? Who is home being a parent to these girls and who's not?"

"That has nothing to do with anything."

"The hell it doesn't."

Patty turned to Kiley. "What did you take?"

Kiley crossed her arms in front of her. "Just some stuff."

"What stuff? What was it that was so urgently needed by you that you couldn't wait until you had the money or until you asked one of us for it?"

"What does it matter what I had?"

"Because I want to know what it is we're not providing for you."

"She had some earrings and a wallet with her. Okay? Do you really think this is helping, Patty?"

Patty threw up her hands. "My God, Greg. You are really a piece of work, you know that?"

"Dad, why did you bring me to see her? All she does is tell me I'm a liar. Every time we talk that's all she has to say to me," Kiley whined.

"First of all, we don't 'talk,' " Patty said. "You refuse to. And second, I'll quit accusing you of lying when you quit lying."

Kiley rose angrily, bumping the table and knocking over her glass. Ice spilled onto the table, and Greg pulled out bunches of napkins from the dispenser to soak up the puddle of melted water. He righted the glass.

"That's great!" Kiley cried. "I'm a liar and a whore and a junkie. Anything else you want to call me? What about you? Leaving us so you can carry on some affair! What does that make you, I'd like to know?"

Greg looked from Patty to Kiley, his face bewildered.

Patty rose and stood eye to eye with her daughter. In a furiously quiet tone she said, "You sit down right now."

Kiley hesitated, then sat. She looked away, affecting a bored expression.

Patty leaned into the table, and her words came out in fierce staccato bursts. "I did not leave the house to carry on an affair, and you know it. If you want to know about affairs, ask your father." Patty felt light-headed, as if the words that came hissing from her had released helium in her veins.

Kiley's face was white and her lips were dry.

Patty rose from her chair just as the waiter hurried over apologizing for keeping her waiting. She squeezed by him with her suitcase and bags and past the people packed into the bar area in their office clothes. As the cool air outside hit her face she started shivering. Then she began to cry. She turned the corner with her baggage and stood up straight, forcing the sobs back down into her throat. She stood there until she regained some composure. Then she bumped her suitcase over the cracks in the sidewalk.

She was early for her flight, so she sat down for dinner at the airport. The salad she ordered arrived but she couldn't eat it. She was trying to make sense of what had just happened. Kiley was like a stranger to her—worse than that, she was like someone Patty didn't even want to know. And with every crisis over the girls, Greg seemed to get more lackadaisical.

She had planned to go over her report on the plane but instead she ordered a bottle of wine and sat back in her seat with the overhead light turned off, closing her eyes in between sips. Did Kiley really think that Patty was the parent who had cheated, or had she just said the ugliest thing she could think of to hurt her? Perhaps in her daughters' minds Patty *was* the unfaithful one—unfaithful to them, which was what they minded most. The girls probably knew what their father had done but would rather overlook it and keep things as they were. If Patty had had the same choice to make for her parents as a teenager she would have voted to keep their marriage glued in place, too. Her parents, though, never would have let themselves come apart in the first place. The rule growing up was don't rock the boat, even if it meant everyone had to eat in silence at the dinner table, pretending that Patty's mother was not silently angry at her father, or that her father was not deliberately ignoring her mother. Patty got in the habit of refusing to acknowledge the undertow of discontent in her house. It had seemed enough that the house remain there for her, her two parents in place as symbols of an order and symmetry that made their unhappiness seem normal.

Some days in her new apartment she woke up missing her girls so much it was as if a part of her body were gone. She missed the way they used to hang out in the kitchen on a Saturday afternoon, drinking tea and joking about nothing in particular. She missed hearing their take on the world—whether they were dishing the hair and clothes of a TV actress or talking about something they had learned at school. She had seen them just once since she moved out. Though she had called them every day, they had trouble arranging a time to get together. Patty herself didn't have much free time these days. But when she had been available, both girls had not, and they seemed unwilling to visit her singly, without the other twin. Maybe they had discussed this ahead of time and agreed not to be separated. When they finally did make a date and she went to pick them up, the atmosphere was strained inside the car.

She had thought the girls would like the place she chose to take them to eat because it had a huge salad bar and good desserts. It was also stylish in bright colors and glass fixtures, one of a number of new places Patty had discovered downtown, and she wanted to share it with them. The girls had toyed with their food and answered her questions about their classes in monosyllables. They were unimpressed with the restaurant. Then she had asked them if they wanted to see her apartment and they had mumbled what she took to be an assent.

Patty's hand had actually trembled as she unlocked her door for them. Through their eyes she suddenly saw how very small was the room which only a couple hours ago had seemed perfectly adequate and snug to her. They acted embarrassed as they politely looked around. She tried to get them to laugh at the miniature kitchen, how you were in effect standing in the living room as you reached in to light a burner on the stove, and how to turn on the tap for water you had to sidle between the stove and the sink. They seemed uncomprehending rather than amused. They wore the same blank expressions when they saw her claw-footed bathtub without a real shower.

"Where do you sleep?" Melissa had asked, almost reluctantly.

Patty had planned on saving the Murphy bed for last, sure it would charm them. But by the time she pushed the button to release its catch she knew it would only make them more aghast. Her fantasy of the three of them growing close again on these visits had been unrealistic. She saw that now. To the girls her tiny studio symbolized everything that had gone wrong in their lives. She imagined them talking snidely about her apartment after they left. Or perhaps they would never even bring it up again between them, as if the fact that their mother lived apart had to be put away like something shameful, a failure that was theirs, too.

Patty wished she could tell them how her new her life felt without its sounding like a rejection of them. Andy had already given her a raise and had dangled a substantial bonus that would be hers when she finished her work on Sunlink. For the first time she knew how heady it was to give yourself over to your work—to make something happen with your efforts and have people recognize it. This seemed important news to give the girls (no one had ever given it to her; her mother's message had always been *marriage, children, home*), but it was news that she couldn't be the one to tell them, at least not now.

Greg, on the other hand, seemed to have renewed his sense of responsibility to his little plot of property. When she had picked the girls up in front of the house she had noticed that everything was pruned to a shocking degree. The rhododendrons, the privet hedge, the mountain ash—all of it cut back to stubs. The lawn was rimmed with a border of raw sod from the edging blade. Everywhere fresh cedar bark dust formed a thick veneer over any exposed bed of earth. There was something almost vicious about the order he had imposed there. Patty had refrained from asking the girls about their father, and they of course had volunteered nothing. She hoped they wouldn't go back and describe her place to him, either.

It took a couple of days before her studio regained its charm for her after the girls had trooped through with their disbelieving, disapproving faces. She would not likely have them back to the apartment again soon; they could eat out together and see movies. Patty didn't have a decent place for them to sit down, anyway. She had one secondhand armchair with a hassock, and two straight metal chairs that went with the bistro table she had bought. The bistro set was outdoor furniture, really. But the armchair was large and wonderfully comfortable and every evening before bed Patty curled up in it with a novel. With the twins over, though, only one of them could sit in the soft chair; the other one would have to perch on a metal one, which even with a seat cushion wasn't very inviting.

She could devise ways to see her daughters, but still she couldn't deny the breach that had grown between herself and them. She wished she could be necessary to them again, regain some of the intimacy she had had with them during their childhood when they would both slip into bed with her and Greg in the mornings. With Greg and Patty curved along the edges of the queen-size bed like a pair of parentheses, their daughters filled up the middle and fell back to sleep immediately. Patty would watch them breathe with their soft snores and fluttering lids. Sometimes she would catch Greg doing the same thing and their eyes would meet over the sleeping girls. It was one of the closest times of their marriage, those wordless moments when they looked at each other without touching over the bodies of their children.

ALTHOUGH SHE had told Morgan he didn't have to pick her up, he insisted. The smell of his car's interior struck her as comfortingly familiar, and she settled into it, emotionally exhausted. Because they talked on the phone almost every day she felt as if they were friends. So when he asked her what was new, she found herself pouring out the whole story of Kiley's shoplifting.

"I know what happened probably shocked the hell out of you," Morgan said, "but kids from good backgrounds pull stunts like that all the time. It's an act of rebellion. You wouldn't believe the crap William put me through when he was in high school. Now he's doing just fine at Stanford. It's a phase."

"I know that. But I feel like I have no influence over anything since I moved out."

"And that makes you feel guilty."

"Of course it does."

"Listen." Morgan reached over and patted her hand. "Your daughters are probably sending you a signal or two, but so what? You must have had good reasons for moving out, and that ultimately sets a positive example for them—that their mother is a person with rights. You can still be a good mother from where you are."

"I don't know. Right now it doesn't seem like it." Yet it felt comfortable to be reassured by Morgan. It didn't even matter that he didn't know her children, or why Patty had left home, or any of the hundred details that would fill in the picture. She felt that he had a gift for moving swiftly to the heart of a situation. He had an executive mentality, one that could sum things up without getting mired in particulars, unlike Greg, who had to be led every step of the way.

Instead of dropping her at the entrance of her hotel, he parked.

"Too tired for a nightcap?" he asked.

"Not at all." She almost added "unless you want to get home," but stopped. He clearly didn't. As he ushered her into the lobby and waited while she checked in, their actions had the power of ritual for her. Already they had a groove to follow: she slid in her key card, he crossed her room to check out the view, and Patty knelt to fetch them drinks from the tiny, undomestic refrigerator. Her hand hesitated between the diet Coke and the Chablis. She opted for the wine, and this time did not need to ask him his drink. Bourbon, straight up.

H er mother was having difficulty deciding between the rose floral and the cream stripes. Patty didn't know why it should matter, since the linen closet at her house was already crowded with bedsheets in every conceivable pattern. But she had learned not to intervene when her mother was making a home decorating decision.

"I don't know, dear. They're such a good buy, maybe I should take both. Could you use a pair?"

"I don't need any sheets, Mother. I have two sets, one for the laundry, one for the bed."

"Oh, that's hardly sufficient. You mean to tell me you and Greg don't have any more than that? I'll get you the cream stripes then, and take the floral for myself."

"I'm talking about my apartment."

"Well, I'm sure you won't be there for long. Thank goodness you didn't take a lease."

Her mother was walking the sheets up to the register. "Mom, if you are insisting on buying me sheets, at least buy ones that will fit my bed. The bed at the house is queen. My apartment bed is double."

"I'm buying sheets for your home," her mother said, pulling out her credit card.

Patty was too annoyed to speak. They left the store and walked in the mall, Cass toting her bag of sheets. The mall had a health fair going on, with cloth-covered tables set up among the ficus trees and varnished benches. They passed tables offering free blood-pressure checks, body-fat testing, and brochures enumerating the early warning signs of cancer.

"That reminds me," Cass said. "I have a biopsy on Tuesday."

Patty stopped and tried to face her mother, who was strolling on. Patty was forced to catch up with her. "A biopsy? What for?"

"Just a little lump they found in my breast. Probably nothing."

"Will you have to stay in the hospital?"

"For a day. Your father will take me."

"I can be there. I'll take the day off."

"Oh, no, dear. Your father will sit there and read his newspapers by my bed. There's no need for you to disrupt your schedule."

"It wouldn't be a problem."

Her mother turned to look at her. Patty usually saw her mother's face as the one she had known as a young child. Age didn't superimpose itself there except in certain moments. This was one of them. Patty noticed the loose skin, the bony nose, the eyes set so much deeper than before. Her mother had always been careful to have her auburn hair color touched up every three weeks, though her complexion had yellowed and dulled beside it. But her mother fought the decline. Her short hair was modishly cut short, her lipstick was a subdued peach. She wore a suit Patty had never seen before, a creamy white jacket with loose pants.

"Patty, you don't need to be baby-sitting me. You need to be spending time with your daughters. You need to patch things up with your husband."

Patty shook her head. "Mom, you don't understand about Greg." She suddenly felt small and vulnerable, pinned under the weight of her mother's judgments again.

"Sit down." Her mother led her to a bench. "How can you just say that a marriage is over, just like that?"

"There are circumstances. Did you ever have this talk with Lynn, by the way?"

"Don't bring up your sister. You and she are not the same, and you know I have disapproved of her divorces. Do you think your father and I always had it easy?"

"I'm sure you didn't."

"That's right, and we didn't just chuck it all out at the first sign of trouble." Her mother smoothed her jacket and looked straight ahead. "Tell me what Greg did."

"All right, Mother." Why should she feel ashamed? And yet she did. "He went to bed with someone else. But you know what? That only started this. What happened next was that I began doing things I hadn't done before, and I like them. I like being able to concentrate on work. I like not having to pick up a house after other grown people."

"And you like abandoning your children?" her mother asked dryly.

"Of course not. But they're growing up and they have to meet me halfway."

Cass shook her head. "They are your children and they are not grown up. They don't have to meet you halfway. They need you to come find them. From what Greg says, things are getting out of control."

"You talk to Greg?"

"Of course I talk to Greg. You don't expect me to stop calling my grandchildren, do you? And when Greg gets on the line I talk to him. Now what is this business about another woman? Is it still going on?"

"I guess not."

"Was he sorry about it?"

"Sorry really isn't good enough, Mother!" Patty's eyes stung with a prick of tears. Her mother had never tried to see her side of things.

"Don't raise your voice to me. I forgave your father many things, including that."

Patty was looking in the direction of the nutrition booth when she heard her mother's words. She kept staring fixedly, wanting nothing to do with them. The nutrition counselor wore a perky little white coat with her name stitched in red cursive letters. She was using calipers to pinch the loose upper-arm flesh of an overweight woman in leggings. Why do people who shouldn't wear leggings wear them anyway, Patty wondered. Don't they know how they look?

"You don't seem surprised," her mother said finally.

"Mom, I don't want to hear about it," Patty said, her voice sounding young and shrill to her ears. "Really. It's none of my business."

"Of course it's none of your business, which is why I never told you, and why I never left your father, and why you grew up in a peaceful home having the security of two parents."

Patty watched the woman stand up and receive a small plastic bag stuffed with flyers. The nutrition counselor smiled after her. The woman left, and Patty wondered if she was going to read the flyers, then change her life. Would she now, after a chance encounter with a metabolically perfect stranger in a white coat, have the courage to act?

"It was not peaceful, Mom," Patty said angrily. "You know that. It was tense."

"We did our best. People are not perfect, Patty. You seem to expect that."

"I don't expect that. Look, Mom. What if Greg and I don't have anything left for each other and all this has made me see that? You don't really think I should live with someone I don't love?"

"I most certainly do. Because I know what you mean by love. You mean something that only exists for a few years in a marriage if you're lucky. After that, things change."

"Mother, I appreciate your help, but I really can't talk about it any more right now."

"You're being selfish, you know."

PATTY KISSED her mother on the cheek in the parking lot. They both acted as if the discussion on the bench had not taken place. It gave the illusion of no one winning, no one losing. But in her car she sat for a long time, staring through the windshield at the cloud-heavy day. She was visited again by the hallucinatory sensation she had had when moving out: her daughters small and alone behind bedroom doors too hot to touch. Finally she pulled out her cell phone and dialed the house.

"Melissa's out with Jason, Kiley's with Will," Greg told her.

"You're letting Kiley go out after what she did last week?"

"Don't second-guess me, Patty. I don't think you're in a position to call the shots right now."

"Greg, you can't shut me out of their lives."

"Who's trying to do that? I called you right away to have a family conference about Kiley's problem at Nordstrom's, and you flew off the handle and spooked her completely. Now she won't talk again. Grounding her isn't going to help."

"She's not some delicate little thing, Greg. She needs someone to be tough with her, and you're not willing to do it. You can't even say the word for what happened at Nordstrom's. She didn't have some 'problem,' she was stealing."

"How can you be so sure? What if she was trying to get caught, knowing it would make us talk to each other?"

"That's ridiculous."

"What's so ridiculous about it? From what the detective said, she was putting things in her pack in plain sight. Even *he* believed that she might just be carrying them around for a while, trying to decide what to buy. That's why he let us buy the stuff instead of turning her over to the police."

Patty was silent, fiddling with her handbag strap.

"Listen, Patty. Let's not fight. Why not come over here and talk about things?"

Patty watched the people loaded with bags come out to their parked cars in the mall lot. She didn't feel like going home to her apartment. Downtown was deserted on a Sunday evening, with all the stores and offices closed. Even the Portland State students were out of sight, squirreled away in their apartments.

"All right, but I don't want to come to the house. I'll meet you somewhere for dinner."

"Robin Hood's in half an hour?"

"Fine."

Patty drove down Powell to Robin Hood's, a generic pasta and hamburger restaurant that their family had gone to ever since it opened near their house twelve years ago. When she walked in, she was reminded of all the times the girls had sat coloring at the tables and interrupting them while Greg and Patty tried to have a conversation. There were candy and prize machines in the lobby and inside deep red booths that accommodated booster chairs. Patty was ten minutes early, so she ordered a glass of wine.

Greg came in wearing a lavender polo shirt and khaki shorts, even though the temperature had dropped ten degrees since yesterday. His hair looked wet from the shower. He slid into the booth opposite her and smiled self-consciously. He must have felt funny coming there, too.

"How was your trip?" he asked.

"It went well." She pulled her sack out and put it on the table for him. "My mother bought you sheets."

"Huh?" He looked at the bag without touching it.

"We were shopping today and she wanted to buy me sheets. Then she insisted on buying the wrong size, which was her not very subtle way of telling me that I belong at the house, where the bed is a queen, and not at my apartment, which has a double."

"A double that comes out of the wall, I hear."

Patty was surprised. "The girls told you about my place?"

"Melissa did. Maybe I pumped her a little. I was curious."

The waitress appeared and they ordered what they always ordered at Robin Hood's: Southwest chicken breast for Patty and steak tips for Greg. "They didn't like being there," Patty said.

"Well, what did you expect? They're having a tough time right now."

Patty looked at the paper cup full of broken crayons next to the condiments. The girls were beyond childhood now, but her mother was right. They weren't grown up yet.

"How's Melissa?" she asked.

"On the surface she's fine, just like always. She asks permission to go out, and she doesn't stay too late, and she acts pretty pleasant around the house. But I don't like this guy she sees."

"You wouldn't like any guy she saw."

"That's not true. Kiley's boyfriend, Will, irks me some, but he doesn't get my back up like Jason."

"Just because he drives a muscle car?"

"He's way too sure of himself. And he's too nice to me, like he's trying to get away with something."

Suddenly Patty remembered what she had thought of a hundred times outside of Greg's presence. "I should have called you to tell you how sad I was about Tim Phelps, Greg. I heard it on the news, and I should have called. I just didn't know what to say."

Greg looked away. "What is there to say?" he asked.

"Did the girls go to the funeral with you?"

"No. I sent them to school."

"What about the lawsuit?"

He shrugged. "It's going to drag on, I guess. I don't care what the school does. I know I'm not going back to teaching."

"What will you do if you don't teach?" She hoped the question didn't sound as skeptical as she felt.

"That's a good question. I can't be with kids anymore, though."

"It wasn't your fault, what happened."

"Thank you."

His statement surprised her. She had never pictured Greg making a big change in his life all on his own initiative. If he was forced out, that would be one thing. But he was telling her that he had decided, independent of the board, to leave. It wasn't like him.

Their meals arrived, and they ate in silence for a few minutes. There was a way in which being here felt like the most natural thing in the world. It was so easy to fall into the habit of being together. Patty had never much taken her mother's advice. But what she had said today had been delivered with such authority that Patty began to wonder if she wasn't right. Was she being selfish? Patty had started out in the right, with justifiable outrage over Greg's infidelity. Now even she admitted that his adultery was not, ultimately, what kept her away. She couldn't claim the high moral ground anymore; neither of them could.

"My mother's going in for a biopsy next week. She's got a lump in her breast."

Greg put down his fork. "Is it serious?"

"I guess they'll find out. You know my mother. I never know if she's in denial, or if she's being brave, or what. She just announces it like she's got an appointment for a manicure, and then refuses to say any more about it."

"Let me know how it goes."

"She said she talks to you quite a bit herself."

"I wouldn't say quite a bit. She's been calling more often lately for the girls than before. I'm glad about it, actually. They seem happy to talk to her."

Patty felt stricken. It was one thing if her daughters weren't talking to her. But it hurt if they were cozying up to her mother. Patty had never seen her mother as a worthy confidante when she was growing up; she was always criticizing Patty's choices. But maybe her mother didn't criticize the girls. Maybe she didn't see the same flaws in them she had seen in Patty.

"I think the girls need to see you more, Patty."

"That's well and good, Greg. That's fine with me. How am I supposed to do that? I called them up yesterday morning and said, 'How about a movie and dinner?' and they were busy. I said, 'How about tomorrow?' and they were busy. I called this afternoon to see if they could squeeze me in tonight, and you told me they were busy. Would you please tell me how I am supposed to see them more often?"

"Move back home."

Patty felt her breath shorten. She would not have a breathing attack now, in front of Greg. But her air started coming in short raspy bursts; she clutched the side of the table. Greg pushed a glass of water toward her. "What's wrong? Are you choking on something? Here, drink this."

Patty shook her head and stood up, trying to quiet her breaths. She tried to talk, to tell him she was all right, that this had happened before. He stood up to help her, but she waved him away and hurried to the ladies' room. Locked in a metal stall, she closed her eyes and concentrated. She tried to make her mind go blank, relax her muscles. Gradually her breaths deepened and slowed. Her pulse moderated. She stayed there for another few minutes, pressing her forehead to the cold door. When she emerged she ran a comb through her hair and patted her face with a damp paper towel. She put on lipstick.

"What happened? I was about to send someone in there after you."

"It's this breathless thing I get now and then. I'm okay."

"Have you seen a doctor?"

"No, it's under control, really." Patty didn't tell him that it was her former home, and her children, and her husband that squeezed the breath from her, and that in the company of strangers she was perfectly fine.

Outside it had started to rain, a fine mist that didn't quite call for an umbrella. Greg had parked next to her, and they stood for a moment behind their cars.

"I'm not moving back to the house, Greg. I started this, and I have to see where it goes."

"I'm glad you realize that, at least."

"What?"

"That you started this. It was like you were waiting for some trigger, almost as if you were hoping I'd do something stupid."

"I'm sorry." Patty unlocked her car and got in. Just as she was swinging the door shut, she remembered the bag of sheets, still in her hand. She didn't want to keep them; they didn't belong in her apartment, and she hated to have anything superfluous there. She sprang out of her car and opened his passenger door. Before she could speak, she stopped, momentarily confused by the heavy smell of tobacco and stale wine; this wasn't Greg's car, was it? Her eyes fell on the overflowing ashtray.

"What on earth? Are you letting the girls smoke?" His eyes shifted, avoiding hers. She remembered his smell the day he came home from seeing Clarissa. But Clarissa lived in Phoenix. Oh, surely not.

"It's not the girls," he mumbled. "Just a friend of mine."

She stared at him, waiting for an explanation. But he said nothing, and had that twitchy, guilty look she had seen that day in the kitchen.

"What I can't believe," she said slowly, "is that you actually asked me to move back home." Then she slammed the car door before he could speak again. She fumbled with her keys, finally getting them into the ignition. As she drove away, she was crying. She still had the goddamn sheets.

Before Patty met Morgan at the restaurant of his hotel she stopped home to change out of her suit and into a short black dress. The steady rain had turned intermittent, like a faucet dripping. She took her umbrella and walked. She liked the tapping sound of her heels on the pavement and the smell of cool air saturated with green from the Park Blocks. By the time she reached the red-suited bellman, she had decided.

They didn't have that much business to discuss, nothing that couldn't have been handled over the phone or by fax. Morgan handed her a file of information on local commercial rentals; Patty flipped through it and offered a few observations. Then they set the file aside and began what they both knew to be a date. It had been two decades since Patty had dated, but she recognized the behavior: immoderate laughter at each other's jokes, a lot of touching of arms and hands, absolute sympathy with the other's point of view. Patty had determined to allow herself this moment of recklessness. Their business project wasn't even halfway done. She shouldn't let this happen until it was all the way done, but then they wouldn't have as many reasons to see each other. For once she wouldn't play by the book.

After the entrees had been cleared, Morgan pushed back his chair and proposed that they have coffee in his room. She agreed.

As soon as they stepped inside he turned to her. She didn't move away as he lifted a hand to stroke her hair. He led her to the bed, patted the space beside him. Patty sat down and tried to smile; she was hideously self-conscious. He was being too strangely formal. He reached around and unzipped her dress. She sat there until he began removing his own clothing, then understood that she was expected to undress herself. Patty had worn a black silk slip and was thankful now for it—it gave her something rather modest to sit in while they were in this awkward, upright position. She began to have misgivings. Not about the act—she had spent a few days calculating its weight, its purpose, its importance at this crossroads of her life—but about her choice of lovers. Underneath the smooth weave of his expensive clothes emerged a man with white flesh as plush and softly dimpled as a baby's thigh. He began to smile apologetically as soon as he had finished kissing her—a kiss that lacked form, the sense of a beginning or end. She was struck by how little the unclothed Morgan resembled his executive self. He seemed not to know what to do; out of pity for him she helped things along more than she was used to. Patty had never been to bed with anyone other than her husband, and this was a large part of the reason she was in Morgan's hotel room now. Patty knew she wasn't divorced, was aware every day of the soft, yarnlike strings tying her to her family. But the laws that governed marital behavior no longer seemed to apply to her. She wasn't married in the old way anymore—with blind loyalty and an absolute sense of what constituted a wrong act. In her present status as a separated woman, Patty thought she was entitled, even obligated, to try this.

Morgan's body over hers was too heavy; he seemed to have no sense that he was crushing her, or that he should lift himself off her and bear some of his weight on his arms. His skin was moist without really sweating. She was grateful that she didn't have a view of their pressed-together bodies; she was sure they looked ridiculous. After a few minutes she realized nothing was happening.

"Jesus," he said, sitting up. "I'm sorry. I don't know what's wrong."

Patty was baffled. What *was* wrong? What was he waiting for? Then she understood, and a slow shame began to creep over her. "It's fine, don't worry," she said.

He was already pulling on his shorts, leaving her sitting on the bed naked.

He wouldn't look at her. "I've been working long hours over this expansion, and I haven't been myself lately. I'm really sorry. You're so attractive, I thought it wouldn't matter."

Patty reached for her slip. Thank God for slips. What did women do who didn't wear them? They had no protection against the world. She stood, and let the silk fall over her like a curtain dropping.

"Please. Don't worry. It's fine," she said. Of course it wasn't fine. They dressed themselves. In her rush to put her slip back on Patty had forgotten her bra. She scooped it off the floor and stuffed it into her bag. She hadn't taken the time to put her hose on right and they were slightly twisted; she felt an uncomfortable pull in her crotch every time she moved her right leg. For his part, Morgan was knotting his tie as if he were headed off to work.

"It's late," she said.

"Yes, isn't it? I had hoped we might have some time tomorrow, but I have a ten-o'clock flight—"

"And I have an eight-o'clock meeting. But you'll be back soon."

"Right. I want to sign that lease by next week."

"So I'll see you then."

"Of course. But I'll take you home in a cab now."

"No, that's silly. It's so close, I'll just walk. I'd like the air."

"It's not safe."

"I'll be fine. It's still pretty early."

"I insist on at least putting you in a cab."

"Well, all right."

They stood under the awning, and the doorman motioned a cab forward with his white glove. Morgan handed the driver a bill and then leaned forward at the waist to wave to her. Sort of a bow. The cab pulled away and began its eight-block trip, for which Morgan had probably paid too much, just to make sure he wouldn't look stingy. Patty's cheeks still burned in the dark. What did it mean when a man—*couldn't?* She had had no experience with this. In high school Greg had been pressed up against her every time they were alone with a hardness so unyielding, so persistent, so entreating and self-renewing, that she took the eagerness of the male organ utterly for granted. Of course, in almost twenty years of marriage they had slowed down, but who wouldn't? When they wanted to, though, there was no problem. She wished now she had paid more attention to those articles in women's magazines that explained this—*difficulty,* how it had nothing to do with a woman's desirability. But Morgan himself said that desire mattered. That he thought he desired her enough to overcome—whatever it was. When it came right down to it, though, he didn't.

She was too weary to walk up the single flight of stairs to her apartment. Patty pressed the button and listened to the pulleys creak and heard the clank of the ancient elevator jerking its way down to her. She wasn't used to the heaviness of the iron gate; it banged closed on her thumb as she entered. She pulled her hand away and cursed, tears springing to her eyes. She examined her thumb under the dim light and saw a blood blister beginning to rise.

As she opened her bag for the apartment key her bra spilled out of her purse and fell to the floor in a pile of lacy froth. She jammed it in her raincoat pocket. Inside her apartment, she curled up in her armchair without reaching for a book or making tea. She could not seem to stir from her position, knees drawn up to her chest, even though she was thinking: *Hang up your dress, wash your face, do your sit-ups.* She did not want to pull down her bed, with its squeaky frame and mattress stale from all the strangers who had laid themselves there.

"WELL, IT turns out that it *is* a little something," her mother said the next day. Her voice sounded normal.

"What does that mean, a little something?" Patty demanded.

"It's not a big lump, as these things go. They think they can get it all."

"What will they do? Just take the lump itself?"

Her mother hesitated. "Probably not. Probably more than that."

"Oh, Mom." The diffuse heaviness she had been feeling since seeing Morgan was now made part of a different, more focused weight.

"They know what they're doing."

"Have you had another opinion? Different surgeons have different theories about this. Maybe a mastectomy isn't necessary."

"My doctor explained it all. He gave me so many factors and statistics and studies my head was spinning. Then he told me what he would advise his own wife to do, and that's what I'm doing."

"But shouldn't you—"

"It's all decided," her mother said crisply. "When are you seeing the girls?"

"Maybe this weekend."

"How long are you going to keep up this foolishness?"

"This foolishness is my life, Mother. Do we have to talk about it right now? I'd rather talk about you."

"And I'd rather not. Talking doesn't help. The only thing that is going to help is those doctors in their green suits. I watched them bend over me when I was getting the anesthetic for the biopsy, and I knew they'd be back. I knew they weren't through with me. It's in their hands now, and I trust them."

"When are you having it done?"

"Tomorrow. They're in an awful big hurry, which I tried to argue about because I have so much to do to the house before the holidays are upon us, although it looks like we won't be having much of a Thanksgiving this year thanks to your—"

"Tomorrow," Patty interrupted. "I'll be there."

SHE HEARD them before she saw them—Greg asking the nurse at the desk which way to Cass Burgess's room. Then she heard one of her daughters say something in a low voice as they moved down the hall. She would know those three voices anywhere—at a distance, muffled by doors, even when they spoke purposely so their voices wouldn't travel, as they were doing now. Patty caught her own frightened reflection in the mirror as she waited for them to arrive.

The girls came over and kissed Patty on the cheek, then went to their grandmother. Cass was sleeping off the anesthetic. Her facial muscles were slack, her unmade-up skin the color of putty. With her hair flattened and her customary bright jewelry and scarves missing, she looked like a faint pencil sketch of herself.

"Gram's going to be fine," Patty said, standing beside them. "The doctors think they got everything. She'll be on chemo for a few months, so she's going to be taking it easy."

"Why isn't she awake?" Kiley asked. She was staring at her grandmother with frank horror written on her face.

"She woke up in the recovery room. Then they gave her something to help her rest. She's been sleeping all day."

"So they think it looks good?" Greg asked.

"So far."

"That's great."

Patty stifled her irritation. All you had to do was look at her mother and see how far from great everything was. This had aged her overnight. And there was no telling how hard the chemo would be. Greg loved to say things were great when he didn't want to think too hard about them.

Her father entered, and he and Greg shook hands as if nothing were the matter, as if they were not in the room with her mother who had just had a piece of her body carved away and disposed of, as if Greg and Patty were not divided from each other, the girls not numb from the confusion of their lives.

"Good to see you, Greg," her father boomed. "How's everything at school?"

"I'm not teaching. The school board is still trying to decide what to do with me."

"Oh, that business. I'd forgotten. Well, they'll come to their senses, I'm sure. Cass is going to be as good as new, girls. She'll be scolding me by tomorrow, just wait. Now let's see. Melissa?" Her grandfather held Kiley at arm's length, squinting at her, pretending to decide which twin was which. It was the oldest joke the girls had known.

"*Grand*pa," they groaned in unison, smiling a little, even now.

"Have you eaten?" he asked them.

"Not yet," Melissa said.

"Well, let me buy you something downstairs. The Salisbury steak's not too bad. Patty, you too. There's no need for you to sit by her side like a Florence Nightingale. Plenty of time for that when she wakes up."

Patty knew her father was trying to keep them all together, and that he was going along not just to pay for their suppers but to chaperon them, make sure the talk stayed inconsequential, see that they ate a meal together with nothing said that was dangerous or real. He was good at being bluff and loud, as good as her mother was with her tight-lipped silences and tart remarks. Greg could handle this kind of scene, everyone trying to put a good face on. Patty knew he'd grow animated, discussing football with her father, and the two of them would tease the girls until her daughters would be forced to shake their heads in smiling exasperation. And really, what was so wrong with burying trouble so you could go on with the next thing? Wasn't that the sign of an instinct to live? She followed them out the door in a spirit of resignation and irony, and—if pressed, she would have to also say—relief. This was her family: her mother, temporarily silenced but still present, still presiding; her father, paying and joking; and, as if there were a magnetic truth to their array, her husband and daughters leading her down the polished corridor with Patty as the last bright point in their constellation.

V

Lorraine had a new job at a place called Malabar's. It was a lot like the Top Hat. She could take the bus to work, but sometimes Greg gave her a ride. One day as he sat at his usual parking spot waiting for her, he heard a motorcycle roaring by and looked up just in time to see Lorraine on the back of it, leaning into the leather-jacketed driver. Greg felt betrayed, then reminded himself just what the situation was.

But the situation was actually unclear to him. He and Lorraine had gotten to be buddies, sort of. As guilty as he had felt when Patty saw the full ashtray, he was telling her the truth when he said the cigarettes were from a friend of his. It didn't all have to do with Tim anymore. Greg thought of this friendship as a kind of vacation from his life. But in truth, he was beginning to feel more and more as if he was faking it when he was home in his split-level house. Of late, he had had no desire to stay in contact with his friends; he returned neither Mitch's nor Wilson Perry's calls. He was getting lax about checking on his mother. He hadn't called Patty's mother at all since the surgery, telling himself that she'd get in touch when she felt up to it. He was there for the girls, but they were making it easy for him to feel he was nominally supervising them. They weren't doing anything outrageous like staying out all night or coming home reeking of pot. He had had no more calls from security officers. His daughters were busy with school and friends, and they were gone so much of the time that it was no problem for him to be, too.

Greg was beginning to think he was being drawn to his true level, where he really belonged. Patty's family, as nice as they were, had always seemed a notch above his own, and he had never gotten over feeling loutish when he was in the Burgess house with its porcelains and knickknacks. Patty didn't go in for that stuff, thank God, but she had always insisted on a certain level of quality in what she bought, a trait Greg associated with her inherent middle-classness. Her father had worn a tie to work and collected a salary. His own had carried a lunch bucket and punched a clock. When Greg had married Patty he had felt she was a safeguard against the fried suppers and cracked linoleum of his childhood. And she had been. She had deftly created just the kind of house he wanted to live in—clean, modern, everything practical and in good taste but not frilly or fancy. Now that she was gone, he felt the house's interior, what he thought of as its soul, was decaying. He got ketchup stains on the sofa and made them worse by rubbing. He jerked on a window shade in a fit of impatience and it ripped loose from its spindle. He even, at this late date in the season, began seeing ants in the kitchen, a problem they had never had before. He supposed it might have something to do with the unusually warm October they were having. Or it might be because he was now the kind of man whose house had ants.

So he didn't know if his being drawn to Lorraine was slumming or a reflection of who he really was. The other day Melissa had picked up the newspaper, open to the classified section in which Greg had circled some jobs, the only ones he thought he might be qualified for.

*"Trucker?"* she had asked him, her voice rising with disbelief.

"It's not such a stretch," he said in a tone that meant mind your own business.

She had put the paper down and not said another word. Later he realized that her reaction might not have been about the lack of status such a job commanded, but the fact that it would send him away from home. To reassure her, he brought it up when they were all sitting around the table in a rare moment of eating dinner at the same time.

"I wasn't serious about that trucker job, Mel," he said.

Kiley looked up with interest from her magazine. "Hey, cool," she said. "One of those cabs with bunks and little microwaves and a TV? Can I come?"

"I don't even think it was a long-haul kind of job. Anyway, I'm not doing it."

Melissa twisted a lock of her hair, a mannerism he had always associated with her edgier sister. Kiley couldn't twist hers anymore, though; she had gotten it all chopped off the other day. Now her hair stood up in aggressive little spikes and was a funny yellow color. Though he thought it was ugly, he had said nothing. On the scale of daughterly rebellions, he could handle a haircut. Kiley looked very different from her twin now, which he guessed was part of her point.

"So what kind of job *will* you get?" Melissa asked him.

"Don't worry, we're not running out of money. The school board's got to pay me until they fire me."

"Maybe they won't fire you," she said soothingly.

"I want them to."

Both girls stared at him. So what? It was time to start being honest.

"How about forest ranger? Can you see me in khaki?" he teased. "Firefighter? Circus roustabout?"

"Maybe Grandpa could take you into his insurance business," Melissa offered, refusing to joke.

"Too dull," Greg said, and he meant it. If he was going to reinvent himself at this late stage, it had better be good. Otherwise, why bother?

"Drug dealer? Plenty of excitement in that," Kiley said.

"As long as you don't pilfer the stock," he said, wagging his finger at her.

She laughed. A real laugh. The first one he had heard from her in weeks. But her comment made him wonder if Kiley could see it in him, too. A deterioration of his character, the peeling away of some veneer he had only pretended went deeper. Greg had been the first in his family to go to college. That didn't mean, of course, that he was any better than the gene pool he came from. Maybe he wasn't even as good; he didn't think he could stomach simple honest labor.

To Lorraine, he represented solidity, stature in the community, even wealth. He didn't disillusion her; in fact, he contributed to the impression by lending her twenty bucks when she ran short. It made him feel like a patron—if you could be the patron of a stripper. Lorraine made him say "exotic dancer." Her job was one of the things he was not allowed to question her about, just as the drinking and drugs were forbidden topics. Rick, too. Though she had never spelled it out in so many words, Greg understood that she would allow him to hang around her only if he was completely nonjudgmental. To tell the truth, her life was beginning to seem normal to him.

The first time he gave her a lift to Malabar's she had asked him with a wicked smile if he was going to come in.

"Aren't you afraid someone will see me and tell Rick?" he had asked.

"Why? Nobody would ever put us together."

He realized it was true. He didn't know if the thought irritated or relieved him.

He had sat at the bar so he wouldn't have to be served by her or another waitress. Later, she accused him of turning his back to her the whole time, but he had seen her. At Malabar's the girls wore gold thongs instead of the little cheerleading skirts they wore at the Top Hat. He knew the shape of her body already, from seeing her in her skin-tight jeans. Now he filled in his mental image with the creamy color of her skin and the way her breasts came to little girlish points.

Malabar's went a step beyond the Top Hat. There was a back room, in which customers could buy private lap dances.

"You're not going to do that, are you?" he had demanded when he saw the sign. He was breaking the rule about butting in, but he couldn't help it.

"Oh sure," she said airily. "It's not like they get real sex from you, you know. It's all simulated."

He guessed he believed her. The fat bouncer always followed the dancer and the customer beyond the door and remained inside with them. Maybe the level of contact wasn't all that different from a dancer getting tips stuffed into her thong after a performance. Why should he care anyway? Lorraine wasn't his wife, or his daughter, or his girlfriend. She was a drunk and a junkie. She lived with some thug of a biker. She had walked out on her kid without thinking twice.

He liked Lorraine a lot. Her crooked smile was somehow sweet, even innocent. When he made the connection between the varnished petal earrings she sometimes wore and the handcrafted picture frames he had seen at Phelps's house he was touched by her stabs at creativity. Maybe she had grown up with a mother who took off with new boyfriends for days at a time, leaving her daughter to fend for herself in their narrow, rented trailer (as Lorraine had said), but the experience hadn't corroded her nature. She said she refused to think about the bad parts of her life, and she wasn't going to tell him about them all, either. What was the point of going through all that shit?

"Do the bad parts include Tim?" Greg asked.

"That's just what I mean," she said. "You keep coming back to it and coming back. News flash, Greg: Tim's dead."

He knew she wanted to shock him. Being shocking was a kind of protective coloration for her; she did it to take the heat off herself and make him uncomfortable instead. But he had seen her cry over her son. Why he wanted her to dwell on that pain he couldn't say. He was half ashamed of wanting it; maybe it was because he was afraid to be there all alone.

She told him he was a brooder. When she thought he was thinking about things that "bummed him out," she'd poke him in the ribs or whistle for his attention, a startlingly loud doorman's whistle she could make between her tongue and overlapping teeth.

One of the things he brooded about was the back room.

"Where do you draw the line?" he asked. "What do you call dancing and what do you call being a prostitute?"

He thought she'd be mad at him, but her tone was matter-of-fact. "Don't be so hung up," she said. "I've got a talent, okay? I know how to use my body; I'm better at it than most people and I like doing it. I don't get hurt, I make people happy, and I make a helluva lot more money than if I was just carrying beers on a tray. Now shut up."

Her answer sounded rational, but it didn't help him. He told himself he would stay away from Malabar's altogether, but he couldn't. His compromise with himself was to always sit at the bar, keeping his back to the private room, and only watching the stage shows out of the corner of his eye. He knew this annoyed her, because he saw how important it was for her to have everyone's attention when she danced. He could feel her need to seduce them all. When she performed he made sure he appeared to be lost in his own thoughts, staring the other way at nothing in particular.

There was a mirror above the bar that aided him in this. It made the club look much larger than it really was, as if the shelves of gleaming liquor bottles multiplied themselves into a liquid infinity. Greg could nurse his beer and keep casual track of what happened in the club by just checking the mirror. He could see the deliveryman wheeling his hand truck loaded with cases of imported beer in from the side door; he watched as a young woman who was dressed like a secretary sat down at a table and filled out an application; and he saw the men in the audience smirk and stare at the women sliding themselves up and down a pole in front of them.

Lorraine did know how to use her body. When you saw her move you realized that most of what made a woman sexy was sheer attitude. Lorraine seemed to love it up there, grinning and strutting and wiggling low to accept a tip. Her routines were a bit more ambitious than the other dancers'—instead of doing the splits with one leg in front and one in back like the other women, she did them with her legs straight out to the sides. He had watched his daughters forever trying to do these "Chinese" splits during their gymnastics years; they had never been flexible enough. He had a moment of being impressed the first time he saw Lorraine sink to the floor, legs sliding out to either side, lowering herself past where the breaking point in her hip joints ought to be.

Greg always chose a moment to leave when Lorraine was backstage. No one at Malabar's ever saw them talk to each other or enter together. When he gave her a ride she always wanted to get out of the car before they reached the parking lot.

"Rick's full of surprises," she said. "Let's just be smart."

Greg didn't feel insulted. He enjoyed sitting alone and ignored in Malabar's. He had come to realize he was one of several regulars. None of these habitual customers acted like they recognized, or even noticed, one another. Each man sat inside a zone of privacy and contemplation where his desires were teased and deferred and where his most secret wishes and disappointments were his absolute own. That kind of loneliness and passivity suited him just now. He had long since outgrown the awkward and embarrassed feelings he had felt upon first entering the Top Hat. Now he took for granted his right to look; it was a business transaction, Lorraine had explained it to him like a patient teacher to a kindergartner. He thought his end of the bargain was better than hers, but she had told him to keep his opinions to himself. So he watched and enjoyed, free and clear.

He was on his knees, trying to reach the nozzle of the vacuum cleaner into the far corners under the passenger seat. He had all four doors of the car open to the clean fall air. The floor mats lay on the driveway covered with rug-cleaning foam.

"Dad, phone for you," Melissa called to him from the kitchen door.

He wiped his hands on his jeans as he went inside. "Who is it?"

Melissa shrugged. "Some woman."

She went back to peeling an apple as Greg picked up the receiver and said hello.

"Greg? Thank God. You've got to help me. I'm really in a jam."

"What's up?" he said, trying to mask the sudden uptick in his pulse with a casual tone. Lorraine was not supposed to call him here. He had never told her not to, but it was one of the things she was supposed to understand, just as he followed rules about how to approach her.

"I need to borrow a few dollars. Could you spare a hundred? You know I'm good for it after my next shift."

There were many replies Greg could not make while his daughter stood six feet away from him at the kitchen counter. For openers, there was the fact that Lorraine had never thought of repaying any of the money she owed him, even on days when she bragged about large tips at work. Then there were the very reasonable questions like why couldn't she ask for money from her boyfriend, and what the hell did she need it for, anyway? There was also the remonstrance he could not make about phoning him at his home on a weekend when his daughters would be around.

"That's not so convenient right now," he said instead.

Melissa glanced up at him, and then down again at the apple slices she was arranging on a plate.

"Shit! Don't give me that. I thought you were my friend." Lorraine's voice was harsh, then wheedling. "Please, please, please, I really need some money right now, and Rick's not home. Just a hundred."

"It's not that I wouldn't be happy to help," he said. He could feel Melissa tense and listening. "It's just that right now's not a good time."

"You fuckhead," Lorraine shouted. Greg pressed the receiver close to his ear to keep the voice in. "Don't bother waiting around for me anymore with that pathetic, shit-eating grin. I can't believe I let you hang around as long as I did."

Greg heard the receiver slam. He took a breath.

"Thanks for calling," he said to the dial tone. "You have a good day, too."

To Melissa, sitting at the table and avoiding his eyes, he mumbled, "Alumni fund-raiser." Outside, he angrily attacked his upholstery with the vacuum cleaner, eradicating any trace of Lorraine Morrison and her filthy ash. When Melissa answered, she had probably heard the loud music playing in the background from wherever Lorraine was calling from. Well, he'd covered himself the best way he could.

*Damn* Lorraine. She was only out to use him, a twenty here, a fifty there, and now a hundred. And coming into his home—even if it was just her voice through the telephone wire in his kitchen. It was his kitchen. His daughter was present. She should know how out of bounds that was. He had allowed himself to get sucked in too far. *Allowed himself*—that was a good one. She was right. He had begged for it.

Despite this, a melancholy begin to steal over him as he vacuumed up the last of the rug foam, leaving the carpet nubby and plush again. Was he now banished? If he showed up with his car in its usual waiting place, would she never again cross the street and climb in? If she spotted him from the bus stop, would she call for Rick and his friends, who carried knives and short lengths of lead pipe in their boots? He didn't know quite what it was he feared losing. The sight of her small rosy breasts he had never asked to touch? A way to relieve his loneliness? His honorary membership in some club he was too cowardly or too sane to join? Yes, yes, and yes.

He tried to put it all out of his mind. Today he had promised to take the girls driving on their learner's permits—their sixteenth birthdays and driving tests were coming up. His daughters had never asked him how his car had suddenly come to smell of smoke. They seemed to have developed a code of silence about any subject that might open questions they didn't want the answers to. But he had resolved that for their driving tests he would purge the car of as many traces of Lorraine as he could. He had even hung one of those scented pine trees she had ribbed him about. It didn't matter now. She wouldn't be around anymore to ridicule him.

The girls were ready promptly at two. You could tell when something was important to them—as driving obviously was. They instantly became courteous and reasonable people.

"Who goes first?" he asked.

"You," Melissa told her twin, climbing into the back.

Kiley took her place behind the wheel, and the sight of her adjusting her mirrors and changing the angle of the seat filled Greg with a sad tenderness. They really were, just now, starting out. They deserved a better teacher than he was.

The driving instruction at least he could do. He was a professional, having occupied the role through twelve summers of teaching Driver's Ed. He knew how to keep his mouth shut and not make a kid nervous. He knew how to look calm, even when they were making him nervous.

"Head out Powell," he said. "Let's go to the mountain." It was a drive he hadn't taken with Lorraine. Right now he didn't want to think about their stupid, juvenile picnics.

Greg offered little words of praise here and there as Kiley accelerated into traffic, kept a careful two car lengths, used her blinkers. He reminded her to rely not solely on her rearview mirror but to use her sideview ones as well. He told her to turn the wheel hand over hand. But she was doing fine and didn't need his help. He found himself relaxing and taking in the scenery as countryside began to replace the strip malls and fast-food joints.

Their family had driven this road mostly during ski season. When they started the girls on downhill lessons in the fourth grade, he and Patty had had two hours to themselves every Saturday while Melissa and Kiley learned to make snowplow turns and stem christies. Sometimes they just went to the bar and warmed themselves up with a brandy, nuzzling each other's wool-socked feet. Other times they used the lesson hours to ski hard, meeting each other laughing and breathless at the bottom of the slopes. Now the car felt unbalanced as the three of them climbed the mountain road without Patty.

They stopped to eat in Zigzag, the sharp scent of pine hitting them as they got out of the car. He felt that if he spun around quickly enough, he would see his wife behind him in her sunglasses and blue Polartec jacket. After the bad taste left by Lorraine's phone call, he was nostalgic for Patty's wholesomeness, her hygienic approach to life.

"We haven't been here forever," Kiley said, as she took a huge bite of her burger at a pitted plank table. She looked ebullient from her driving. Sauce dribbled down her chin, and she swiped at it good-naturedly.

Melissa was more subdued. In spite of Kiley's shoplifting incident and the sudden spiky hair, Melissa was the one these days who seemed most unlike herself. It was her listlessness, the way she looked worried all the time, never laughed. Now she sat picking the lettuce and tomato out of her hamburger and refusing to eat, calling her meat "too bloody."

"Send it back," Greg suggested.

"No, I'm not hungry." Greg realized that her rounder face was now, in fact, the thinner one of the twins.

"Are you sick? You look kind of pale," he said.

"I'm fine."

Greg looked sideways at Kiley to see if her face would register anything that might give him a clue about her sister. But she was scanning the dessert menu, taking herself out of the conversation.

Greg and Kiley each had the blackberry pie à la mode. Melissa sipped her seltzer.

"Your turn," he said, trying to elicit some excitement from her as he handed over the keys. "Try not to kill us."

"Thanks," she said. "You didn't worry about that when Kiley was driving."

"You'll do great," Greg said, patting her arm. "I was just joking."

Melissa was more hesitant than her sister behind the wheel. Though traffic on the two-lane highway was light, she waited until there was no car in sight before she pulled out. Then she accelerated too abruptly and sent a spray of parking lot gravel flying behind her.

"Way to peel out, Mel," Kiley said.

Melissa bit her lip and said nothing. He had coached anxious drivers before and knew that it was useless to tell them to loosen up. What helped was encouragement for everything they did right, and step-by-step instructions when a tricky maneuver was coming up. Right now, Melissa was inching along behind a log truck. He let her do so for about five minutes, then he began to feel impatient.

"Do you want to practice passing?" he asked.

"No, that's all right," she said. "I'll just wait." They drove along behind the truck, which moved to the right for them whenever the

shoulder was wide enough. No one said anything in the car, the silence making Melissa's decision seem the more pointedly wrong.

Kiley exhaled noisily from the backseat.

Melissa's eyes flashed in the rearview mirror. "Why don't you
drive if you think you're so good at it?" she fumed.

"Happy to," Kiley said.

"Settle down, you're doing fine," Greg soothed her.

A couple of cars were lined up behind them. After another minute
during which the log truck rode the shoulder, the car behind shot by,
passing both Melissa and the semi. In a few seconds, the second car
followed suit.

"Don't take the hint or anything," Kiley said.

"Your sister will pass when and if she's ready," Greg reproved
her. "You're not the driver now, Kiley."

"That's for sure. If I were, we wouldn't be going twenty-five miles
an hour," Kiley grumbled.

"All right, already, if it makes you happy," Melissa said defiantly,
suddenly accelerating and swerving out. Before Greg had a chance
to tell her to drop back and get a view of the oncoming traffic, before
he could warn her about inclines and blind spots, they were in the
wrong lane, a jeep headed toward them.

"Get back in!" Greg bellowed. After a long second in which
Melissa seemed frozen by her predicament, she did as he commanded, braking hard and squeezing back in behind the truck.

Kiley said, "Oh, my fucking Lord," slumping dramatically onto
her side in the backseat.

Without a word, without signaling, Melissa pulled abruptly over to
the shoulder and turned off the car. Greg reached over to reassure
her. She jerked away from his touch and wrenched her door open. He
found her in back of the rear bumper, doubled over and puking, as
the car cooled in ticks.

H e couldn't help himself. Monday he was back in his parking spot by the Dumpster. At eleven o'clock Lorraine entered the bus kiosk and sat with her legs crossed, smoking in short, impatient puffs as she swung her foot and watched down the street. He turned on his blinkers and hazard lights, and his front and back wipers. He made his radio antenna go up and down and caused his car alarm to chirp. Finally, she crossed the street, trying to bite back a smile.

"You fucking idiot," she said, as she climbed in. "The idea is to be inconspicuous."

"You were ignoring me."

"Duh."

He fanned five twenties in front of her, crisp from the cash machine. She hesitated, then folded them into her jeans pocket.

"I needed it Saturday," she said by way of thanks.

"What for?"

She squinted at him through her smoke.

"Gin. Weed." She paused to gauge his reaction.

He kept a poker face.

"Heroin." She blew smoke at him. "Bail. Wonder Bread. Does it really make a difference?"

It was his turn to shrug. "Just curious." He started the car.

"Is she cute?"

"Who?"

"Your daughter. Was that Melissa or Kiley?"

"Don't call me at home," he said.

"Not even if I get tickets to the World Series?"

"Not even."

"Not even if I've got the winning Lotto ticket I bought with money you loaned me and I want to share?"

"Not even."

"Not even if I want to tell you you've got credit on account for a special dance in the back room?" She traced a decaled gold fingernail along his chino-covered thigh. He felt a jolt—a less explosive charge than the electricity that had come straight out of the ground last summer, but with the same haloed, life-unhinging force.

"Don't call me at home to tell me," he said, then paused. "But I'm listening now."

THIS TIME he swiveled on his barstool to watch openly when it was Lorraine's turn onstage. She wore thigh-high boots, and little red nylon trunks with wide suspenders that ran over her chest and somehow covered her nipples without slipping off. The song was "Light My Fire." She sported a plastic firefighter's hat that clashed badly with her dyed red hair, which had always reminded him of the color of barbecue sauce. The number was as corny as they came, but Lorraine seemed oblivious to that as she gyrated around the pole and insinuated a length of fire hose between her legs. She saw Greg looking and winked at him as she peeled the suspenders off, and then in a flash somehow rid herself of the trunks. The rest of the show was a lot of ass-wagging in her thong.

Maybe Greg was becoming inured to the whole thing. Or maybe it was just the stage part that bored him, the exaggerated fantasy element of it that struck him as cartoonish. When he sat with his back to the action and a waitress brushed by his elbow to get drinks from the bar, when he was that close to a mostly undressed woman who was not even looking at him, who was for the moment unconscious of her body and his gaze—that's when he grew excited.

Then he saw Lorraine disappear into the back room with a beefy middle-aged man—sort of a Phelps type—and Greg felt the blood vessel at the side of his neck begin to jump. He glanced at the Budweiser clock above the bar and folded his napkin into accordion pleats while he waited for the man to come out again. Six minutes later the customer emerged, looking the same as when he went in except for perhaps a slight glistening at the temples. Or maybe Greg was imagining the shine from this distance and in this dim light.

"YES, SIR?" the bartender said, coming over.

Greg leaned forward. "How do you arrange for a private dance?" he asked in a low and unexpectedly hoarse voice.

"I can take care of that for you," the bartender said smoothly. "Do you have a dancer in mind?"

Greg nodded. "The one who was on a few minutes ago—'Light My Fire.' Her."

He had no idea what he had set in motion as the bartender moved to the end of the bar and cocked his head to the bouncer. They conferred briefly, and the bouncer glanced without expression at Greg before disappearing into the back room. In a minute he emerged, and nodded from his post to the bartender. The bartender came over to Greg and said he could go back. Greg left a five for him on the counter.

The bouncer opened the door for him and gestured for Greg to take a seat in a kind of upholstered banquette before an area of polished tile floor. In a few moments Lorraine emerged from a curtained-off area. She was wearing a black catsuit that made her legs look skinnier than ever. When she saw him, she raised her eyebrows.

"Fifty dollars, please," she told him, holding out a hand.

"I thought you said I had credit," Greg mumbled, peeling off more new bills. Thank God he had the cash on him.

She smiled flirtatiously and went to whisper something in the bouncer's ear. He glanced at Greg with more interest this time and left the room. They were alone.

"You do have credit," Lorraine said to him over her shoulder as she went behind the curtain again. "But I had to charge you something in front of the Tank. You paid the basic rate, but I'll give you the deluxe dance."

The lights dimmed into total blackness. She let him sit there for half a minute in the dark. Then a pounding disco music came on, filling the whole space with vibration. A second later, a strobe slashed across the room illuminating a sudden Lorraine dancing in front of him, her body weirdly speeded-up and jagged in the light. He had had a momentary fear, sitting on the banquette, that he was not going to be able to watch her without laughing, that the whole one-on-one of the dance would strike him as silly and embarrassing. Now he was lost in a confusion of senses. She was there and not there, her flesh appearing out of the leotard a limb at a time: first a bare arm, then another. Flashes of torso, small breasts that teased him with the insubstantiality the strobe produced. Finally the body was a whole nude, but not whole, never all knitted together—it was a fractured, dismembered nakedness. The eyes were closed, the neck twisting away from him as if in pain. The body did not so much pulse with the music as it seemed to writhe, to fly apart. Then he felt the pressure of her, the softness of skin against his face. Madly he tried to lap his tongue against it, against the bleached, colorless nipple that appeared and disappeared, against the curve of a waist that cut away from him. When he got his hands on it, around the body itself, his senses warred: what felt solid in his hand blinked away in the maddening strobe. She—not she—then she again—pressed against his straining cock, grinding against him, then leaving him, then coming back, teasing him. Finally, relief as her fingers loosened him from his pants, the comfort of closing his eyes to the shards of light so that he was only a darkness himself—and her mouth—a velvety enveloped nothingness, a heaven he floated in until he could no longer sustain it, and he was forced to let the groan come shuddering loose from some terrible, final place inside himself.

He welcomed the surprise of the kiss on his lips, the human touch of it, her tongue pushing open his mouth, prying it open, really. When his mouth filled at first he didn't understand why. The song was over and she had melted away from him. Silence and no one. His skin humming and crawling in the dark. He had to swallow, and understood that it was himself he tasted, a gagging second of his own salty cum. He felt his way to the door, and when it opened he blinked at the odd, still glare of the lights from the stage.

"Everything okay?" the bouncer asked in a businesslike tone.

Somehow he nodded, and made it back out into the world.

H e felt cured of her, debased beyond any sexual fascination, humiliated to a lucid calm. After three days during which he did not show up waiting, did not go to Malabar's, she called him.

"Most of my customers repeat, you know," she said when he picked up the phone.

"I've been busy."

"Bullshit. Didn't you like it?" He realized she wanted to hear praise from him, that her voice held an edge of hurt.

"It was fine. Really. I've just been tied up. I'll probably see you sometime next week."

He didn't think she would call again, but the next week one of his daughters answered the phone and said it went dead after a couple seconds. The day after that, he was home watching television when the phone rang and he listened to the machine pick up and record silence. Later when he played the tape back he discovered that it wasn't silence after all; he could hear, when he turned the volume all the way up, the faint rattle of music and laughter in the background and a short exhalation of breath, like an emphatically released drag on a cigarette. At least she had the decency to remain silent when he didn't answer, a sign that she understood the rules. In time, she would realize that Greg had withdrawn from the scene. She should be glad about that. So should Greg. But he didn't feel glad just yet. He felt empty.

HIS DAUGHTERS were about to turn sixteen. He had examined the problem for days. How to celebrate without Patty? Or, if she would consent to be together with them, how to celebrate with her? As it turned out, Patty took matters into her own hands.

"Would it be too awkward?" she asked when she called. Her voice seemed friendly.

"Of course not," he said, pleased that she was not so far out of their orbit that she could not imagine them all sitting down to dinner together. He asked the girls if they wanted to bring their boyfriends, and was relieved when they both immediately and without joint consultation said no.

The morning of their birthday he rose early to prepare French toast. The girls straggled down with none of the giddiness he associated with them on this day. Even turning fifteen, they had not been able to maintain a teenage mask of cool. Today, though, they had no problem looking indifferent. He planted kisses on their cheeks and made them sit while he worked. In spite of his bustle and cheerful cursing over the skillet, the air in the kitchen seemed thick with gloom. Patty had always made a big deal over their birthday, fearing that an ordinary celebration would not be big enough for sisters who had to share everything, even the moment of their birth. When they were little she had waked them up with singing and lit candles arrayed on some elaborately decorated cake. Greg remembered seeing the girls bolt up amid a tousle of sheets, faces flushed from sleep, and stare with wonder at the tiny tongues of flame their mother was bringing them. He didn't have a knack for effects like that, though he had been happy to play his supporting role.

Today, though, he was in charge, and from the looks on their faces, high expectations were at least something he need not worry about.

As he poured them juice and brought their plates to the table, Melissa slid a small wrapped package over to her sister. It was the twins' tradition to exchange gifts over breakfast.

Kiley unwrapped the paper and opened the jeweler's box it contained. She extracted the watch, a delicate oval face with a thin black leather band, and dangled it between her thumb and forefinger. "It's great, thanks."

Greg winced inwardly for Melissa at her sister's flat tone, the way she put the watch back in the box and snapped the cover down without even trying it on.

"Here's yours," Kiley said, putting a box of similar size in front of Melissa.

Melissa had two bright spots of color on her cheeks as she used her fingernail to slit the tape on the paper. Inside glinted a silver Nordstrom's box.

"You didn't steal it, did you?" she asked when she saw the box.

The air in the kitchen solidified like glass. Greg stood still with his spatula, waiting for it to break.

"What a bitch you've turned into," Kiley said, slamming her fork down and backing her chair away from the table with a bump. Greg watched her grab her backpack from the counter and storm out the kitchen door.

Melissa stared miserably at the unopened box.

"Not a very funny joke," Greg said, sitting beside her in Kiley's empty chair.

"Did you see how she acted when I gave her mine?" Melissa cried, her voice rising and breaking. "She always acts like it's me who starts things."

Greg nodded. He didn't have much of an idea what the deeper currents were between the girls, but anyone could see how far lately they had come apart, going their separate ways after school and never huddling together anymore in the same bedroom.

"I saw," he said, feeling for once that talking to his daughter was easier than he thought, a matter more of listening, really.

"Let's see what she gave you," he said.

She seemed on the point of refusing, perhaps mostly out of the habit of not following his suggestions, but then she reached for the box. A pair of plastic skull earrings grinned up at them. Melissa tried to maintain her tragic composure, but her mouth tugged up into a smile.

"They're really awful," she said.

"Kiley would like them," he pointed out.

She laughed.

"Just trade," he urged her. "You must have liked the watch you got her."

"I spent a ton on it," Melissa agreed with regret.

"Well, then." He surveyed the platter of untouched French toast. "And nobody wanted my breakfast, either. How about it? I put orange juice in the batter, just the way—"

They looked at each other and smiled ruefully.

"Well, we'll see your mother tonight," he said, getting up to start the dishes. Melissa helped him scrape plates into the disposal.

"I'm sorry, Daddy. I'm just not hungry," she said as her breakfast slid into the sink.

"You're never hungry lately. What's the matter with you? When's the last time you had a checkup, anyhow?"

She didn't answer, but he continued anyway, thinking that now when they were alone was a good time for him to express his concerns. For what it was worth.

"You mope around, you look tired all the time—even now, when you just got up. I mean it, I think you should see a doctor. Maybe you've got mono. I had it when I was in college. I could barely drag myself around for three whole months."

He thought she was ignoring him, but he glanced up in time to see his daughter's face collapse in on itself the way paper does when it cannot resist the airless space created by a fire. He reached out for her, and she buried her face in his chest, heaving huge sobs against him.

"What is it?" he murmured, scared that his ability to say the right thing would vanish, that she would wheel around and follow her sister out the door to a place he could not reach her. "Tell me, honey. What?" He was on the point of guessing—*Is it your mother and me?—Is it the fight with Kiley?*—but feared there was something so violent and new about this crying that supplying words for it would lead her away from telling him its source. So he just let her cry into him, petting her hair as if she were a cat, hoping that if he left an opening, she would creep toward it.

She shifted away from him, and he let her go. In a matter of seconds her face had puffed into an unrecognizable mask of itself, wet and smeary, with slitted, red-rimmed eyes. She was still crying in small shudders.

*Please God,* he prayed, for in that instant he needed a God to back him up, one who was a father himself. *Help me to not screw up.*

"Oh, Daddy, I'm sorry," Melissa said suddenly, pitching herself against him again and sobbing anew. "I'm so sorry." Her crying became hysterical, a series of little gulping screams. He reached over to turn on the tap, got some cold water on his hand, and cradled her face with his palm. She began to quiet a little then, and he continued to wash her face with his hands—he had no cloth handy—cooling her by degrees. This was the way he had washed her as a toddler, never squeamish about wiping away snot with his fingers because she was his child.

Her eyes were closed. He smoothed her hair back with cold water, lifting it away from her hot, sticky face.

"Whatever it is, Melissa? Whatever it is, it's going to be okay. Sit down and tell me and I promise we're going to fix it." He waited, and she seemed to unclench a little. She stood there swaying with her eyes closed for maybe two minutes, and he found a patience within himself he didn't know he had. He could wait. He would remain rooted to this spot in the kitchen for as long she needed him to, and wait.

Finally she said it, at first with her eyes closed, and maybe it was because he couldn't see her eyes that he didn't hear it right. Then she looked straight at him and said it again, so there was no mistaking it.

He had imagined everything else, girlish hurts and problems—flunking a subject, getting suspended for smoking a cigarette in the school john—but somehow, in spite of the boyfriend, in spite of the scene with Kiley over the pink compact of pills, he had not allowed this thought to occur to him.

"You're pregnant," he echoed, trying to make it just words. He felt as if floors were falling away beneath him, as if he had started on the top level of an elevator and the cables had suddenly given up their tension. His stomach bucked once, and he willed it steady.

Now that she had said it, she seemed calm. Her breathing quieted. She stood very still and studied some point behind him.

"Okay"—it was his turn to take a breath—"let's sit down." Questions crowded him, and he discarded each in turn. Not *who*—that was clear. Certainly not *how*. *When* would be important, but not yet. They were still on the *what* that lay in front of them.

"You're sure?" he asked. "You've had a test?"

She nodded.

"Jason knows?" He didn't know why he was able to say the boy's name so calmly. He didn't know why he wasn't speeding down the street in his car to find Jason, smack him up against the wall, hit him again and again, until there was no more Jason left. He did know why. He was looking at her.

Melissa's mouth twisted up again until she got control of it. "I don't want to be with him, Daddy. We broke up."

Something on the back of his neck tingled. His fantasy came back, Jason's eyes, terrified against the wall. Jason, reduced under his fists to nothing, a grease spot of annihilation. "He didn't . . ." Greg shook his head to clear an image. "He didn't *make* you have sex, did he, Melissa?"

"No, it wasn't like that," she said in a low voice. "We both . . . you know."

Greg nodded, experiencing a surreal moment of relief at learning his daughter's sex had been consensual. The relief, however, lasted less than a second. She was sixteen. She was pregnant. She didn't love the boy.

"And so . . ." he began, trying to get her to fill something more in, give him something to grasp at.

"I want to get an abortion, Daddy."

He thought that this statement should produce relief, too, the way it had when Patty had announced that she would get one, saying that they weren't ready. If she had wanted to have the baby then he wouldn't have argued, though the thought had made him go slack with fear at eighteen. But she hadn't wanted to, and so he followed her lead, feeling lucky that his girlfriend was so sensible and calm, that she didn't lay a guilt trip on him, that she made it easy on him, in fact, telling him when and where they would go, how much money they would need, what rules they needed to follow after that.

Greg wasn't that high school boy now, the one who had never held a newborn, his own flesh, a baby whose milky gaze stared at him without knowing what it saw, needing from him everything he had to give.

He wasn't that raw, inexperienced boy trying to save his skin and fix things with the least possible fuss. He was a father whose babies had been soft squirming weights in his arms, requiring his vigilance, his devotion. The little moon faces turning to follow his voice had compelled him to pour a stream of whispered promises into the tiny whorled ears. Seeing them tight asleep in their bassinets was enough to send him off daily to a job he didn't particularly like, because they needed him to go, to earn, to be their dad. Now one of those babies was right here, miraculously grown into a person. And Greg had lived enough to know that some things could not be "fixed," not really. So the word "abortion" produced no wave of relief, even though he knew this child of his was not ready for a baby of her own, did not even have what Patty had had, the backing one way or another of the baby's father.

"Can I ask," he began hesitantly, "why you and Jason broke up?"

She made a face without speaking and left a silence. "Why is a crooked letter," she said, lifting one corner of her mouth. It was Greg's own joke coming back to him, the way he used to tell the girls they had asked enough questions when they were little and pestering him. He waited. This wasn't a joke.

"I was never friends with him the way Kiley is with Will," she continued finally. "We never really had anything to say to each other. I mean, I liked being with him and all, but mostly it was . . ." She trailed off.

Greg filled in: his car, his body, his cool, his laugh, his control, his status. All the things Greg had immediately recognized and distrusted. All the things he had failed to warn Melissa adequately about.

"Is it wrong not to tell him at all?" she asked.

Greg was lost on that one. He needed Patty, but not in the old kind of way, the way of deferring to her plan. He needed her to think with him, and with Melissa. Not to tell them what to do, but to look at this thing a hundred ways until they knew it, and had not missed anything.

"I don't know," he admitted. "Have you told your mother?"

Melissa's pupils seemed to grow and shrink. She shook her head. "I feel horrible enough without having someone yell at me."

That's when Greg realized that all these years he might have given the girls something different from what Patty gave. He had always credited her energetic involvement with them, her sterner hand at discipline, all the ways he knew she showed them she loved them. He was a failure a hundred times over at parenting and everything else, but here was a tiny way in which he had not failed. Melissa had chosen him. Even if she had just chosen the parent who was in the kitchen with her at the moment she was ready to break down, it amounted to the same thing. He was the one who had been there. And she had not been afraid of him.

hat evening Patty showed up at the restaurant with a cake box in her arms. She was wearing new clothes, a dark green jacket and black skirt. Every time Greg saw her now—at the hospital, at Robin Hood's—she wore something he had never seen before. It confused him, that moment when he caught sight of the woman first, and needed an extra beat to recognize his own wife in her. Greg had forgotten that Patty didn't know about Kiley's haircut. Her eyes widened when she saw it.

"Wow," was all she said, touching one of Kiley's gelled quills. She kissed the girls and gave them both cards.

"These are from Grandma. She's sorry she couldn't give them to you herself tonight, but she's weak from a chemo session. She wants to be better by Thanksgiving and have us all over." Patty glanced at Greg.

*Sure,* he shrugged. Thanksgiving at Cass and Walter's was what they did. He didn't know if Patty was just giving in to her sick mother by continuing the tradition this year or if she was softening, beginning to admit that they were still a family, the four of them. He wanted her to soften, he had never stopped wanting it, even when he was sitting in Malabar's, bizarrely linked in friendship or obsession to Lorraine. But he was all done having that secret life. He hadn't seen Lorraine for days. Her telephone hang-ups had stopped. He had made a clean break from all that.

Kiley ripped her envelope open, no doubt expecting money to fall out. "A savings bond," she said. "Good ol' Gram." Her tone was a mix of amusement and disgust. Then she got an idea. "Hey, you can cash these things in early, right?"

"If you want," Patty said. "It'll be worth a lot less."

Both girls looked at her, seeming to expect more resistance. Greg was surprised, too. How unlike Patty to roll with that, not to argue about what Grandma would want them to do.

"Just don't mention cashing it in when you write her a note," Patty said.

The waiter came then and hovered a second while they decided if they were ready to order.

"You all go ahead," Patty said. "I'll be ready." It was what she always said. Decisive about everything else, Patty for some reason could not choose from a menu in a new restaurant. It was a family joke. Now, after the girls had ordered pasta, and Greg his steak, the waiter stood with pen poised, ready for Patty's order. To beg time, she asked him to repeat his specials.

"Oh, God, I can't decide. I'm between the trout and the swordfish." She smiled apologetically as she bit her lip and scanned the menu for clues.

They waited, the girls shifting with embarrassment. Greg didn't mind, except, as usual, he knew what she really wanted. It was this strange thing that happened to them when they went out to dinner. Patty would get paralyzed by her choices, while her real desire was somehow obvious to Greg.

"Have the trout," he advised her now, because it came so automatically to him. "You can have swordfish anytime."

As soon as he said it he was afraid she'd be mad, that he had overreached from his estranged position. Instead she looked relieved.

"You're right. Trout," she said, smiling at the waiter.

The girls seemed to release a collective breath. Patty avoided his glance, and Greg knew why. It was such a married moment they had just had, the telepathy, the ritual flurry of her helplessness and his sudden gesture of control. It was still a mating dance, after all these years.

"So? Tell me!" Patty demanded. "Did you pass?"

Greg had picked the girls up after school and had driven them to their tests. The examiner had taken both girls out together, which Greg had wanted to object to, but he had decided to stay out of it. If the girls wanted to protest the twin treatment, they were old enough to. He had wanted them to be tested separately because he was beginning to see how the new Kiley made Melissa nervous. Kiley's recently acquired rock-and-roll mannerisms, her ironically drawled "Dude"—as if she was purposely parodying a rocker, except she was also in the role, too—left her sister awkwardly silent. Especially now, Greg felt protective of Melissa.

"Of course we did," said Kiley.

"Some of us barely," Melissa added.

Patty raised her eyebrows, waiting.

"That tester was a complete jerk," Kiley defended herself.

"So you thought you had to show him," Melissa retorted. She turned to her mother. "He told Kiley he was docking her for not slowing down at a yellow light. So of course she can't keep herself from going faster, because she's mad, and ends up zipping right through another one."

"But you passed," Patty said to Kiley.

Kiley reached into her pocket and flipped her license over to Patty. Greg had already seen it: the sullen expression she would have to live with for the next four years.

Patty inspected it without commenting on the picture. "And you?" she asked Melissa.

"You didn't tell your mother," Greg said.

Melissa looked at him, panic widening her eyes.

"About your perfect score," he said quickly. He wasn't trying to needle Kiley. But he had almost not believed it when he heard about Melissa: the scared rabbit of a driver who had almost killed them last weekend had aced her test.

"For some reason I wasn't nervous at all," Melissa marveled, shaking her head. "I just kept hearing Daddy's voice: check your mirrors, hands at two and ten, remember your blind spot."

Greg thought she was making fun of him as she imitated his coachlike pointers. But then he caught Patty's glance at him—friendly, grateful, amused—and realized with surprise for the second time that day that maybe he wasn't such a useless father after all.

"Well, I'm proud of you both," Patty said. "I can hardly believe how grown up you're getting."

Greg and Melissa exchanged a glance. They had agreed that they would invite Patty to the house after the dinner to tell her. Kiley would probably shut herself in her room to listen to music, or head out to find Will. If Patty came, they weren't worried about getting her alone. But Greg wasn't at all sure Patty would agree to come over. And if she did, he was dreading the scene ahead, perhaps even more than Melissa was. After all, wasn't he supposed to have been preventing crises just such as this by his full-time parenting of the last two months?

He wasn't prepared to defend himself, didn't think there was a defense. One reason he couldn't work up any outrage over Melissa's pregnancy was the degree to which he believed himself implicated. He couldn't say exactly what he should have done to swerve Melissa away from this disaster—for he thought of it as an accident, like a matter of being mowed down by a huge truck she had wandered in the way of. Curfew, rules, she had had all those. Clearly, the trappings of parental control were not sufficient, unless he went so far as to chaperone his daughters' dates, riding along in the Camaro or bicycling behind Kiley and Will. But really, what would suffice? After all, Kiley had had no trouble getting herself pills—whether for acne, as she'd said, or for what Greg now pretty positively suspected, contraception. And if not pills, there were, as she had pointed out, condoms available from the fishbowl in the school nurse's office. (How urgently he now wanted to recommend the condoms to Kiley over the pills because of STDs—except he didn't want her to need any of it, pills or condoms, and didn't see how he could offer such advice in a way that didn't automatically make it permission.)

What, then? Would things have gone differently if he had never messed up their family life, beginning with the two hours in Clarissa's hotel room? Or maybe it really had begun the day he sent the boys back out onto the field after the rain stopped, so they wouldn't waste ten precious minutes of practice before their first big game. Because the day Tim began dying—wasn't that the moment Greg began systematically shredding everything in his own life that mattered most?

And yet, he couldn't quite believe that if lightning hadn't struck, the girls would still be virginal and safe, locked into their smooth young bodies like perfect carvings of ivory. Look at him and Patty. There had been no crisis, no free-falling parent creating the rush that propelled their own bodies toward each other.

It grew on him slowly, the idea that maybe he and Patty should have talked about their abortion with the girls when they found Kiley's pills. Maybe telling them about their own mistake, how it could happen so easily, how they knew all about heavy breathing in the back of a dark car, on a blanket in the woods, a basement couch. That they—did they?—wished they had waited longer. (But he had never wanted to wait. He had only made it through those blurry, frustrated years with the help of Patty's sweet body, the discoveries he made in it, the places he claimed there as his alone.) To tell his daughters that he and Patty understood longing, had not themselves been able to resist it—did that warn the girls away from having sex? He didn't see how.

But maybe if they talked about how the abortion felt. Except, he didn't know. He hadn't felt. He had gone to the bank, driven, waited, bought doughnuts, kissed Patty goodbye at the door to her parents' house, where she was going to put herself to bed. Had he asked Patty how she felt? Or had he just tried to cheer her up, say funny things? He couldn't remember. He couldn't see much about the day at all: its weather, the expression on Patty's face, or if he had caught a glimpse of his own eyes in the mirror. All he remembered was being scolded for getting powdered sugar on the car seats, and how, like counting out the money, dusting off the sugar seemed something to focus on.

He poured Patty another glass of wine. She seemed happy tonight, loosening in the old way.

"Can we have some?" Kiley asked. She nudged an extra wineglass toward him.

"Oh, I don't think—" he began, but Patty interrupted him.

"Let them have a tiny bit, Greg. Sixteen's a big day."

He poured an inch into Kiley's glass, and held the bottle over Melissa's. Their eyes locked and she shook her head. It could mean that she felt sick; she was only toying with her pasta. But it could also mean that she was keeping her options open, was beginning to think of the pregnancy as a pregnancy: no wine, no coffee, no aspirin or other over-the-counter remedies. He himself had said they needed to talk about everything, keep an open mind. Did he really want that? Did he want his daughter to go to one of those alternative high schools for pregnant girls where AP English, if it was even offered, was on the curriculum along with courses on diapering and prenatal nutrition? Did he want a baby to come into the house, a house Patty didn't live in, and might not ever return to? Or, barring that, have his daughter grow a baby she would not hold when she delivered it, or hold once and then hand over to smiling, solicitous adoptive parents? This last he could not imagine. If it was to be a baby, it would be his grandchild. If it was not allowed to become a real, breathing baby, if the coded cluster of its early cells was to be suctioned (he forced himself to think exactly, think the word) away, he could live with that, if Melissa could, if that was what she wanted. But no strangers would take a birthed child from his daughter, who would, he knew—he knew her—love it tenderly on sight.

"Well?" Patty was looking at him.

"Sorry—what?"

"I asked you if you wanted to tell the girls what their presents are."

"You go ahead," he told her. They had conferred earlier about this on the phone.

"Well, we got you these," she said, pushing two small, flat boxes toward them, "but the main present is that we're going to pick up the cost of adding you to the car insurance as long as you're in school."

"Awesome," Kiley said.

Greg wondered about the "we," if Patty meant it the way it sounded, that they were back together, or would be back together, down the road. Then again, he supposed that separation agreements and divorces could accommodate arrangements such as deciding who kept up the teenagers' car insurance.

Melissa unwrapped her flat box first. It was a gift certificate for a department store—not, Greg noticed, Nordstrom's.

"Thanks," Melissa said. Greg could see how hard she was trying tonight, the tight smiles she was mustering.

"I looked at things," Patty said. "But I just didn't know what you needed." She didn't say "I just don't know you anymore," but that's what it came out sounding like, and what everybody heard, judging from the silence that fell.

"But I also wanted you to have something that you would remember," she continued. "I thought you each might want to pick a piece of jewelry of mine, next time you—come over."

"Cool, Mom," Kiley said, clearly in a good mood because of the driver's license, the savings bond, the free insurance, the gift certificate, and now the chance to pick something she might actually like. Greg couldn't help noticing that the girls had, in fact, traded back their presents to each other. Kiley's skulls dangled from her head. Melissa wore the dainty watch. They seemed to have declared a truce.

"Can I have that pineapple necklace you got when we went to Hawaii?" Kiley asked.

Patty hesitated, her gaze darting to Greg. He had bought her the gold pineapple after a morning when they had made silent, furtive love under the covers as the children slept on in the next room of their rented condo. What did it mean when she started giving those trinkets away?

"Sure," Patty said. "Melissa? What do you want?"

They all looked at Melissa to see what she wanted from her mother. She opened her mouth to speak, then closed it. Greg's stomach muscles tightened for her, to help her keep control, not cry now, not yet.

"Um, earrings?" she finally said, her voice cracking a little on the word.

"Sure," Patty said softly, studying her. "I'm sure we can manage that."

**VI**

Maybe it was because she sensed something was up, or maybe it was because the wine had lowered her resistance, but when Greg proposed that they eat the cake at the house, she agreed. She also, if she admitted it to herself, was feeling very sentimental and emotional today, the day her daughters turned sixteen. The offer to give them some of her jewelry had been spontaneous, because she realized, as she watched them open their gift certificates, that the things they bought at the store—new shoes, jeans—would wear out and get thrown away. She wanted to give them something for this birthday that would last forever, something that would bind them to her. When inviting them to take something from her, she hadn't even thought about specifying limits—what if they wanted her pearls, a graduation present from her parents, or the diamond studs Greg had given her the night before their wedding? But they had chosen in the spirit she had offered: a keepsake, something of value, but nothing she couldn't part with.

Greg suggested that Melissa ride in Patty's car on the way to the house, and Patty was glad for the chance to steal private, sidelong glances at her daughter. She saw what Greg meant. Something was going on with Melissa, that much was clear. She looked, all of a sudden, delicate: thin and white and transparent.

"Don't you feel well?" she asked her.

"I wish people would stop asking me that," Melissa replied crossly, staring out the passenger window so Patty could no longer see her profile.

"Sorry," Patty said dryly. Her new philosophy with her teenagers was to back off. She wanted them to know she was interested and loved them, but really—her mother's advice aside—did parenting mean that you had to be their verbal punching bag? Patty thought not. The girls had to learn that their moods did not qualify them to abuse others.

"Sorry, too," Melissa said softly, seeming to address the window. If Patty hadn't been listening, she might have missed the words altogether. But she was listening, and patted her daughter's knee in response. They said nothing else the rest of the way.

When she turned into the driveway beside Greg's car, cutting the wheel in a radius that her wrist remembered by itself, Patty's breath speeded up—just for a few seconds. Everything was so powerfully familiar, as was the feeling of belonging that emerged all at once from some storage area of her brain where she had stashed and half forgotten it. Now the sharp outlines of her life here came rushing back, jabbing her heart with a series of quick, rabbitlike beats. And yet, things were different, too. Greg, for instance, at dinner seemed a more definite character somehow. She couldn't automatically assume she knew what he was thinking now; there was a process to his thoughts that forked in new directions. For the first time since she had known him he seemed not to need her. It changed everything. She felt freer in his presence, and also, strangely, that she had to work harder. This transformation touched her house, the backdrop of most of their life together. It wasn't the same place she had left because she didn't know her place in it.

Patty saw Greg get out of his car and peer toward the stoop, and she followed his gaze toward the dark, shadowy shape he was staring at.

"What the hell?" she heard him say, and Patty looked again and saw that the shape was alive, that it was the figure of a woman rising up on all fours from where she had been curled.

"You're home!" a voice shrilled, morbidly high and sweet, full of exaggerated cheer. "I've been waiting for hours!"

"Lorraine, what is this?" Greg said grimly, moving toward the step. "Are you drunk?"

"Oh, sweetie, no, nothing like that!" she sang out, rising and swaying. She steadied herself with a hand on the screen door. "I just missed you, is all. It's been so long since you've come to see me, I thought you were mad. Are you mad? Don't you like me anymore?"

Patty's heart was thudding halfway out of her chest. She had instinctively stepped forward and gathered each girl close with an arm, and they had melted into either side of her, compliant and mute. The three of them watched this thin, wild-haired woman (or was she a girl? She sounded like a girl) stagger toward Greg. She tripped on the step and fell forward into his arms. He backed up under her weight and lowered her to the ground, after which he took a step away.

"Whoops!" she shrieked, her giggles a brittle, tinkling cascade. She got herself up into a sitting position, her arms clasped around her drawn-up knees as if she were posing for a photo on the beach.

"At last I meet the family," the woman said, for Patty heard, now that she dropped the shrill falsetto, that the voice was rough, an older voice, though the body was that of an undeveloped adolescent—thin legs in spandex, a long, baggy sweatshirt.

"Greg, what's going on?" Patty finally gathered enough breath to hiss. "Who the hell is this?"

"Tim's mother," Greg replied tersely, frozen and staring at the woman sitting on his walk.

Patty gawked in confusion. It took her a moment to get Tim's name back, then connect it with the present. She remembered Greg's telling her that the boy's mother was missing.

"Tim's mother, Tim's mother," the woman crooned, or taunted. "I have a name, you know," she said over her shoulder to Greg, scrambling to her feet and lurching toward Patty, her hand extended.

"Lorraine," she announced, dropping her hand when Patty kept both of hers tightly wrapped around her daughters' waists. "I'm Lorraine, and I'll be your unexpected guest tonight," she said in a mock waitress voice, then giggled. That's when Patty first noticed the purplish bruise that covered half the woman's face, and something that looked like a spatter of blood on the front of the sweatshirt.

"You must be Patty," Lorraine said. "Except—" she glanced at Greg before returning her gaze to Patty—"I thought you flew the coop. I thought that's why our boy here has been so lonesome and needy-like. Why he came out of nowhere and started sniffing all around me."

Greg suddenly gripped both sides of his head as if he were going to pull it off. Then he wheeled around and took a menacing step toward Lorraine.

"Get out!" he roared. "Get the fuck off my property!"

Lorraine shrank away from him, instantly deflated by his violence. Then she seemed to puff herself back up with contemptuous bravado.

"Your property," she said in a fake admiring tone, turning her head to take in the rhododendron bush, the low azaleas, the blocky wall of privet hedge. She smiled and nodded as if she now understood everything. "Oh, yes. Your property. It's very nice."

Patty had never seen Greg in the mode he entered next, straining to keep his self-control, hands trembling in front of him.

"Greg," Patty said. "She's been beaten."

His hands dropped to his sides and he turned away. After a few seconds during which they all stood silently, a tiny intermission, Greg turned back and approached Lorraine. He examined her face. Then he said, "That's not my problem, Lorraine."

"I didn't come here for your sympathy, you dickhead!" she screamed at him in sudden tears. "You think I think you'd care? You with your big, showy guilt over my son, just so you can hang around me and get your rocks off?"

Greg winced as if she had hit him in the face.

"You're high as a kite," he told her, his voice professionally calm, like a psychiatrist's, or a high school principal's, someone paid to comment on the troubling behavior of others. "Whatever he does to you, you somehow agree to. You said so yourself."

"I didn't agree to this!" she screamed, lifting her sweatshirt and displaying a series of shallow zigzag cuts to her skin that had dried in almost a herringbone pattern, as if someone had been trying to merely decorate Lorraine, not wound her. "I didn't agree to be tied up and have a goddamn knife held to my throat!"

Patty finally shook herself out of her paralysis. "Let's go, girls," she said. "You're coming home with me tonight."

"That's not necessary, Patty. I can deal with this," Greg said, staring at the cuts as if mesmerized.

"Oh, I'm sure you can, Greg. But that doesn't mean the girls have to be here to watch you do it. I think they've seen enough."

"Let her go, Greg," Lorraine sneered. "She's not about to stick. I know the type."

The blood rushed to Patty's face. At that moment she could have physically attacked this woman herself. Instead, she pulled the girls with her in the direction of the car.

"Ouch, Mom, let go," Kiley said, shaking herself free.

"Maybe Dad needs us," Melissa said.

"You heard him," Patty replied, her words clipped. "He can deal with it."

At that moment a motorcycle roared around the corner. Patty heard Lorraine cry out, "He's going to kill us!" and at first she thought Greg had gone crazy. But when she looked back at Greg, she saw him and Lorraine watching the street, transfixed.

"Get in the car!" Patty shouted, pushing the girls together into the backseat. She jumped in and turned the key. She backed out of the driveway with a squeal of the tires. Before she shifted and gunned the accelerator, she caught a glimpse of the heavy, rounded bike, the broad back of a leather jacket, the dull black half-helmet that reminded her of a World War I soldier's.

She was already dialing 911 from her cell phone, reporting her address, saying that she didn't *know* what was about to happen, but that they had better get there fast before someone got killed. Her thoughts were coming in quick flashes, like slides you clicked past swiftly on a projector, trying to find the one you wanted.

When she had gone two blocks, she pulled over and turned to the girls. "One of you drive. Go straight to Grandma's house. Don't tell her any of this. Say you wanted to visit her on your birthday—say anything—you're celebrating your licenses—whatever. I'll keep the phone with me and call you there." She slid out. Kiley opened the back door and stuck her head and one leg out.

"But Mom—"

"Do it! Go! I'm headed for Stan and Betty's. I'll be okay. The police are coming. Just go. Wait for me to call you at Grandma's."

Melissa had already gotten out of the other back door. She came around and got into the driver's seat.

"We're going," she said calmly. "Get back in, Kiley." Kiley shook her head in bewilderment, then followed her sister's orders. Patty watched Melissa pull away smoothly, with Kiley sitting up in back like a rich old lady being taken for a ride by her chauffeur.

Patty tried to run, but her heels hobbled her. She stopped and pulled them off, jamming them into her bag, along with the phone. Then she sprinted along her old jogging route, hugging the soft edges of the manicured lawns. Out of the corner of her eye she saw the scenes from the lit picture windows—her neighbors, sitting by lamps reading their magazines, on their couches watching television, maybe someone wondering aloud whether it was finally cold enough to lay a little fire.

Then she saw Stan and Betty's lights. Stan, who couldn't speak without making a sly, winking comment about wayward husbands and strict, supervising wives. Betty, who called Patty "dear" and used to cut slices of chocolate chip banana bread for Patty's girls after school, carrying them next door on flowered paper plates.

Patty's own house was dangerously silent. The motorcycle was still on the drive, as was Greg's car. But the house was dark, as if no one had entered it yet. The front lawn was a black, deserted square, its neat border shrubbery transformed in Patty's mind to hulking, huddled-over shapes.

Patty pounded on her neighbors' door.

"Stan! Betty! It's me, Patty." They were slow to open. When they did, they peered out at her.

"Patty! Are you back from your trip? Wonderful to see you. Come in for a cup of tea, dear," Betty said.

"The police are coming," Patty said, trying to regain her breath. They gaped at her.

"I need you to direct them to my backyard. I think Greg's being attacked, and maybe this other woman—it's too complicated to explain now. Could you just watch for them please?" She wanted to grab Stan—staring at her now like a friendly, befuddled Ronald Reagan—and shake him into some kind of useful action.

At that moment Patty heard Lorraine's shrill scream from her backyard.

"There, do you hear that?" Patty looked wildly around her and spied an iron spike stuck in Betty's garden that supported a heart-shaped enamel plaque reading *Birds and Bees at Work*. She grabbed it and brandished it like a spear. "Watch for the police!"

She hugged the side of her house as she crept along, staying in the shadows. As she got closer she heard a soft methodical grunting, like someone working hard at lifting bales of hay or shoveling a ditch. Lorraine's voice was a soft keening now.

At the corner of her house, Patty inched forward and saw Lorraine on her knees in the grass rocking back and forth, crying, *"Oh Jesus oh Jesus oh Jesus."* The biker in the black jacket stood over Greg, who was lying in the grass. He still wore the helmet. Silver glinted from his boots in the dark as he rhythmically kicked Greg, who buckled each time like a jackknife. Patty couldn't tell if the grunting was coming from Greg or his attacker. She fingered the dull point on her iron stake and didn't know what to do. The man was protected from head to foot with leather. She doubted that even a knife from her kitchen would help her. She backed away into the shadows and returned to the front of the house, groping for the phone.

"Emergency," the female voice answered briskly. "What is your name and the address you are calling from?"

"Patty Goodman, 84 Fircrest. *Please,*" Patty whispered as loudly as she dared. "Someone is beating my husband—the backyard—I'm not sure he's even conscious anymore, he's—"

"We have squad cars on the way, Mrs. Goodman. Do you know the assailant?"

"No. Please hurry. I've got to go."

"Mrs. Goodman, can you stay on the line with—"

"I can't," she whispered, clicking off the phone.

As she neared the back corner of the house, Patty heard the biker's voice for the first time, rough and low, calling Greg a motherfucking faggot, saying he was going to cut Greg's balls for messing where he shouldn't have.

She heard Lorraine's voice scream, "Don't!"

"Shut up, you worthless cunt, or I'll cut you next."

Patty strained to see what was happening; if he was about to stab Greg she would have to shout, create a diversion, anything to buy a minute until the police came.

It was Lorraine who saw her, stopping her crying to focus on Patty's face. She had opened her mouth as if about to speak when the biker turned to follow her gaze.

"Son of a bitch," he said, advancing a step toward Patty and her garden stake. "It's a Charlie's Angel," he jeered.

Patty saw the shapeless face and scraggly goatee. He might have had some blood smeared around his nose, it was hard to tell.

Suddenly the whole backyard was lit with a floodlight, making them all freeze like actors on a set. At the same moment, police rushed from behind and immobilized the biker, locking his arms behind him in cuffs and taking the knife. Lorraine fell away to the ground, where she lay in a sobbing heap.

The biker was being shoved past Patty by another officer. As he got closer, Patty could see that he did have a bloodied and swollen nose. He grinned a half-metallic sneer at her, saying, "Which angel are you, baby?" as he shuffled by.

An officer was turning Greg over on the grass. A siren grew louder, obliterating everything, and then was cut off in front of their house like the snarl of a cat.

"Mrs. Goodman?" someone was asking. She ignored the voice and rushed to Greg. His whole face was bathed in blood, and he was breathing with a strange clicking sound. As she said his name, trying to make his eyes open, a white-uniformed paramedic pulled her away and moved in with his kit. Another took up a position opposite, and they began a rapid-fire exchange of vital signs, lifting the skin of an eyelid, ripping Greg's shirt open to press a stethoscope to his chest.

A tall officer was tugging on her elbow, but Patty couldn't pull her eyes away from Greg. He was completely limp as they lifted him onto the gurney.

"Are you Mrs. Goodman? Ma'am, we've got to get a statement from you. We need to know what went on here tonight."

As if Patty knew. As if she knew the first little thing about it.

"They're taking my husband," she said, twisting away from him. "I've got to ride along. Please."

The police officer and paramedic conferred. Then he nodded to her. "You can go in the ambulance. I'll follow to the emergency room and we can talk there."

A female police officer was half hugging, half dragging Lorraine forward to them. Lorraine had her eyes closed and was mumbling a strange string of syllables.

"Do you know this woman, ma'am? She won't identify herself."

"Lorraine somebody. The dead boy's mother."

The officers exchanged rapid glances. "There's a dead boy?" the tall officer asked sharply.

"No—I mean he died a while ago. Timothy Phelps."

"You'd better stay here with me for a few minutes until we get this straight. I'll give you a ride to the ER after that. Don't worry, the paramedic said your husband is stable."

Patty watched the white suits hurry Greg away on the gurney. The swarm of uniforms in her backyard was thinning out. The female officer and the tall one remained with her and Lorraine. Patty closed her eyes and tried to compose her thoughts.

"Start with this woman," the tall officer said.

"I don't know her. My husband does—we live apart. We came home from my daughters' birthday dinner—"

"Your daughters?"

"I sent them to my mother's when the man on the motorcycle came."

It was all a swirl, of strange, improbable fact. She had to go back to Tim, how Greg had wondered about who his mother was, how Patty knew nothing else about any of it until she arrived at her house tonight (how easily the pronouns came to her: my house, my husband) and found a crazed, drunk or high woman on her steps. Maybe she had come to Greg for some kind of protection—you could see how she had been hurt, the slashes, the bruises. And then the biker, and driving the girls away—

"Maybe you could just drop me at Leonard's," Lorraine suddenly piped up. "I'm so tired of all this." Her head lolled onto the female officer's shoulder.

"Leonard's?" the tall officer asked Patty. She shook her head. No idea.

"Okay, that's enough for now," he said, snapping the aluminum cover of his notebook shut. "I'll need more from you later, but I know you're anxious to get to the ER."

"Give me just a minute, will you please?" Patty hurried over to Stan and Betty, who were posted outside their house in their cardigans and slippers.

"Thank you both," Patty said.

"Oh, well." Betty's voice was weak. She had seemed on the point of saying "Anytime, anything we can do"—which would be her cheerful reply if Patty had thanked her for lending a casserole dish or for picking up their newspapers when they went away for the weekend.

"Five squad cars," Stan said in a wondering voice. "We sent them right to your backyard."

"Well, all I can say is thanks," Patty said. "You're probably pretty mystified—I don't know the whole story myself. The short version is that the woman was running away from her boyfriend, that biker, and I think she came to Greg for help."

Betty looked troubled. After a pause she said, "Well, we hope we'll be seeing more of you around here, dear."

"Greg needs a keeper, you know," Stan added, trying for his old jovial tone.

Patty had no reply.

VII

Greg took an odd comfort in having his face against the grass and dirt. It wasn't imaginary anymore, his fall, his descent. Here was the tangible, material force he had called down upon himself—hadn't he? Unlike the lightning, which had struck as a kind of cosmic joke, wasn't this the conclusion to something Greg had started himself? Lorraine equaled Rick. Rick equaled this beating. He knew it, maybe he even craved it. How far? How much of himself did he think was demanded in sacrifice? It didn't matter. He might have invited it, but he couldn't stop it.

After the first few minutes, he ceased to feel pain. He did this by lifting himself out of his body, so he could pay attention to other things: Lorraine's voice crying for someone, the bark of a dog, the sizzle of a star, the way blades of grass grew deep as a forest you could wander through, lost.

From his perspective, floating just above the earth, he could see Tim over by the garden, weeding with his back to him. *Thank God you're okay,* Greg said to him. *Leave that now, you've done enough.* Tim grinned over his shoulder and said, *Just let me finish this part.*

*I'm almost through.* Greg couldn't believe it: Tim, in his backyard again. Just a kid in gym shorts doing some yard work. *Come say hello to your mother,* Greg said. *She's going to be so happy to see you.* Tim replied, *In a minute. Tell her I'm on my way.*

Greg tried to tell Lorraine that Tim was here, but she couldn't hear him; she had her hands over her ears, screaming. Then he looked back to find Tim, but saw nothing but the garden in moonlight, its perfect rectangle of bark dust and silvery hosta leaves.

*There's no reason to leave,* Greg called out, searching for him in the lacy dark absences of the dogwood's branches. *We haven't even talked yet. Your mother's just scared. She'll be okay.*

"YOU'LL BE okay," a nurse was telling him, as she held his wrist, studying her watch. "Do you need something to help with the pain?"

He stared at her.

"Do you know where you are, Mr. Goodman? You've been asleep."

He looked around him. It was morning. "I'm in the hospital," he replied, as if answering a quiz question.

The nurse nodded. "You've had some injuries, but nothing that won't heal. The doctor will be in to talk to you soon." She busied herself across the room, and then Greg thought he heard her rubber-soled footsteps retreat. He raised his head to check, and pain shot through his body in so many directions that he had no idea what on him was broken. He laid his head back down, breathing rapidly.

She appeared at his side again. "Pretty sore?" she asked. Greg nodded minutely. "I can give you something with codeine, if you want. Or ibuprofen? Your choice."

"Ibuprofen," he said. He needed to feel everything clearly. He needed to know where the edges of things were, including the pain.

"Okey-doke," she said cheerfully. When she stood by him to brace his head up and give him the pill, her broad motherly face dissolved in black dancing spots as the pain spasmed through his shoulders and back. He sank back into the pillow, eyes closed.

"Just rest now," she said. "Your wife was here a minute ago. Maybe she popped out for a coffee."

Greg lay there and tried to piece last evening back together. There was Lorraine at his house, making a scene, horrifying Patty and the girls. His despair, then, that the consequences of his—what?—his *lusts,* he guessed—but was that what it was, really? Wasn't it something more like fear, the fear of going ahead with his life?—were being played out at his home, before his family, where they would see what type of person he really was and leave him for good.

Then, what? The fabled Rick's arrival. Lorraine had never mentioned he was so ugly; Greg had pictured a tattooed body-building type, not the piggish, goateed mutant he turned out to be. Greg's awareness split, then: one part of him noting the departure of Patty and the girls, the other trying to think what to do. There wasn't time to get into the house; Rick was already charging toward him and Lorraine. Greg thought if he landed the first punch—and his fist *had* connected, he saw the spurting blood, from this the first punch he had thrown since maybe eighth grade—he'd have the upper hand. But the blows began, teaching him otherwise, Greg at the mercy of a kind of street-fighting viciousness he couldn't begin to defend himself against: kicks to the groin and his kidneys, an elbow to his windpipe, Greg's hopelessness against the helmeted, leather-armored, unrelenting blows.

Someone was with him. Greg opened his eyes and saw Patty. She frowned down at him.

"I'd like to tell you the other guy looked worse," she said.

He smiled weakly.

"Sometime you're going to have to explain what all that was about," she said.

"I'll explain what I can," he said. Through a swollen eye he examined her; she looked wan and drawn. "The girls?"

"They're okay. They're at my mother's. At least Kiley's okay. Melissa's got a bit of a situation on her hands, doesn't she?"

Greg tried to read her face. "She told you."

"She was waiting up for me last night. Quite an evening I had, all in all."

"Did you yell?"

"Yell?"

"Melissa was afraid you'd yell. Did you?"

Patty reflected, as if she was trying to picture herself. She shook her head. "I cried. We spent half the night, both of us, crying. By the time we were through, I don't think we knew exactly what we were crying about. There were so many things."

Greg let that settle on him, three words drifting down like feathers zigzagging to earth, their deceptive lightness. So many things.

"I'm sorry." He closed his eyes.

"I'm sorry, too."

He opened his eyes, surprised. "For what?"

"For walking away from the girls."

They were quiet for a minute, Greg breathing against pain.

"Melissa told me she wants an abortion," he said.

"She told me that, too," Patty said.

Greg reached his hand up, saw it outlined against the sun leaking in from the window blinds. She took it, her wrist lying across the stainless-steel guardrail of the bed. Her wedding ring glinted in the light.

"Are you—was it the right thing? When we had one?"

"We." Patty smiled thinly.

"You."

"Damn right, me," she said. But she still held his hand. "You've never asked me that before."

"I'm asking."

Patty looked up at the ceiling, at the holes in the acoustic tiles. "The right thing?" She shrugged. "It felt like the only thing. I've never been sorry. Sad, once in a while, but not sorry."

"Maybe that's why we had twins."

She met his eyes. "You know I've always partly believed that?

That the baby came back to us. Like she took a ride on some karmic
Ferris wheel for a few years, and that when we said 'yes,' she came
back to earth with her sister."

"Did you tell Melissa that? About the first pregnancy?"

She nodded. Then she said, "She's going to make an appointment.
She wants us both to be there."

"I'll be there," he said.

WHEN PATTY drove him home the next day, his broken ribs taped, his
eye sutured, a flaring bandage across his nose, he saw his house, im-
possibly ordinary in the daylight. His recycling bin was still at its
place by the curb from where it had not been brought in; his mail-
box housed two days' worth of credit card offers and sale flyers. Patty
had told him about the neighbors gathered in little murmuring groups
in the street as the last of the police cars pulled away, the phone mes-
sages of concern that just barely concealed the titillated hunger for
details. When Greg went to replay them he heard also the message
from Joy Scinterro, Channel Nine News, who had plucked his name
from the police reports.

"Greg—please call—I was so worried when I heard about your—
accident." She left the station number, her cell phone number, her
home number, and her pager number.

He was still musing over her recorded voice, its message erased,
when the phone rang and it was her real voice. She must have had a
station intern dialing the hospital every hour to see when he was released. He had turned off the phone in his hospital room and asked
for no visitors to be allowed in except family.

"Greg—how *are* you?" she asked in her softly insistent tone.

"Is this an interview?" he asked.

"Well, no, but . . . Greg there *is* a story here, of course you know
that," she said confidingly. "As soon as I saw the police report I
started digging. Your assailant is involved with some very bad
people—he's got a record as long as my arm. He's part of a group of

bikers who deal weapons and drugs. Their trademark is cutting people they don't get along with—I can't believe you're okay."

"Gee, thanks," he said. His mind flashed back to the strange pattern of slashes on Lorraine's stomach. How they were cuts meant to
toy with her, how they might have been made slowly, one at a time.

"Of course, I'm so relieved; I just meant that this guy was very
dangerous."

"I think I know that."

"Greg. *Lorraine Morrison.* I know who she is." Joy's voice became
a conspiratorial whisper.

"Congratulations."

"Oh, come on, Greg. Give me something. Tim's mother running to
you for help? Greg Goodman almost getting killed protecting her?
Give me the back story, *please.* I can make it look very, very good for
you. Greg, the public *deserves* to know about this; you're already in
their hearts."

"Sorry, Joy."

"Did you know Lorraine Morrison was charged with possession?"
Greg was silent. His ribs stabbed at him.

"She made a deal, checked into a rehab."

"Good." But he already knew that, had scooped Joy Scinterro on
her research. He had asked the police how he could get in touch
with Lorraine; they had given him the number of the rehab facility.
Greg had had to lie to a string of hospital personnel in order to get
through to her; even posing as her brother he had trouble. When finally he heard her on the line her voice was flat and colorless. It had
none of the gravelly jokeyness he was used to. He congratulated her
for going into detox. She snorted. And he remembered the truth in
her voice once when she had told him about just wanting to sit on
some steps and watch everyone else go by. Sit it out. She had been
straight before, he knew, and she hadn't liked the feeling. Maybe
when she was straight she brooded. Maybe she had to keep whistling
just to keep her mind off things. And after so much whistling, she'd
tire.

Joy tried one last gambit. "A story like this might help your case with the school board. I hear they're close to a final decision."

"Fuck the school board. That's my one statement on the record."

PATTY STOOD before him, her arms folded across her chest. As he listened to Joy he had watched her walk from the living room to the kitchen as if she were disoriented and needed a map. She hadn't sat down; she hadn't touched anything. Now he was the one to rise and start gathering scattered newspapers and stray articles of clothing to make a space for her.

"Don't straighten up on my account," she said.

"You're not at home. I can see that."

"Because I didn't immediately start cleaning?" she asked, her mouth twisting up with wry (or was it bitter?) amusement.

"Because you're not taking possession of anything. Not even a chair." He swept some stuff off a rocker and gestured to it with mock formality. "Won't you sit down?"

"No, thanks. I've got to run. The girls and I are going to take my mother out to lunch."

"Oh." Trying not to sound as disappointed as he felt.

"It's been good for them to see so much of each other. It cheered my mother up a lot. Kiley took one look at that turban she wears now—her hair's gone, you know—and said, 'Grandma, when did you become a Sufi mystic?' It broke right through everything."

Greg smiled.

Patty hesitated. "Listen . . . I was thinking the girls might like to stay there for the rest of the weekend. They could help out, grocery-shop or whatever. Their energy would do my mother a world of good. And in a funny way, I think the girls could use some neutral ground right now."

"Away from their insanely accident-prone father."

She shook her head. "Just until we figure out the logistics of this."

Something plunged within him. He wanted to be back in his hospital bed, the nurse saying, "Your wife's here," and him allowing himself to believe it, dazzled by sun reflecting off a wedding band as she held his hand.

"So what you're saying is . . ." he cleared his throat.

"I still need time." She shook her head. "It's too much to process. I've changed, you've changed . . . maybe that's in our favor. I don't know. I don't know anything for certain right now."

He nodded, hoping that the warm mist he felt swimming in front of his vision wasn't apparent to her. She didn't need to know how sorry for himself he was feeling right now.

HE TOLD her he would be all right alone. He didn't mean it, but he thought he should at least pretend, so she could go to her mother, who needed her, and to the girls, who most certainly did as well. After she left, Greg felt completely taken apart, deconstructed, the pieces of himself scattered so far he didn't think he'd ever find them. He was afraid of his own house. He was afraid of his neighbors' faces. Of the mirror. Of silence. He picked up the phone to call Wilson Perry, and put it down again. Did he really have any friends? He stood breathing hard in front of the kitchen bulletin board where Patty used to pin grocery lists and school memos in some other life and pondered this. After a few minutes he decided, yes, Wilson was a friend. Patty, too, he surprised himself by thinking. She was his best friend. He should tell her that. Then shrank from the thought. What if she had nothing to say in return?

He struggled into a jacket and went out to the backyard. Nothing, no sign of chaos, apocalypse. No weeping Lorraine, no Tim hunched with his back to them. Only a coiled hose, securely pinned against the wall; a gas grill, shrouded in plastic.

He started walking then, slowly, with no destination, and perhaps because of the cold, he saw no one outside. The wind had sharpened itself on its journey through the Columbia Gorge. By the time it hit the east side of the county it was like a blade that scraped the sky a clean, hard blue. Greg hunched for warmth into his jacket, walking in the street. For some reason when his neighborhood was conceived no one had thought sidewalks were necessary, only curbs. He had never questioned this before, had always traveled these blocks enclosed in his car. Now, at ground level, he felt how curious it was that there be no space for someone on foot, how vulnerable the children were as they walked back and forth to school. He remembered, suddenly, scuffing back and forth himself with a book bag and a lunchbox. How it felt to be a child, buffeted by forces like slamming doors and raised voices and school bells and the wind from passing cars. How he had determined to grow up to be louder and stronger and in charge and behind the wheel.

He was still capable of fooling himself, thinking he had no plan when in fact he had been headed for Phelps's house all along. He stood in the street and stared at the real estate sign for some time. Sale pending. The house looked empty already, the curtains open to a black interior that even from here looked hollow. A stray newspaper had blown against the foundation. Phelps had settled the lawsuit; Greg had had a letter from his insurance company last week. What would he do with his money, that and the proceeds from the house? Greg tried to picture him on a beach somewhere, sipping a drink—or on a ranch in Wyoming, or on a cruise ship—and had no luck. There could be no vacation for Phelps, no place he could come to think of as home. He was unlucky in a way that Greg hadn't even gotten near. How he must have loved Lorraine, to coax sobriety from her, nurse her withdrawals, stand before the dress racks, choosing. It's conceivable that she loved him back, to wear the presents he brought, keep it up for as long as she did. Greg was suddenly certain they had had their happy moments, shoulders touching over Tim's crib, ogling the infant eyelashes and parted lips, shushing each other, saying, *Be quiet now, just let him sleep.*

# A Trick
of Nature

Suzanne Matson

## A Reader's Guide

# A Conversation with Suzanne Matson

*Elizabeth Graver is the author of the novels* Unravelling *and* The Honey Thief. *She teaches with Suzanne Matson in the English Department at Boston College.*

**Elizabeth Graver: What was the initial seed of this novel? Did the story surprise you in any way as it progressed?**

Suzanne Matson: A few years ago my mother sent me a clipping about an incident in my old neighborhood involving some kids who were struck by lightning at football practice, one of them seriously hurt. I started thinking about the almost mythological proportions of such a freak accident—the Zeus-like incursion of the lightning bolt into the middle of something as mundane as a suburban football practice. Then I began thinking about my old neighborhood itself, a working class suburb where the public schools were decent but where sports reigned supreme. When I was a kid I couldn't wait to grow up and live in the city—as soon as I was in college I lived in a series of downtown apartments. But now, twenty years later, I'm back in the suburbs, raising my own kids. I was struck by the irony of this—how wanting a house and a lawn seems almost inevitable when you've got small kids. You want them to have freedom to run and explore, but in a protected, bordered way. So I guess the seed for the book began with the lightning, and how even in lives and places that are supposedly *safe* there is no guarding against the unexpected. There are no truly safe places. I guess if something surprised me during the writing it was how emphatic that notion became for me: marriages aren't *safe*, in the sense that you can count on them to stay the same, and the tidy suburban lot you tend on the weekend is only a symbol of your desired control over nature.

**EG: Your first novel, *The Hunger Moon*, was narrated from the points of view of three female characters. *A Trick of Nature* has, at its heart, the perspective of a man. What challenges and rewards did you encounter in writing from Greg's point of view?**

SM: I really liked writing from inside Greg's head. He's forthright, he wants things to be simple and clear, and when they're not he gets kind of pissed about it. At the same time, his nature is to hope for the best. The hardest part about adopting his point of view was not that he was a man—for some reason, that didn't seem difficult—but that he was largely unconscious about his limitations. I wanted his vision to grow as the novel progressed, but I didn't want him to have any unrealistic breakthroughs. He has a habit of denial that I couldn't cure him of. As a result, I had to show the readers things about Greg that Greg couldn't see himself.

**EG: I remember that, as you were working on this novel, Patty's perspective was one you added fairly late in the game. What made you want to add her point of view?**

SM: For one thing, I needed another angle on Greg; her understanding of him was in many ways deeper than his own. And yet, as she fell into the habit of taking control in the marriage, she stopped seeing him fully. I think that's a real danger in a long marriage, that the partners have a version of the other in mind that doesn't grow; as a result both can get stuck in their roles. It may be a comfortable trap for a while, but I wanted to show how after they were married for almost two decades there were bound to be ways in which Patty's and Greg's roles had grown static and binding. This is especially true for Patty's character. She was difficult for me to get at until I realized how much buried resentment she had. Once I understood that, she began to get more complicated for me.

**EG: In many ways this is a novel about middleness. Greg and Patty are entering middle age, and they live what appear to be, at first, fairly middle-of-the-road suburban lives. And yet, as you show, their world is full of unexpected cracks, sutures—like the lightning that strikes Timothy Phelps. What drew you to this world? Are there other writers of suburbia or middle age whose work inspired you?**

SM: Well, what drew me was the fact that in some ways, this is my world. I came from the kind of place Patty and Greg live in, and I wanted to document it. And, as I said, now I'm a parent in the suburbs. But yes, there are literary models for what I wanted to do. In particular I love Updike's Rabbit novels. I had only read *Rabbit is Rich*—and that back when I was in college—when I started writing *A Trick of Nature*. I knew right away that Greg Goodman was in some ways a kinsman of Harry Angstrom: they both have self-conceptions framed in terms of a sport, neither is interested in looking too deeply into his personal relationships until those relationships begin to crumble, and neither has a deeply thought out value system or a religious faith. I didn't allow myself to read the rest of the Rabbit novels until I was done writing my novel; I didn't want to feel too influenced. But when I sent the book off to the publisher I read the whole Rabbit tetrology as a reward. I was struck anew at the similar emotional blueprints that make up Greg and Harry.

**EG: Fathers play an important role in *A Trick of Nature*. While you primarily focus on Greg's role as a father to his girls, we also see him—through his memories of his own father—as a son. How does Greg's past inform his current life as father and husband? How does it inform his reactions to Timothy Phelps and his father?**

SM: I see Greg as emotionally undernourished. His father was an un-evolved, unsatisfied person who took a lot of his frustration and bitterness out on his son. Greg is a much better parent than his father was—more open, more emotionally generous. But because he's afraid of duplicating his father's harsh parenting, Greg tends to abdicate when it comes to disciplining his teenage daughters. When things get emotionally volatile, he'd rather leave the unpleasant confrontations to Patty. In Tim Phelps, Greg sees a kid who reminds him of his younger self; his impulse is to bolster him if he can, run interference with Tim's gruff father. Greg is even aware of this impulse, and it leads him to remember what it felt like to be an adolescent boy—how important the equations of power and vulnerability are then, and how sports for him became a safe place to channel anger and aggression. As Tim's football coach, Greg has the ready-made language of the pep talk to try to support Tim; he belatedly realizes how limited and one-dimensional a language it is.

**EG: Lorraine Morrison is a particularly intriguing character, both in terms of her own story and in terms of what she allows Greg to explore. How do you understand her place in the book?**

SM: She's the wild card. Greg needs to track her down, both out of curiosity, and for reasons he can't quite fathom himself. When he does find her, he's fascinated by her utter disregard for all that he takes so seriously—home, family, stability, reputation, and parental responsibility. As Greg begins to question the shape of his own life, the apparent freedom of hers looks alluring. She's not free though, as he begins to understand the longer he knows her.

**EG: You write very convincingly about what it's like to parent teenaged twin daughters, coach football, and work at a place like the Top Hat—all experiences you've never had. Can you describe how you go about filling these fictional worlds with such rich details?**

SM: For the football stuff I had to consult my husband, my brother, and some male friends. It's not a game I'm particularly interested in. What does interest me is football's power to bind men together—not all men, but certainly many of the men I grew up with and the boys I went to school with. I wanted to try to get at what that male enthusiasm was all about, see if I could understand it for myself. The same goes with the strip club. What sends a particular man there as a regular customer? I've never been to a strip club, but by asking myself questions about Greg's motivation in going there, I was better able to picture the setting, as well as his growing sense of comfort in that dark and anonymous atmosphere. It became increasingly clear to me that, for Greg at least, it wasn't as much about sex as it was about loneliness. It seemed like a place you could be attracted to if you were feeling unmoored. As for parenting teenage daughters—I just tried to remember what it was like to be one: mouthy, reckless, emotional, immoderate. I declared myself an adult at fifteen, much to my mother's horror. My own sons are still small, but I can imagine how bewildering it will feel one day when they're telling me they're grown up, and I'm still seeing kids in front of me.

**EG: What are you working on now?**

SM: It's a new novel—no title yet. I always have to get to the end of a book before I can find a title. This one has just one point of view instead of the multiples of *The Hunger Moon* and *A Trick of Nature*, but I follow my character through three stages of his life: when he's nine and a significant family loss occurs, to when he's in college and struggling, to the final section when he returns as an adult to his hometown in New Hampshire to try to deal with his father's Alzheimer's disease. My character has a successful life in Los Angeles and has been estranged from his father for years, but it falls to him to make his father's living arrangements. It's been fascinating to follow a character over the course of thirty years; I love how complex the layers of time and memory become, the opportunities you have as a writer to use that.

# Reading Group Questions and Topics for Discussion

1. Greg Goodman is often quick to judge other people—and to find their actions wanting. He passes judgment, at various points, on his friend Mitch, on his daughters and wife, on Lorraine Morrison, on Tim Phelps's father. But the world is also judging Greg—most notably for his role in Tim's death. Do you think Greg's understanding of right and wrong changes over the course of the novel? As a reader, do you find yourself passing judgment on Greg? On the other characters?

2. The twins, Kiley and Melissa, are fifteen when the book begins, and going through many changes and awakenings of their own. How do the girls' experiences echo Greg's and Patty's? Do you think Greg and Patty are good parents to their teenaged daughters? How might they have been better?

3. A *Trick of Nature* is filled with rich descriptions of place, from the Goodman's suburban house, to Patty's studio apartment, to the club where Lorraine works. How do the various characters' reactions to these places reveal their inner fears and longings?

4. When Patty finds out that Greg has had an affair, does she react in the way you'd expect her to? What surprises you about Patty? What do you admire in her? What do you see as her weaknesses or limitations?

5. Lorraine Morrison lives in a very different world from Greg, but at the same time, the two characters have a great deal in common. How do you understand the nature of their relationship and the emotional journey they take together?

6. Joy Scinterro, the Channel Nine News reporter, appears sporadically throughout the novel to ask pointed questions of Greg. Why do you think Suzanne Matson included her in the book?

7. At the end of *A Trick of Nature*, we read that Greg "felt completely taken apart, deconstructed, the parts of himself scattered so far he didn't think he'd ever find them." Who is this new Greg? What does his future look like? How do you understand his relationship to Patty at the novel's close? To his daughters? To himself?